I0702859

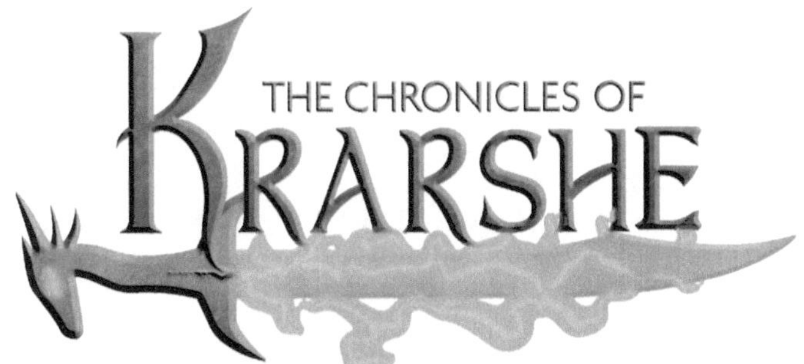

THE HEARTS OF MEN

VOLUME 1

By A.S.K. Florian

Illustrations by Yosheki

The Chronicles of Krarshe: The Hearts of Men, Volume 1

Copyright © 2024 by A.S.K. Florian

This is a work of fiction. Names, characters, businesses, places, events
and incidents are either the products of the author's imagination or
used in a fictitious manner.

Artwork copyright © 2024 by Yosheki (https://yosheki.carrd.co)
Cover art by Yosheki
Cover design by Campbell Karanian
Interior design by Vic's Lab, LLC (https://www.vicslab.com)

Printed in the United States of America

First Edition 2024

ISBN-13: 979-8-9909237-0-6

Dedication

To my cousin, for constantly badgering me
to put this story on paper.

In memory of my mother, for giving me
the strength and courage to pursue it.

PROLOGUE

The old man rubbed his brow, massaging away his fatigue. The wisps of mystical light twisted and wound through the air around him in an endless tangle, flowing through the empty study, bathing the otherwise dark room in a pale blue glow. "There must be at least one..." he said. "There MUST be." He took off his spectacles and cleaned them with a corner of his robe. As he set them back in place, he said again with renewed vigor, "I KNOW there must be someone."

The wisps of light continued to dance around the old wizard as he caught one in his fingers. His eyes became unfocused, reflecting the events the strand of light contained as it wriggled its way through his gentle grasp. "No, not him," he said after a few minutes, releasing his grip. He caught another, repeating the process again and again. The same way he had done countless times.

"Ah, this is hopeless!" he shouted, flopping down into a chair that materialized behind him. "Maybe there isn't any—No, NO! You can't speak this way. No, there must be someone. I know it!" He looked over by the door. "Don't give me that look,

Wilfred!" he said, pointing a thin, bony finger toward the figure by the door. "You KNOW I hate when you look at me like that!"

The doll sat there on the floor, staring lifelessly at the wizard with its button eyes.

A moment passed.

"You're right. I must keep trying. There is no other option." The wizard stood up, his chair vanishing into the ether. He caught another luminescent strand. "You know, Wilfred, there are times when—" He stopped. "... This... This is it! Aha!" The wizard danced around as the mystical lights all faded away, leaving him standing in the middle of the now-furnished study, a single wisp in hand. "I knew it! It was just a few months! ... Or was it a few millennia?" He thought for a moment. "Bah! Doesn't matter! We found him, Wilfred! I told you I wasn't crazy!" he shouted, eyes wide, pointing at the doll once again.

The doll slowly tipped over before flopping onto the book it sat upon.

"Ahh... A wondrous find, in all of the different times and paths." The wizard sat at his desk, laying the mystical wisp of light upon it. "Now, let's see... Hmm..." He traced his fingers over its length more slowly than he had previously and his eyes unfocused again. "Bit tumultuous, this one. Hmm... There is some trouble for us, but it's unavoidable." The wizard came out of his trance and turned to the doll. "Yes, Wilfred, I'm certain. I know it—err, will know it later. Why do you never trust me?" he asked, exasperated. With a sigh, he returned to his investigation. "Mmm... Without a doubt, this is our best opportunity. I have found and will find no better options. Or so I will discover. Okay!" He released the mystical wisp and walked over to the table littered with books and stood before the doll. "Bring the other two. There is much to discuss. Or, is being discussed? Nevermind. Just summon them here so we can begin! I need to fabricate the talisman. I'll clean the room."

The old wizard turned and looked around the room, now cleared of books and other equipment. An ornate table sat in the middle of the room with three fine chairs around it. "Good. I hate cleaning. Hmm? You haven't summoned them yet, Wilfred?"

The doll sat upright in one of the chairs, motionless.

"Fine, I'll just do EVERYTHING around here. Or, have done everything..." he thought for a moment before waving, dismissively. He stared down at the doll. "Oh, you're right! His name. Hmm." He appeared at his desk once more, tracing his fingers along the glowing strand. "His name... Mmm... That one's a bit tricky. It seems his name is..."

* * *

"Don't be foolish, Krarshe!" His father's voice shook the walls as it echoed down the stone halls.

"I'm not being foolish, *do'a*!" Krarshe retorted. "You are being closed minded! Or perhaps just a coward!" He glared at his father, his vibrant blue eyes shone with rage.

"Krarshe, please try to understand. There is nothing to gain from living amongst them," his mother said as she tried to calm Krarshe and his father.

"It is pointless," his father said sharply. "Listen to me when I say you will only be met with hate and disgust. At best, they would simply fear you!"

"You don't know that for certain!"

"Krarshe..." his mother started.

"I have lived long enough to see their treachery and malice!" his father interjected.

Krarshe could see the same fierce blue-eyed anger in his father's eyes; there was no getting through to him. Krarshe was out of arguments, or too weary of fighting to think more on it. It was clear no amount of reasoning was going to get through to his parents. He turned away from them and inhaled deeply, too frustrated to say any more.

There was a long silence.

Their home had been filled with bickering and quarreling for the better part of an hour. The sudden quiet was unsettling. Krarshe expected his father to shatter the quiet with either his voice or a blow, but it never came.

His father spoke softly, with indignation. "Fine. Do as you wish. If you will not listen to reason, then there is nothing left to say."

Krarshe relaxed, realizing the confrontation was over. He thought about how to respond. It wasn't the reaction he expected, so anything he had prepared would just incite another argument. "I will be all right, *do'a*," assured Krarshe finally. It was the only thing he could come up with.

Another pause. "... I know, *do'e*. I have no doubt that you will survive out there," said his father quietly. His voice was hoarse from their yelling match. "Wisdom with you, Krarshe." He turned and retreated into his chambers.

Krarshe just nodded toward his father and turned to his mother.

"He's just worried about you," she explained. "Not physically, but your heart. Remember, your *do'mro* lived among them for a time too, and he was told all of the stories growing up. I worry too, Krarshe," she said gently as she pressed her forehead against his affectionately.

Krarshe smiled, closed his eyes, and focused on his mother's embrace. It was warm. Loving. "I know."

Krarshe, too, had heard his grandfather's tales growing up in his infrequent visits. Tales of the vast hills of sand and stone beyond the mountains to the east, where the sand crawled with enormous, subterranean beasts. Tales of huge trees in forests to the south, their boughs twisted and tough, a fortress for the elves. His grandfather's stories were endless and the results of a lifetime of exploration. The world seemed so large in his stories, so full of adventure. Adventure that Krarshe now sought.

His mother released him from her embrace to look him in the eyes. "My *do'e* is too kind and gentle of heart." She smiled at him. "We'll be here if you decide to return."

Krarshe nodded.

"You should take those little metal pieces your *do'mro* brought back."

"Okay," said Krarshe.

"Oh, and bring back a souvenir when you do. I'm sure it'll cheer up your *do'a*."

Krarshe chuckled. "If I can find something. You know how picky he is."

"And me one of those pieces of cloth... A 'dress', I believe it's called? You know how much I find those interesting," said his mother. Krarshe looked back to see a wide grin on her face.

He shook his head, exasperated. "Yes, yes, I know."

"And what of Ari? Did you let her know?"

"No. If I did, she'd want to come too. You know how she is." Krarshe paused for a moment, thinking on it more. "... She'll be fine."

"That habit of yours..." she sighed, shaking her head.

Krarshe stepped outside and looked over the mountainous landscape. The sun was well past its apex, now near the horizon. The shadows of the hills and mountains were beginning to stretch and reach across the valleys. He breathed deeply the mountain air, the cool sensation filling his lungs, making him even more eager to start his journey. His mind was a whirlwind of thoughts. Where should he go first? To the coast, to try the seaside cuisine his grandfather spoke of? To the deep forests, to seek out the fae? To the action in a big city? His options seemed limitless.

He was pulled from his thoughts by his mother's soft, soothing voice. "Go with Wisdom, *do'e*."

Krarshe looked back. The joyous smile on his mother's face was gone, replaced with a lonely one burdened by sadness. Or was it concern? Krarshe wasn't entirely sure. But loneliness was part of any journey, for both of them. He had already accepted that and her lonesome expression would not deter him.

"I'm off, *fusu'a*."

CHAPTER 1

K rarshe sighed heavily as he stared up at the clear blue sky, his vibrant blue eyes wincing a bit in the sunlight. He sat there enjoying the placidity of the sky, watching the lone cloud go by as he absent-mindedly kicked and dug at the edge of his wagon with his boot, trying to get the caked mud off of them from when he helped push another wagon in the caravan out of a ditch the day before. The yelling and screaming seemed so distant as he watched the cloud drift by. Krarshe sighed again. "Must be nice..." he said.

Am I really envious of a cloud? Krarshe thought.

"Yer turn, ol' man." A gruff voice snapped him out of his reverie.

Krarshe turned to look at the man standing next to his wagon. He was balding, stout, and about as coarse as his voice would have led one to believe. His leather jerkin was in bad condition, likely damaged from years of use, and most certainly fitted well before the years of brew took their toll on his gut. Krarshe stared at him blankly for a minute as the meaning of the words didn't register immediately. His thoughts were still on that one strangely envious cloud.

An ear-splitting scream drew his attention to one of the other wagons as one of the bandits was getting rough with a female traveller. Krarshe couldn't bear to watch such a stomach-turning scene again, so he averted his gaze and gritted his teeth in reluctant acceptance of his own uselessness. His eyes came to settle on a cluster of bandits huddled around the body of an adventurer, one of the caravan's hired escorts. One of the bigger, brawnier bandits in the cluster stood over the body, gloating as he rocked his axe back and forth, turning the adventurer's head left and right where it was lodged. The others were sifting through his belongings like rats picking through garbage looking for food. Krarshe looked off in the distance, the few adventurers who escaped alive were mere dots on the horizon.

Why did we even hire them? Krarshe wondered to himself.

"Oy, ol' man. Hurry up. Ah doh't have all deh." The bandit next to his wagon pointed his sword at Krarshe, this time more insistently than before.

What a rusty piece of junk. Does that even have an edge anymore? Krarshe thought. *I figured people would treat the elderly better, but I guess I misjudged them.* He heard another cry from the woman from before. *At least a sword to my throat is better than that...*

"Right, right. Just give me a moment, eh?" Krarshe said, reaching into the back of his wagon. "These old bones don't move as quickly as they used to." He pulled out a leather pouch and tossed it to the bandit with a clink of metal.

The bandit clumsily caught it, almost dropping his sword. He hurriedly tore open the pouch to count the three silver coins. "Dis it?" He was clearly disappointed, his grip on his sword tightened.

Another gangly bandit sauntered over, carrying a sword he foisted off one of the adventurers' corpses. "Dat all yeh got off dis ol' man? Not bad," he said to the heavier bandit, readjusting the sword he had leaning over his shoulder in an exaggerated manner.

"I dunno. Is it, ol' man?" the fat bandit said, pointing his sword even more aggressively at Krarshe. The tip was so close he could smell the old, rusty metal of the blade.

"Honest, that's all I have," Krarshe pleaded as earnestly as his meager acting skills allowed. He pulled the cloth covering his wagon back a bit to show the bandits the contents. "All I have left to offer is this."

"Wheat?"

"Yes, I'm a wheat merchant. I got this from the east, out in Gagerith."

The two bandits looked at each other. They turned away and started murmuring to each other. Krarshe couldn't really care what they were saying. He was just tired of dealing with bandits who didn't have a modicum of intelligence. He looked over the rest of the caravan. Or rather, what remained of it. Bandits continued to harass fellow travellers for money and goods, beating those that tried to defend themselves. A few of the merchants were dead, having attempted to protect their goods.

Mistake, thought Krarshe. *Usually better to just let them have it.*

Finally the bandits turned back to him. "We'll be takin' dat too," said the stockier one. "An' deh wagon 'n' horse."

Krarshe sighed. "Thank you for sparing my life. I'm most appreciative, kind sir." The words were sour, but he did his best to sound sincere. Bandits like being made to feel important.

"Yeh, now gitouda here behfore we change our minds."

Krarshe climbed down from his wagon. A few steps away, he turned around quickly back to the wagon. "Almost forgot my staff. You wouldn't be needing an old man's walking stick, right? I know you're not that heartless, kind gentleman."

The bandit sneered a bit at him. *Uh-oh, did I lay it on too thick there?* Krarshe wondered. Then the bandit gestured dismissively and Krarshe grabbed the staff. He gave a brief, shaky bow as the bandit turned and yelled to the others about his haul.

* * *

Krarshe limped and hobbled his way down the uneven dirt road, looking back periodically to check how far he'd travelled from the caravan. When he was certain the bandits couldn't see him anymore and that he wasn't being followed, he un-hunched his back and stretched.

"That posture is rough." He held his stretch for a minute before breathing a sigh of relief and tossing his staff aside. He threw his black traveller's cloak open and reached into his old, worn brown robes and pulled out a leather pouch. He opened the drawstrings and checked its contents.

"One, two, three... Hmm... Seven Remonnet gold roses, three Remonnet silver roses, four Imperial gold seals and two silver seals, eleven Remonnet copper roses, and seventeen copper gerins. Well, no idea when I'll be travelling to Gagerith again without a horse, so I should probably exchange those gerins. If I can find an honest broker... Wait, where is—" He frantically started dumping the contents of the pouch onto the ground. A small metal plate fell to the ground. "Phew, thought I left that in the wagon." He picked up the plate, which had his name and merchant details engraved on it next to an official Remonnet rose insignia, and stuffed it back into the pouch. "Would be problematic trying to enter the city without my identification plate."

He took a moment to gather all of the coins and put them back in the pouch. "I should be set for a while," he said, tossing and catching the coin pouch, listening to the coins jingle within. He looked up at the sky again. The lone cloud was a long ways away, nearly to the Molduhr mountains now. "How nice to not have to travel by foot..."

I wish I could fight like this so I could have dealt with those bandits. Krarshe held up an old, boney hand toward the cloud. *Who knew being an old man would cause this many problems?*

Krarshe shook his head. "That would cause too much of a scene, Krarshe," he told himself.

Krarshe sighed again. "I feel like I've been sighing too much lately," he said to no one in particular. "Well, let's head back to the city. I'm sure I can find some other work before I run out of funds. Hopefully something other than a merchant this time."

Tucking his coin pouch away again, he continued down the road.

* * *

Krarshe closed in on the huge stone walls of the city of Remonnet. The massive fortified city sat on the Silver River. Its towers jutted out from the wall on both sides of the river, controlling the waterway and guarding entry into the city from its banks. Armed soldiers patrolled its walls and peered out over the battlements. Krarshe could make out scorch marks on the walls: cosmetic scars from battles past that weren't important enough to repair. He looked up to see the flag of Remonnet, a thorny rose, fluttering in the slight breeze.

Krarshe got in the line of carts in front of the Imperial Gate, the entrance closest to the trade district which was strictly used as a merchant's entrance. As he waited in line, he looked around uneasily, now conscious of how out of place he appeared. Surrounded by merchant carts, he was the only one in this line travelling by foot. The other peddlers kept shooting him inquisitive glances or scoffing. Hopefully the guards didn't give him as much trouble as the merchants did. He unclasped his cloak and draped it over one shoulder, both because it was too warm and to make himself feel less awkward just standing there.

"Next!"

The line shifted forward slowly. *Ugh, this will take a while...* Krarshe thought. He looked around, trying to find something to keep his mind busy. This would be far too painful to sit through, with only the thoughts of his own awkwardness.

He looked at the cart ahead of him, but the contents of the cart were covered by a cloth. It was standard practice to protect it from the elements and hide them from curious thieves. *Too bad.* He turned to the cart behind him. His eyes met the merchant riding the cart, apparently watching Krarshe himself. The man just smiled, nodded a bit in acknowledgement, and

then looked away, trying to pretend that he wasn't staring. Krarshe didn't care, he knew people were looking at him. He turned back toward the walls. He was just barely in the shadow cast by the fortifications and would accidentally blind himself if he shifted slightly. The walls really were tall enough to make you feel insignificant. He couldn't imagine sieging this city and how impossible it must seem.

"Next!"

Krarshe looked back at the cart ahead of him and watched it pass through the gates. Apparently he had distracted himself enough because it was now his turn. He slowly approached the stationed guard. The guardsman had his helmet off, revealing his reddish hair that was darkened with sweat. Krarshe didn't envy having to wear heavy armor on such a hot day. The shade did little to help them escape the heat of the season of Sirnus, but they were likely thankful for the reprieve from the sun. Upon seeing Krarshe, the guard looked around slightly, almost imperceptibly. Krarshe just disregarded it and offered his plate.

"You're a merchant?" he asked.

Krarshe nodded. "My caravan ran into a bit of... trouble on the roads."

"Only a bit?" the guard asked jokingly, as he gestured to the absence of Krarshe's cart.

Bit rude to laugh about a merchant losing his cart, isn't it? Krarshe thought. "A group of bandits hit us pretty hard. Killed most of the adventurers we hired as escorts. Had to give up my cart and horse to get here alive," he explained.

The smile fell from the guard's face. "Oh? Would you mind giving me a few details about where? I'll submit a report and see if we can deal with them."

"Couldn't have been more than a few days walk from here. We had reached the river's bank already along the Imperial Road, and had passed the fork toward here."

The guard nodded. He turned to a couple guards leaning against the wall to the side who were dousing themselves with water from a bucket they had. "Jauc, come here."

A young guard, startled, jumped up and ran over, water dripping down his face. He attempted to wipe it with his forearm, but the metal of his armor just smeared it messily. "Sir!"

The guard relayed Krarshe's story to the young guardsman. *Is he old enough to be a guard?* Wondered Krarshe, studying the young soldier. *What is he? Fifteen maybe? Either way, he's young. Maybe that's why he's serving at a checkpoint.* Krarshe shrugged and looked back as he waited. He noticed the irritable looks the other merchants were giving him, fanning themselves with their hands or tapping their feet impatiently. While he understood the importance of dealing with the bandit threat, holding up the line like this made the handling of the situation feel poorly managed.

"Right away!" The boy crossed his fist in front of his chest formally in a salute and took off through the city gate.

"Okay," the red-haired guard said, turning back to Krarshe. "It shouldn't be long before they've been brought to justice. Do you have an inventory list? Or, can you tell me what goods you had? Also, if you know where you'll be staying while here, we'll be able to get your goods back to you."

"That won't be necessary," Krarshe said, holding up a hand. "I didn't have much. And, honestly, I was planning to step away from the business of travelling. It's hard to do at this age." The wheat would have probably brought in a good profit, as the conflict had halted any formal trade with Gagerith, the leading grain producer in the region. It was quite lucrative for independent merchants, but was no small feat to get it across the mountains into Remonnet. But he was done with the merchant business, emotionally, and wanted to just cut all ties with it. Frankly, he was too disinterested at this point to want to find a good buyer.

"Very well. Do you grant Her Majesty all rights to the property then?"

Krarshe nodded.

"I guess that's that then. Thank you for reporting this..." The guard looked at the plate again. "Karashee?"

"'Krarshe'," Krarshe corrected.

The guard continued looking at the plate, puzzled. "Karshe?" he attempted, still struggling with the pronunciation. "I'm not sure I've seen a name like this before."

"It's—" Krarshe paused. "I'm from the north."

"Doesn't look Talyrian, and you certainly don't look to be from Dher Molduhr."

"Farther north. Outside of Armia."

The guard looked at Krarshe again, his eyes narrowed, clearly skeptical. He shrugged slightly and returned Krarshe's plate. "Well, wherever you're from, Karshe, enjoy your stay in Remonnet. Make sure you exchange your merchant plate for a civilian plate if you decide to quit the merchant life and settle down here."

"Of course," replied Krarshe, giving up trying to correct the guard's pronunciation and slipping the plate into his robes. "Do try not to die of exhaustion in this heat."

The guard chuckled and nodded to Krarshe. "Next!"

* * *

Krarshe made his way through the huge stone gate into the city. Without goods, he was able to skip past the secondary checks, freeing up potentially hours of his day. The hustle and bustle of it was dizzying, almost nauseatingly so. There were dozens of carts lining the edges of the exaggeratedly wide street. City guards looked through the contents of every cart, looking for contraband, verifying each merchant carried only what their identification plate permitted them to sell. One merchant argued with a guard as one of his barrels was carried away by another pair of guards, likely something in violation of his merchant plate. Another merchant handed a stack of coins to one of the guards, the tax on his goods. All in all, it was a tedious and exhausting process that took far too long. A loose chicken almost flew right into Krarshe as he looked around, followed by its seller almost crashing into him as he chased after it. Krarshe focused on where he was going after that reminder. If there was one good thing about losing his goods, not dealing with all the chaos here was it.

He hastened his pace, not wanting to dally and get run down by a cart. He turned down a side alley, then down another, and finally into the open plaza of Feyfaire; the primary market district in Remonnet.

The plaza was alive with commerce. Vendors called out to passersby and customers haggled with merchants. Novice adventurers tried to make their case to veteran armorers. Young apprentices ran to and fro, as they weaved around patrons trying to fulfill their master's demands. Smooth-talking jewelers enticed every young maiden that passed by with charming words and glittering gold. Countless food vendors pushed their wares, as their fires released both alluring sizzling and the most delectable fumes. The myriad of smells from the food stalls hit Krarshe like a great wave, making his mouth water. He hadn't been able to eat since his encounter with the bandits the day before.

Krarshe paused for a moment to think, then shrugged. "Not like I have anywhere to be," he said aloud, not that he could hear himself over the noise that filled the plaza.

He passed stall after stall, appraising the selection. Bean dishes, fruits, vegetables. None of them appealed to Krarshe, not with the growing ferocity of his hunger. As he passed one stall, a large slab of meat was slammed on a table in front of him. After recovering from the shock, he gazed at the slab of meat, glistening enticingly.

"You rook rike yer crayvin' somethin' hearty."

Krarshe reluctantly redirected his gaze to the man behind the table. Staring back at him was a large, hulking individual, two large teeth protruded from his underbite, pale green skin. The eyes, though, made Krarshe hesitate to reply; fierce, focused, like a hunter.

Krarshe finally spoke up after what felt like an eternity. "S-sorry, just been a long time since I've met an orc as a vendor. Don't your folk tend to come down here for mercenary work?"

"Yeah," the orc said in his deep, gravelly voice. "Usually. I couldn't deal wif it anymoor, though. This war. It's a roosing fight regardress of who you fight for. No honor in that." He looked down at his hand, lost in thought. When Krarshe was about to interrupt him, he looked back up. "So, you buyin'?"

"Ah, yes. How much will this buy?" Krarshe pulled out his coin pouch and fished out two copper roses and put them on the table.

The orc hacked off a slab of the meat, the table shook with the force of his blade, and handed it over to Krarshe at the end of his large knife. "Enjoy."

Krarshe nodded and took the meat. He wasn't sure what it was. Venison perhaps? He didn't really care, food was food. Walking away from the stall, he tore into his purchase, eager to fill his empty stomach. It was pretty obvious that the orc was a mercenary, but Krarshe was pleasantly surprised by his skill with cooking as the meat's juices spread the succulent flavor throughout his mouth.

After feverishly finishing his food, Krarshe knew he had to find lodgings. Ideally, he'd be able to get into a nearby inn before they filled up. He wasn't keen on travelling all the way to South Bank for somewhere affordable, and wasn't really interested in smelling fish all night. He could always cross over to Stormbridge, but those prices were exorbitant. Not quite as bad as Castle Ward, but he now had to think economically. His money would likely last a while, but not if he was spending forty silver roses per night. A place in Feyfaire was his only real option.

Once again, he found himself hurrying through the plaza, wiping his greasy hand on his robes. As he was looking around, trying to recall which inn was closest to the plaza, he felt a force slam into him, knocking him to the ground. "*Krun!*" Krarshe grunted as he made contact with the hard stone street.

"Armand!"

Krarshe saw a boy in a white jacket run over. Rubbing the back of his head after hitting it against the cobblestone, he looked down at what hit him and saw another child in matching attire.

"Guh," the boy on top of him grunted, lifting himself off Krarshe. "Curses upon you, you dreg! Watch out!"

I'm at fault?! Krarshe thought. He pulled himself up to a seated position. Getting a better look at them, maybe "boy" wasn't right. They looked to be in their teens, though he couldn't be sure. Judging ages wasn't a skill he was particularly good at. Maybe around the same age as that young guardsman from before. What he was good at though was noticing small details.

"Remonnet Magic Academy?" he said, reading the emblems on their jackets.

The second boy, who he could only assume was the rushed one's friend, nodded. "Sorry about that. We're just trying to buy our spellbooks before they run out."

"Yeah, and we're going to miss them if we keep sitting around here!" barked the boy, Armand. He stood up, bowed the briefest of apologies, and took off into the plaza, nearly knocking over a vendor carrying a stack of boxes.

"Armand!" the other boy yelled out. He let out a sigh, bowed to Krarshe, and ran after his friend.

Krarshe watched them disappear into the crowd. He wasn't aware that there was a magic academy in the city, though he wasn't surprised. Being the capital of the Remonnet province, it would be strange if it DIDN'T have one.

"Oh, curses," Krarshe exclaimed, remembering he was in a rush himself. He jumped to his feet and took off into the streets of Feyfaire.

* * *

Krarshe flopped into his bed. He managed to find a room in the Five Barrel Inn, but it wasn't as cheap as he was hoping for. Eight silver roses a night, but it did include a meal. Better than the alternatives. He rolled over on the lump-filled mattress and stared at the ceiling, the din of the streets fading away alongside his quieting mind until he was unsure if there were still people outside.

What now? He wondered.

He raised his hand toward the wooden ceiling, studying it, noticing each wrinkle. He curled his hand into a fist, one finger at a time as the joints cracked as each pulled itself into his palm. He thought back on his day. The sweaty guard at the gate, the orc merchant... That delicious meat.

And that brat who ran into him.

Krarshe sat up abruptly. Those kids. The emblem on their jackets. A magic academy. Yes, studying magic. He couldn't become a guard, he had no interest in working for any faction. He was just a merchant, not a role he wanted to play again. The thought of selling the same products time and again, to the same people time and again. No. But, to learn spellcasting. Yes, this was it. He was already acquainted with magic; it was part of his life before setting out on his own, but he didn't know how people here used it. If he became a mage he could have dealt with those bandits. He might have stood out a bit as a spellcaster, but not enough to cause a stir. No more than an adventurer at least. He'd just blend in with the other mages from around here.

This was perfect. Not only did it sound interesting, but it also would help him down the road. And it was another facet of life in this world he wanted desperately to see and explore.

19

Krarshe pulled his boots back on. If they were buying spellbooks, then it must be a new term. He shifted his foot in his boots until it felt that they were on properly and dashed out of his room. Downstairs, he weaved between the empty dining tables and cut across the room to the front desk.

"Excuse me!" he called out, trying to get the attention of the innkeeper.

"Yes-yes," called a voice from the back room. Out stepped the plump form of the innkeeper's wife. Her round, soft-featured face gave a warm smile as she dried her hands on her apron and approached the counter. "What can I help you with?"

"I was just wondering if you could tell me where the Remonnet Magic Academy is," Krarshe asked hurriedly. He knew it probably wasn't in Feyfaire. Probably in Castle Ward, or maybe even all the way in Stormbridge. Hopefully not, as it'd probably be too far to make it there at this time of day. And, judging by the rush of those two kids earlier, classes would probably be starting soon. If he missed the chance to enter now, he'd have to wait for longer than his finances would allow.

"The academy? It's over in Castle Ward. Just head toward the castle's plaza, then turn down the east main street."

"Thank you!" Krarshe gave a slight bow.

"You better hurry, it's getting late."

Krarshe didn't say anything in response. He quickly waved a hand in acknowledgement and ran out the front entrance.

Krarshe ran through the busy streets, nimbly evading fellow pedestrians. He chuckled a bit to himself, seeing the astonished faces of those he ran past. *Must not be used to such an old man being this quick on his feet,* he thought. Admittedly, it was likely pretty strange, and he knew he'd exhaust himself much quicker, but he didn't care. He had a mission, and the gawking of strangers wasn't going to faze him.

He made it to the plaza just outside the walls of the castle in what must have been record time. Krarshe took a moment to try to catch his breath as he surveyed the quiet square. He'd only been here a handful of times, and there were numerous streets leaving the plaza. Unlike the ever-busy streets of Feyfaire's markets, there appeared to only be a few individuals mulling about here. The sunlight was beginning to stretch down the street from the west, reaching through the center of the cobblestone plaza, casting long shadows that grew ever so slowly. He had to hurry. He found the widest street heading east and guessed it was the one the innkeeper's wife was speaking of. Not having time to think on it more, he sped down it.

He continued running down it for a few minutes, passing numerous homes as well as a sparse few high-end stores which were already closed for the day. Gradually, Krarshe's dash slowed to a jog. He began to second guess himself, seeing nothing but small houses of what he assumed were wealthy merchants and lesser nobles. Finally, he came to a full stop and tried to assess his whereabouts. There were a few well-dressed men across the street who watched him quietly. Him, a disheveled old man, wearing his old cotton merchant robes. He suddenly felt very out of place as one of the gentlemen leaned in toward the other, clearly whispering something, eyes fixed on Krarshe.

Krarshe took a deep breath, brushed the long stray hairs from his face and called out to them. "Hello sirs! Perhaps one of you two gentlemen could lend this old man some assistance!"

The man who was whispering to the other stood upright. "Hail! What could I do for you?"

At least he seems nice? Krarshe thought to himself as he walked within talking distance. As he approached, the gentlemen backed up slightly, trying to hide their repulsion. *Maybe not.* "I was looking for the magic academy. Perhaps you could give me directions?"

"Of course. Continue down this road. At the next street on your right, its gates should be in view," said one of the noblemen, pointing down the street.

Krarshe gave an exaggerated bow. "Thank you ever so kindly. You have saved this man this day." Oddly enough, like bandits, rich folk like to be made to feel important.

"Yes, yes, we were happy to be of assistance. Now, we must be on our way," said the gentleman with a slight bow, more of a nod. The two men continued down the street, perhaps a bit faster than they had previously. Krarshe watched them briefly, wondering why they seemed in such a hurry to get away from him. He lifted his arm slightly and sniffed.

"Mmm, maybe that was it," Krarshe said with a laugh. "I should have probably washed myself off a bit, it's been a hot few days…"

Not much he could do about it now. Knowing how close he was, Krarshe decided to walk the rest of the way. The sun had just perched itself atop the city walls, so he should have plenty of time. Plus, running into the academy, panting and tired, would probably garner similar reactions as those of the nobles. Perhaps worse. People, he found, hold first impressions very important. Too bad the smell was unavoidable. He'd just have to not get too close to them.

Krarshe turned the corner and, nearly immediately, stood before a great iron gate which bore the same design as on those boys' emblem: a staff with a thorny rose coiling up it, along with the words Remonnet Magic Academy split between the top and bottom of the emblem. He let out a sigh of relief and walked in.

The academy wasn't much to look at, once past the grand gate. It consisted mostly of one large, unassuming building. A few large windows dotted the walls, but it was too dark to see in. It also had a smaller, connected building jutting out toward the entrance. There appeared to be a large open-air enclosure attached to the back of the building, walled in with stone and plaster over twice the height of a human. There were also a couple smaller buildings within its walls, but nothing that impressive. One of them had what appeared to be a large smokestack protruding from it, and the other had numerous smaller windows that appeared to be on two floors. None of the other buildings appeared to be in use, or open to the public, so he walked around while looking for a place he could inquire about enrollment.

This is a lot more desolate than I expected, Krarshe mused, walking through the bleak, barren stone enclosure.

As he made his way toward the large, central building, he passed the smaller attached building. Inside, he saw a young human girl standing behind a counter, clothed in similar garb to those two boys from the market. Walking in, Krarshe saw numerous items lining the walls and shelves. He walked through the maze of items, gawking at the sheer quantity. Scrolls, staves, wands, armor, clothing, alchemical equipment, and things so alien to him that Krarshe wasn't even sure what they were or how to describe them accurately. Krarshe guessed that the academy ran this store, likely leveraging their expertise to sell magical equipment. Perhaps employing the students helped them pay their tuition fees. After all, it wasn't uncommon when he was travelling to see students and apprentices pay for their mercantile education with labor.

"M-may I h-help you?" stammered a small, fragile voice from behind him. Krarshe turned to see the girl had stepped out from behind the counter and snuck up on him.

"Oh, I'm not looking to buy. Sorry," responded Krarshe. She looked down slightly, seemingly dejected. "B-but, you could answer a question for me." At this, she perked up again, *How strange people are,* he thought.

"Absolutely!" she said excitedly, before quickly shrinking back to her timid self. "W-what k-kind of question d-did you have?" She didn't appear comfortable dealing with customers, but desperately wanted to be helpful. He thought he saw her shoot a glance toward the store counter, but he wasn't sure.

"When do classes begin for the year?" Krarshe asked. "Or, rather, when is the deadline for enrollment?"

The girl stared at Krarshe blankly, her eyelashes catching the few strands of chestnut-colored hair that hung as bangs in front of her face. "E-excuse me?"

Did she not understand Krarshe's question? As he was about to respond, she spoke up again.

"I'm s-sorry," she said, brushing the bangs out of her face to free her eyelashes, to no effect. "I just didn't expect that question." She laughed awkwardly. "Enr-rollment ends tomorrow evening."

"Fantastic!" Krarshe's excitement startled the meek girl. "Where could I enroll?"

Another blank stare. This was getting old. "U-umm..." she stuttered, bringing her hand up to her lip pensively.

"Aren't you a bit old to be enrolling in this academy?" came a sharp remark from behind the counter. Krarshe turned to see a man step out from the back of the shop. His appearance was as sharp as his tongue: jet black hair pulled back into a ponytail revealing his receding hairline, tall, thin in face and body, his nose almost as pointed as his chin. Everything was sharp and clean, save for his long, unkempt eyebrows.

Whoa, those eyebrows... Krarshe tried not to focus on them too much. He cleared his throat. "Is that a problem?"

"We expect a lot from our students," he said, placing, almost slamming, a book onto the counter as he made his way out from behind it. "I don't think a man of your age would be able to handle it, is all," the man scoffed. "And I don't allow naps during my lectures. Not even for my elders." He grinned mockingly.

Krarshe looked over to the girl from before. She was looking down, staring at her feet. She looked terrified of this man. Or maybe she just wasn't sure what to do in this situation. He felt a bit bad for her, as she had tried earnestly to help him, and this supposed teacher was stomping all over that effort.

Krarshe took the hint. "I see, my apologies." He sighed. "I guess I missed my chance, eh?" He let out a laugh, and glanced over to see the girl smiling gently, with a tinge of pity.

Having diffused the situation a bit, Krarshe said, "Thank you for your assistance, young miss." He made sure to emphasize those last two words, making clear that he was addressing the young girl alone, disregarding the teacher. He bowed deeply to her, causing her to nearly stumble while trying to bow back to him. As Krarshe turned to leave, he thought he caught a glimpse of a sneer on her instructor's face, clearly bitter about being ignored. Krarshe couldn't help but smile.

* * *

Krarshe walked leisurely back to the inn. "Too old, huh?" he muttered to himself. After a long pause, he continued, "Well, I guess that leaves me with few options. I'll do it better this time. I learned a lot from this first go at it."

As he entered Feyfaire, he turned down an alley he knew to have several clothing stores. The sun was all but down now and the street lamps were beginning to be lit, so he wouldn't be able to be picky. He made his way through the still-busy streets of the trade district and stepped into the first clothing store that appeared to be satisfactory and approached who appeared to be the last employee still working at this time.

"Excuse me, I was wondering if you had any clothing for young men here."

The man looked up from the shirt he was mending. "Certainly, just a moment." He placed the shirt down and hurried over to Krarshe. "What are you looking for?"

"Nothing special. A shirt, pants, shoes, the necessities, basically."

"You said for a young man?"

Krarshe nodded.

"Do you know anything more? I wouldn't want to sell you something that won't fit the boy."

"Ah, yes. Sorry," Krarshe apologized. "About this tall, this wide." Krarshe gestured with his hands. Judging by the puzzled look on the tailor's face, maybe he didn't explain it well enough. "I-is... Does that make sense? I'm sorry, I'm not sure how else to explain this."

The man smiled. "It's a bit tough to estimate, but I think I can provide you with what you're looking for. Maybe for certainty, we'll err on the larger side. Better to be loose than not fit at all," he said with a laugh. Krarshe joined him with a chuckle.

The man went to the shelves in the store and started combing through the piles of shirts before pulling one out. It appeared to be a plain white, or perhaps off-white, linen shirt. He held it up, evaluating it before draping it over his shoulder. He repeated the process with additional shirts and pants before bringing them over to Krarshe for judgment.

After inspecting the selection, Krarshe holding each one up, feeling the texture of the material and giving them a tug to test the stitching, he settled on a few basic pieces of clothing. The shoes were a bit more difficult, as there was no way to try them on to judge feel and the employee wasn't a cobbler, leaving him unable to discuss them in detail, so Krarshe just chose one that seemed to be in the best condition. In all, it cost thirty-eight silver roses. Not bad for a complete set of clothing, let alone ones that were this durable.

By the time he finished his purchases, the sun had set completely, and the night crowd now filled the streets. Many of the stores began closing shop for the night, and some of the less-savory street vendors began to set up shop. People were beginning to get rowdy. Makeshift outdoor taverns were setting up boxes and stools to serve as tables. A few men staggered through the streets, clearly having been drinking for a while now and not looking to stop yet. He watched one of them make a pass at a woman setting up the makeshift tavern, only to be smacked hard enough to be knocked to the ground. His buddies just laughed at him. Another two men were getting into a heated argument, the premise unknown to Krarshe. Before he knew it, a fight had broken out between the two. Everyone just cleared the way for them, egging them on, booze in hand. The streets of Feyfaire at night were no place for the faint of heart.

He heard one vendor yelling over the noise of the crowd about some cheap food. Speaking of food, dinner would probably be finishing up back at the inn, so if he didn't want to have to pay for another meal at a street vendor, he'd have to hurry back. Gathering the clothes firmly in his arms, he rushed to the inn while trying his best to avoid the rowdy crowds.

* * *

Krarshe made his way down the street toward the academy, carrying a burlap sack with the clothes he bought the night before. He looked around, searching for the perfect spot. He found a small back alley that appeared to have a small alcove, out away from the street. He checked once more to see if there was anyone watching him, but the streets were silent, nothing to disturb the morning mist floating gently above the ground.

He stole down the alleyway and went into the alcove. He noticed a cat, lounging on a box at the back of the alley. At his approach, the cat opened an eye sleepily and yawned.

A witness! Thought Krarshe with a grin.

He took a deep breath and closed his eyes. He focused, thinking, visualizing.

An elf, he thought. *It's probably less work down the road.*

"Hmm..." he said, thinking harder.

Male, definitely male. His mind wandered for a brief moment back to the attack with the bandits. *I'm not sure how it would go otherwise. Young, maybe seventy? Or eighty? Let's just split the difference and go with seventy-five.*

He opened his eyes for a moment, inspecting the shoes he bought the night before, and closing them once again. Krarshe continued his visualization for a minute.

Krarshe exhaled, and nodded. "Okay. No turning back, Krarshe," he said to himself, keeping his eyes closed.

Krarshe breathed deeply again.

At that moment, a bright light filled the alcove. The cat awoke with a fright, crying out before taking off down the alleyway.

A moment later, a handsome young man, an elf, stepped out of the alley. His unkempt blond hair shone bright in the morning light with an almost blue hue, his eyes a deep vibrant blue. He tugged at his clothes, and looked down at them. "Not bad," he said, admiring them. "They feel as nice as I thought they would, and fit well enough. Except these shoes." He looked down as his foot shifted in the shoe as he kicked the toe against the stone pavement. He checked the worn-out robes in the burlap sack he carried. Digging around in them, he pulled out his leather coin pouch and stuffed it in the pocket of his pants.

"Okay," he said proudly. "Let's go to school."

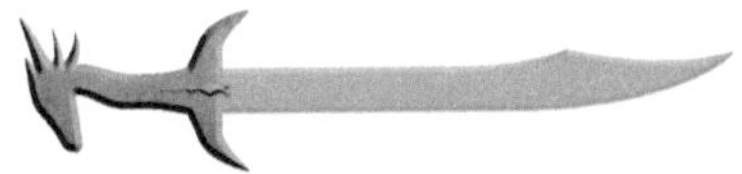

CHAPTER 2

Krarshe walked through the gates of the academy just as the morning sun crept over the city walls and spilled into the corner of the academy's barren stone courtyard. He never found out where to go for enrollment, but he figured he'd just look around. The store run by the academy was locked, seemingly not open yet. With no other obvious options, Krarshe wandered the school grounds, trying to find someone while not appearing suspicious.

After maybe ten minutes of meandering about, Krarshe saw someone moving about in the store. He made his way over to it as he saw the teacher from the day before open the door from the inside.

"Oh! Good morning," he said when he saw Krarshe. "How may I help you?"

"I wanted to inquire about enrolling in this academy," said Krarshe.

"Enrollment, eh?" the teacher asked, raising an unkempt eyebrow. "Cutting it rather close, classes begin tomorrow."

Krarshe nodded. "I just arrived in the city. The rains last week made the roads difficult to travel."

"This time of year can be difficult, yes. Where do you hail from?"

"Up north. Outside of Armia," Krarshe said, remembering how the guard reacted yesterday.

The teacher looked at him for a moment, seemingly considering Krarshe's response. "... That's quite a journey. What country is it?"

"I'm certain you wouldn't know of it. It's small, and doesn't get much recognition as being an independent kingdom. You could traverse it in a day by foot and not even realize you walked through an entire country," Krarshe said, trying to get off of the topic.

There was a long silence. Krarshe shifted uncomfortably, hoping this wild-eyebrowed man would just let it be.

Finally, the teacher spoke. "Well. As long as you speak the language here in Remonnet, there shouldn't be any issues. And, of course, that you have accepted currency for the tuition."

Krarshe smiled. "Of course. What is the tuition?"

"Thirty gold roses for the first term," the teacher said flatly. "You'll also need a spellbook and uniform. We can provide these, for an additional fee. While the uniform can only be bought here, you can search for a copy of the spellbook wherever you wish. Also, if you need lodgings, we can provide that as well."

Krarshe was stunned. Thirty gold roses was a staggering amount. Enough for a whole fleet of carts with horses. "H-how much for the—" Krarshe began to ask.

"A spellbook will be an additional five gold roses, the uniform is thirty silver roses, and a room in the dormitory is fifteen gold roses for the whole term." He rattled off the prices as though he had done it a thousand times. Maybe he had.

Krarshe nearly fell over. *This MUST be extortion. He must think I have no concept of money in this kingdom,* he thought. As he was about to speak, he thought he saw a brief smirk on the teacher's face. But, when he took full notice, the teacher had the same serious, stern look he had from the start.

"If you don't have the funds right now, that is fine. You can pay them tomorrow before the class begins. I understand you must be tired from your journey," said the teacher, smiling, a mask of compassion.

"Uhh…" Krarshe wasn't completely in control of his thoughts yet, still unsteady from the shock. He composed himself and responded, "Yes, I'll need to wait until tomorrow to pay. I assume I won't be allowed to attend classes if this debt is still outstanding."

The teacher nodded. "That is correct. Would you like to enroll now then?"

Krarshe breathed deeply, swallowing. "Please."

"This way, then." The teacher gestured with a flourish, his black coat billowing as he turned and outstretched his arm. "Marcus!"

Krarshe spotted a student in the back of the store, carrying a box. He halted, still carrying the box. "Yes, Professor Owyn?"

"Bring me some enrollment papers. Quickly!"

Marcus dropped the box and ran for the back room.

Owyn turned back to Krarshe and again ushered him in. "Do you know how to write?"

"Not in the common language, no. I apologize."

Owyn held up a hand. "No apology needed. It happens quite often with foreign students. Can you read?"

Krarshe nodded. "Well enough." If he wasn't able to, he wouldn't have gotten anywhere as a merchant.

"Very good. I'll handle the writing then, if that's fine." Marcus came back, breathing a little heavy, and handed a piece of parchment to the teacher. Owyn took it to the front counter. Taking a quill from the corner of the counter, he wet it and readied the fine tip just above the top of the page. "Now, if I can just get your name."

"Krarshe."

Owyn's quill touched the page, but froze almost immediately, before even writing the first letter. The ink began to pool on the page before he responded. "Krarshe?"

Krarshe felt his throat tighten slightly, his brow furrowed unconsciously. "Yes," he confirmed. The hesitation after hearing his name was not that uncommon, but this may have been the first time someone pronounced his name properly in the years since he was last home. It was strangely unsettling.

The teacher turned to look at Krarshe. Krarshe kept a straight face, giving no indication of his concern, his blue eyes staring back steadily at the sharp-featured teacher. "Right, Krarshe." He resumed writing. "Any last name?"

"... No, sir."

Once more, the teacher looked at Krarshe, his eyes narrowing slightly. "A commoner, eh?" He turned back to the paper and finished writing. "Rare to see one of you enrolling in our academy."

Krarshe could see why. At thirty gold roses for a single term, excluding all the extras, it would be nearly impossible for commoners to afford it. He wasn't even certain if he, himself, could afford it.

The two of them went over the specifics of the school, rules, rights, and other details of his enrollment. He elected to forgo the dormitory and spellbook. He bought the uniform, as he had the money on hand, and got one that seemed appropriately sized. After what felt like hours, the sun now illuminating nearly the entirety of the courtyard, it was finished.

"And with that, you are officially enrolled," said Owyn with a humorless smile. "Now, do be sure to collect your fees before tomorrow. Classes begin at dawn."

Krarshe nodded. Taking the school uniform he had just purchased, he left the campus.

* * *

"Definitely extortion," Krarshe muttered to himself. "There's no chance I'm staying on the campus. I'd be better off walking here every day. And I'm not spending money on that spellbook. I'll see if I can find a cheap one in Feyfaire." Krarshe continued to fume quietly to himself like some sort of madman. While irked about the ridiculously high price of admission and the resulting barrier to entry, he was largely concerned about his finances. He knew he'd have to find a good rate of exchange on his seals and gerins if he was going to even come close to being able to afford the tuition alone. Bartering was part of his former merchant job, but currencies were a different story entirely. And, as he had just experienced with Owyn, his apparent age made him an easy target for swindlers.

Krarshe paused at the entrance to the plaza in front of the castle. It was mid-morning now, and all of the aristocrats in Castle Ward were scurrying around the plaza, seemingly making themselves look busy to their fellow aristocrats. *What do they do all day?* Krarshe wondered. As he watched the crowd, he noticed a guard near the castle's entrance eyeing him. Krarshe realized he probably looked like a pickpocket scoping out his target. He wasn't that well dressed after all, and it'd be weird for a child to be watching a crowd of nobles and lesser aristocrats. He decided he should probably move on before they took action against him.

He started toward Stormbridge, as it was likely his best bet for a good money changer. Or at least an honest one. Feyfaire had many of them, but most that set up there would undercut anything you brought in. Being the merchant district, there's high demand for money changing, but it resulted in borderline criminal exchange rates. Castle Ward probably had a few, but they often dealt with nobility. The chances of them taking a child seriously were slim, and it was almost guaranteed he'd be accused of stealing it. And South Bank... Well, he'd more likely be robbed before he even arrived at the broker.

"Ugh..." Krarshe groaned. It was a long way to Stormbridge, a trek he wasn't looking forward to. He was even less excited to come all the way back to Feyfaire for another inn. "This is becoming more of a hassle than I had anticipated." Not wanting to drag this out any more than he had to, he picked up the pace.

As he made his way west toward the river, he noticed Castle Ward was very clean. Feyfaire always had a bit of garbage lying around, but you could mistake Castle Ward for an abandoned city if it wasn't for the high-class citizenry meandering around. He saw some noble women in dresses far too elaborate to be comfortable, looking at jewelry in the window of a store, ridiculing the shabby craftsmanship of it. He passed two well-dressed men, commenting on the state of the ongoing war. Based on what he could catch as he passed by, the queen of Remonnet was meeting with someone from Talyra, and the men didn't sound too happy about it. These aristocrats really did meander around this district endlessly.

Seriously, what DO they do all day?

Before he knew it, Krarshe was able to see the Silver River's banks. The river cut right through Remonnet, with Castle Ward, Feyfaire, and South Bank on its southeastern shore, and Stormbridge on its northwest. From where he stood, he could see the great stone arches of Stormbridge, from which the district got its name. Despite supposedly being hundreds of years old, the bridge was in nearly perfect condition. Krashe wasn't sure if it was because of manual maintenance or if it was protected by magic, but its care was of utmost importance. It was perhaps the biggest, most well-known landmark in Remonnet.

The bridge was fairly busy as Krarshe began to cross it. Carts rolled down the middle of the bridge, bringing food from the farmlands outside Stormbridge, or carrying finished goods to be sold in Feyfaire. The outer edges of the bridge were filled with pedestrians; some carried sacks, filled with smaller trinkets to sell at a street stall, while others just appeared to be travellers making the long trip to and from the trade district. Krarshe stopped to peer over the low stone wall of the bridge, looking down at the water. Some fishing boats floated by with their hauls, heading toward South Bank. Even well over a hundred feet from the water, he could see the size of the catch they had. Krarshe's stomach growled. *I'll have to have some fish later,* he thought, his stomach growled thinking about one of his favorite dishes.

As Krarshe neared the end of the bridge, he caught the smell of smoke and the distant sound of metal clanging. Separated from Castle Ward, the northern part of Stormbridge housed most of the industrial production. The southern half of Stormbridge, however, was residential and commercial. All things considered, this was probably Krarshe's favorite district of Remonnet. He just wished the inns here weren't so expensive. He made his way toward the financial district in Stormbridge, where he was likely to find a money changer. It didn't take long to find one near the bridge. If people came from Feyfaire looking for a better rate, this would be the first spot in Stormbridge they'd come to. This business had prime real estate, and thus likely wouldn't have survived if it cheated its customers. Krarshe opened the door, the chiming of the bell welcoming him in.

"I'm in th' back! Gimme justa moment, eh?" a hidden voice called out from past a door behind the counter.

Krarshe slowly walked in and headed toward the counter. Even though it was near midday, there were numerous candles illuminating the room. In the light, the place seemed dusty, and the room was eerily quiet, a sharp contrast to all the noise from the nearby industry. He saw a scale on the counter and a pile of stones cut into precise blocks. There was a large tome opened next to a quill. Peeking at it, Krarshe saw a bunch of numbers scribbled down at weird angles all over the page. The writing was too messy to read, and too scattered to follow what it was for.

"What can I do for yeh?" asked a voice, startling Krarshe. It was an older man, largely bald, with a few stray long hairs from the sides brushed over the bald spot. His scraggly, pointed beard and mustache were as white as the rest of his hair, save for a dark streak down the length of his beard. He slowly stroked his beard, demonstrating how it had grown accustomed to its shape, as his tired, gentle eyes quietly evaluated Krarshe through a small pair of eyeglasses.

Krarshe cleared his throat. "I'd like to exchange these for roses," he said as he pulled out the seventeen copper gerins and placed them on the counter.

"Seventeen copper gerins? Let's see..." He picked them up and looked at them carefully, holding one between his wrinkled fingers as he studied it. He then picked up his quill, wet it, and began scribbling on the book, seemingly starting wherever the tip hit the paper. "That'd be... Umm... And current rate..." he muttered, speaking his thoughts as he wrote. The broker paused for a minute, bringing the quill tip to his lip as ink dripped down it to his chin and followed the black streak in his beard. Krarshe's face contorted a bit in concern before twisting itself into a stifled smile at the peculiarity of the old man.

"I can give yeh thirty-eight copper roses," he said finally, punctuating the page with a large drop of ink. He looked back to Krarshe.

"That's fair," Krarshe said, nodding. "Could I also exchange this?" He took out a single gold Imperial seal and pressed it into the counter.

The broker snatched it up not a moment after Krarshe took his finger off the large gold coin. "I-is this... An Imperial gold seal?" He looked it over several times, turning it over, rolling it between his old, ink-stained fingers. The large gold coin shown brightly in the light, the series of interwoven triangles and concentric circles, all encircled by a serpentine design emblazoned upon its surface glinted in the sunlight. He went down behind the counter and came back up with a small trinket. He put it up to his eye, revealing the lens it had, and looked at the coin through it.

A minute passed before he finally spoke again. "Where'd yeh find this?" he asked as he looked at Krarshe inquisitively.

Krarshe saw this question coming. Imperial seals were rare, much less a gold one. "My father was a travelling merchant. He came across it during his travels, and held on to them in case he ever found himself in dire need." Seemed believable enough.

The old man pursed his lips, not having a counter remark he could respond with. He placed the seal back on the counter and ran to the back room. Krarshe heard a crash of books and boxes, followed by more noises as he rummaged through the back room. Finally, he came back, covered in dust and dirt. He blew off the cover of a book he carried and opened it up. He flipped through the pages, scanning them for a minute before he finally stopped. His long, thin finger pointed and slid across the page as he read and mumbled the words, taking quick glances at the coin through the small lens.

He put the lens down and closed the book. "This," he started, "this is, undoubtedly, an Imperial seal. Doesn't 'pear to be a forg'ry neither." He stroked his beard again, tugging on it slightly as he thought.

Krarshe stood there, awaiting a response that never seemed to come, just silence. This long silence went on for several minutes. The broker began pacing slowly, staring at the floor as he tugged on his beard. Every so often, he'd stop and look as though he were about to say something, only to continue his pacing. Pacing, stopping, pacing, pausing, beard-tugging. This dance seemed to continue for an eternity.

Krarshe was getting impatient. "Umm... Excuse me?" he called out, raising a hand meekly, almost afraid to break his concentration.

The broker stopped, and turned to Krarshe. "Fifteen gold roses," he said bluntly. His eyes weren't the soft, gentle eyes that Krarshe saw before, but cold, hard eyes of a businessman.

This was way more than Krarshe expected. He knew that Imperial seals were rare, but this exchange rate was hugely in

Krarshe's favor. And, this was likely after the broker attempted to make a better deal for himself.

"Is this the rate for each of them?" Krarshe asked.

The old man froze. "E-each?" he asked, stammering.

Krarshe pulled out two more of the gold seals. As he put them on the counter, the old man's eyes grew wide, his mouth fell open. Krarshe looked up at him, snapping him out of his trance.

He cleared his throat. "Y-yes. Well." He paused and sighed. The broker nodded slowly, surrendering. "Yes, fifteen gold roses for each." He chuckled slightly. "Would've done less if I knew yeh had more. Clever lad," he said with a smile.

Krarshe returned the smile. "Well, then if I could get those forty-five gold roses."

"Of course," he said, as he returned to the back room. "Anything else I can do for yeh, mah lordship?" he called back in jest.

"I think that would be all," replied Krarshe, as he began to pace around the room casually. He looked out the window, watching people and carts alike begin their journey across Stormbridge. He heard a few coins hit the wooden floor, followed by a "Five curses!" and a groan as the broker crouched to pick them up.

"Actually," started Krarshe, "I have a question."

Another groan of relief. "Certainly."

"Why are these Imperial seals at such a high rate? Not that I'm complaining." Krarshe smiled.

"A bit of a silly question, eh? Prolly because they're not minted anymore," said the broker, still shuffling around in the back. "Not since the empire collapsed nearly a century ago. They were the only ones who knew the process. Not like yeh can use normal forgin' methods." Krarshe heard some clinking from the back room. "The design makes forg'ries real hard, wi' that level of precise detail."

"Oh... I wasn't aware," Krarshe said, slowly, rubbing the back of his neck bashfully through his blonde hair.

The broker came back to the front room, dropping a sack on the counter with a clink. He raised an eyebrow. "Yer a strange one, lad. Yeh been kept locked up or something?"

The two laughed.

"Well, thank you for enlightening me," Krarshe said.

The old man nodded and said, "Of course! And thank yeh for gracing me with riches."

Krarshe tied the sack to his belt and went back out into the city.

* * *

"Three 'na half gold roses."

Krarshe stared at the merchant blankly. *What is this outrageous price?!* He thought. He looked at the spellbook, the last copy he could find anywhere in Feyfaire. The leather-bound tome looked to weigh several pounds, nearly as big as the crate the street merchant used as a counter, and had a strange collection of symbols stitched into its cover. He had no idea what it said, but the merchant assured him it was the book the academy used. *For this price, I wouldn't be surprised if I'm being deceived... No way this is worth three gold and five hundred silver,* Krarshe thought. His experience told him not all merchants were honest.

"C'mon, boy. 's almost time ta close shop," the merchant said, looking toward the sun as it crept down closer to the top of the city walls. His hairy arms twitched and flexed their large muscles as he rhythmically tapped the crate impatiently with his index and middle fingers.

He was right, it was getting late, and Krarshe still hadn't secured any lodgings. The idea of buying this ridiculously priced book bothered him though and he just couldn't bring himself to pull out his coin purse.

A hand slammed down on the makeshift counter from

behind Krarshe. "Sold!" Krarshe looked back to see a teenage boy with short, messy brown hair behind him. The curls and waves of his hair accentuated the freckling on his youthful face. Krarshe wasn't entirely certain, but the boy appeared to be slightly shorter than himself and similarly slim. Removing his hand from the table, Krarshe saw a pile of rose coins.

"Ah-ha! Fantastic!" shouted the merchant with a grin. "See? That's how ya need'a be!" The merchant handed the boy the tome. "Well, I oughta be a closing up. Wish ya luck, lad," he said to Krarshe as he began to collect the few wares he still had.

Krarshe turned to glare at the sudden customer who stole his prize out from under him, his face not hiding the scorn he felt. The boy, despite what he did, seemed remorseless, his face maintaining its innocence.

"Are you also a student of the academy?" he asked.

Krarshe looked down at the book in the boy's hands. "Yeah..." He was still too frustrated to look at him in the face.

"Sorry, sorry. I didn't mean to take it out from under a fellow new student." The boy's face remained jovial. "Perhaps we can share the book? What's your name?"

"Krarshe," he muttered.

"Karsh? What an odd name," the boy said with a smile. "My name's Tibault. Pleasure to meet you." Tibault reached his hand out.

Reluctantly, Krarshe took his hand and shook. *He's as innocent as his face,* he thought, frustrated that he couldn't maintain his anger. He disregarded the mispronunciation.

"You have to be one of the only elves attending this academy. Do your parents hold land in Remonnet?"

Krarshe shook his head. "No."

"Surely you can't be from Thalas'anir, right?" Tibault asked, pressing Krarshe for an answer.

"N-no. I'm from the north. Outside of Armia."

"Oh, okay. Seems strange that you'd be sent this far for schooling. Are there no other academies up north?"

Krarshe was growing tired of this interrogation. He needed to find lodgings soon, and this was eating up his precious time. He decided to try and force the issue and started walking down the street, slow enough for Tibault to follow, but quickly enough to convey that Krarshe had somewhere to be.

"I wasn't sent down here, actually. I came here by choice." Krarshe looked to see if Tibault was following him, which he was. *Must be the talkative sort. Not inherently bad, but always tiresome.* "I decided to enroll on a spur of the moment."

"R-really? That must be a first!" Tibault laughed. "I don't know anyone who enrolls in this academy by choice. My parents forced me, personally. 'You will not shame the Dumont name!'" Tibault mimicked, wagging a finger like one scolds a child. He laughed even harder than he did before. "You see, my family... I come from a family of mages. If I didn't go, they'd probably disown me." Tibault stopped walking for a moment. "Probably if I fail too," he said solemnly, barely above a whisper. Krarshe couldn't tell in the dimming light that illuminated the street what kind of expression Tibault wore, but he thought he saw a slight flicker of concern in his brown eyes.

"Well! I'll just have to not fail, right?" Tibault, back to his happy self, laughed again, running his hand through his curly brown hair as if to comb away his somber thoughts.

Krarshe and Tibault walked in silence for a while. The sun was all but set, and the street lamps had almost all been lit. The raucous night crowds would be out soon. He heard a yell behind him and turned to see Tibault on the ground, the spellbook falling to the ground opened.

"Curses, I hate Feyfaire. The stones here are so uneven," Tibault said, rubbing his knee.

Krarshe reached out a hand to help him up. "Yeah, the streets here are especially dangerous at night, and not just from the people. I've certainly received my share of scrapes and bruises." Tibault took his hand and stood up. While he dusted himself off and checked for any injuries, Krarshe went and picked up the spellbook. He flipped through a few of the dingy, yellowed pages. They were filled with strange symbols and characters he didn't recognize. "What language is this?"

Tibault made a few forceful blows against his pants and looked up. "Honestly, I don't know. I hope they'll teach us how to read this, or I'm in trouble."

"We BOTH would be," Krarshe corrected. The two laughed.

"All I know," Tibault started, "is that it's whatever language the spells are in."

"They're not in the common tongue either?"

Tibault shook his head. "Certainly not. Again, I don't know what language it is, but whenever I've heard my parents cast spells, I can't understand a word of it. They won't say what it is either."

Krarshe closed the spellbook and studied the stitched characters on the cover again before handing the book back to Tibault.

"Well, I should be going. It's a long way to Castle Ward," said Tibault.

"Are you staying in the dormitory?"

"No, no. That place is ridiculously expensive. It'd be a mistake for anyone to stay there. I think only those from wealthy families outside the capital stay there. Mostly nobles, you know? My family lives in Castle Ward."

"Oh, you're one of those aristocrats," Krarshe said. *That would explain the lack of hesitation buying the book. Rich folk.*

"I mean, my father is a lesser noble, barely worth acknowledging. We only received a title in the past couple generations. But yeah, I guess so," Tibault said with a shrug.

"Never would have guessed."

"Most of the students at this academy are. The academy has a reputation for being very prestigious," stated Tibault.

"Is that why the prices are so high?" Krarshe asked.

"Are they? I wouldn't know, actually... I've only heard from others how ridiculous the dormitory is," Tibault admitted as he looked away, clearly averting his gaze from Krarshe. "Wait. Did YOU pay by yourself?"

Krarshe nodded.

"Wow. That's incredible. You're not a noble, and you paid for it yourself?" Tibault shook his head in disbelief.

So the prices WERE exorbitant, Krarshe thought. *Perhaps it's intentional as a barrier to entry for commoners?*

Tibault interrupted Krarshe's thoughts. "I really must be going. My parents would be furious if they knew I was still in Feyfaire at this time."

Krarshe looked around. The night crowd was in full swing, with drinking, gambling, fighting, and the like. "Yeah, you better get home. Again, Feyfaire can be pretty dangerous at night." A roar from the masses erupted as a drunken fist fight began. "For multiple reasons..."

Tibault watched the two burly men across the street exchange blows for a minute. "Yeah. Well, Kash, I'll see you in school tomorrow," he said with a toothy smile.

Krarshe nodded as Tibault ran north, disregarding that the pronunciation was getting worse. "Now," he said, "I have to find an inn."

As Krarshe headed toward the city walls in hopes of finding a cheaper inn away from the central plaza, he thought back on the spellbook. What language was that? The fact that the son of a mage family wasn't sure means it must not be a language most people use. Whatever it was, it was clearly not talked about publicly. Krarshe continued to think on it as he walked through the dimly lit streets of Feyfaire.

* * *

The inn's dining hall was abuzz with the drinking crowd. Bottles clinked and mugs clomped on the wooden tables as guests made merry the night with the assistance of ale. Krarshe sat quietly at his table, awaiting his food. Because of his time with Tibault, he ended up having to put off his dinner until all but the most dedicated drinkers remained in the hall. He ended up having to settle on The Easy Lute, one of the less-known inns in Feyfaire, but a high quality one. The price reflected that too, at seventeen silver roses a night for two meals, a private room, and a hot wash basin brought to the room every day. Krarshe was mildly put off by the price, but it wasn't all bad. It helped that he was able to negotiate a discount for an extended stay, so he wasn't paying full price.

A bard was playing to the side of the room, strumming a lute, likely what gave the inn its name. Based on his familiarity with the other inn staff and several of the patrons, Krarshe assumed he was either an employee or a regular musician. He began reciting the opening verse *The Five Curses*, one of the more common songs he'd encountered in Armia, when a voice came from behind him.

"Your food, sir," said the waitress, placing his plate of pork, beans, and some sort of green vegetable that Krarshe wasn't sure what it was. Some kind of local produce, he guessed. They had sold all of the fish Krarshe had wanted so badly this afternoon, so he had settled on this. He looked at his plate disappointingly only for a moment before looking at the waitress. She had dark brown eyes that matched her dark brown hair, which was pulled back into a ponytail and secured by a small red ribbon. Her smile was enough to warm the heart of any weary traveller. This certainly made up for the lack of fish and extra cost for the inn.

"Thank y—" Krarshe started before being interrupted by a crash. He and the waitress looked over to see another waitress, a catfolk, quickly trying to pick up the dropped mugs and clean up the broken bottle. Her orange ears, tipped with white, drooped slightly atop her short orange-red hair, clearly distraught over her mistake. Her orange tail, touched at the end with white like her ears, hung low, curled behind her as she crouched down.

"Oh! Na'kika, wait. Let me help you with that," Krarshe's waitress said, running over to the catfolk girl. He watched the two of them clean up the mess as the room returned to its cheery atmosphere. The catfolk Na'kika continued to look sullen, her tail and ears giving away her emotions.

Krarshe took a bite of his pork while he watched. It wasn't the best food he'd had, but it would do. *It was worth the price to be served by such pretty girls,* he thought. He shook his head at his own thoughts, trying to dismiss the charm they had cast upon him.

His waitress returned to the table as Na'kika took the mugs and shards of the broken bottle into the back. "I'm sorry about that," she said, slightly out of breath.

"Not at all. Was she okay?" Krarshe asked. "She seemed troubled."

"Yeah, she'll be fine. She's new, and isn't used to making mistakes. They'll happen, so it's a lesson that'll be good for her to learn."

"Indeed," Krarshe said. "It seems her ears and tail do most of the talking for her."

The waitress' expression changed, more sullen than Krarshe was expecting. "She..." She looked around, and then leaned in closer to Krarshe. "She lost her tongue, actually. Apparently her village was raided by some mercenaries on their way to Rolith. Most of the villagers were killed, her parents included."

Krarshe was horrified. He knew there was a war going on, but this savagery was as bad as the bandits. Maybe worse. "But why would they take her tongue?"

"I'm not sure, to be honest. She doesn't talk about what happened much, not that she can. She usually tries to communicate with gestures, but specific details are hard. She doesn't know how to read or write either, being from a small village." The waitress sighed, bringing her hand to her cheek as she wistfully watched Na'kika bring another few mugs and bottle out. "Maybe it's because of how important their tongues are. You know, with how catfolk show affection through licking," she whispered to Krarshe, even quieter than before, to the point where he could barely hear her over the roar of the room. "I don't know, honestly. It's cruel, whatever the reason. And to such a sweet girl."

Krarshe wasn't sure how to respond. He just quietly watched the catfolk girl nimbly make her way through the busy dining hall. Aside from the mishap a moment ago, she was quite agile, a trait very common among catfolk. At least, from what he had heard.

"Well, if there's anything else you need, just let me or Na'kika know," said his waitress, flashing that alluring smile. She certainly knew how to keep customers coming back to this inn.

What a devious tactic, thought Krarshe as he watched his waitress leave, her pale blue skirt swaying with her hips as she walked. He turned to look at Na'kika again. She seemed in better spirits than before, but her ears and tail told a different story. One of sadness. More than just dropping some cups and ale.

Krarshe turned back to his plate. School began at dawn the next day, and he had a long way to walk. It'd probably cause problems with Wild Brow if he was late on the first day. Krarshe smiled to himself, thinking about the look that teacher would make if he called him that to his face. With that pleasant imagery entertaining him, Krarshe dug into his food.

CHAPTER 3

Krarshe sat at a long, worn table, resting his head in his hands as he watched his fellow students trickle into the classroom. He had gotten there significantly earlier than the rest to ensure he could pay the matriculation fee before class started, but misjudged what time class started. He let out a great yawn and turned his attention to the window, watching the front gates through heavy eyelids. The classroom was the biggest room in the front of the building, giving a great view of the stone courtyard as the morning sunlight climbed over the walls of the academy. He had been there since before the sun came up, and he had counted each stone of the courtyard pavement as the sun reached it. It was up to seven stones.

Krarshe turned his attention away from the window and looked over the students who had arrived. There was a group of three girls, all whispering and giggling amongst themselves. The shine and careful grooming of their hair led him to believe they were probably aristocrats like Tibault. A couple of boys entered together, chatting about something that Krarshe couldn't quite make out from the back of the room. Their hands made gestures which led him to believe it was something lewd, only strengthened when one of them nodded toward the group of girls before laughing.

The room filled faster and faster as the sunlight reached the eighth stone of the pavement. It became loud in the dingy, dusty classroom as more and more students talked and gossiped and joked. Krarshe was beginning to miss the past hour or so of silence that he had taken for granted. There were two things he noticed as he observed the room: first was that everyone seemed well-groomed, and the second, that everyone seemed to know someone. Everyone was talking with a companion. Only Krarshe sat in the back by himself, quietly watching the class.

"Karsh!"

Krarshe looked to the entrance and saw Tibault waving at him. His hair was smooth, combed back flat against his head, no longer the curly mess it was yesterday. Without the disheveled locks of hair hanging in front of his face, the scattering of freckles across the bridge of his nose were even more prominent. Krarshe gave a hesitant wave to Tibault as he walked over to the table and sat down on the seat next to Krarshe. He dropped the spellbook he had snatched from Krarshe on the table in front of them, halfway between him and Krarshe.

"You're here early," he said, brushing his hair back with his hand carefully. A stubborn curl stuck up, not willing to fall in line with the rest.

"Yeah," Krarshe muttered, looking out the window again, away from Tibault. "I had to pay my tuition still." He watched as the Professor Owyn stepped out from the store to yell something to a few students that just entered the premises, causing them to speed up toward the school building. "Apparently 'dawn' doesn't mean the same thing to everyone."

"It doesn't?" asked Tibault absentmindedly, still fighting with the stray curl before another one joined the revolt.

Krarshe turned to look at him, sleepily watching the boy fight with his hair. Rather than responding, he turned back to the window. Owyn had disappeared from the courtyard. A moment later, the two boys who were outside came running into the room, panting, followed by Professor Owyn.

Everyone quieted down and stood up. Krarshe just sat there for a moment, watching, before he noticed Tibault nudging him and gesturing for him to stand. As Krarshe stood, every student bowed and greeted the professor in unison, "Good morning, Professor." Krarshe attempted to follow, always a step behind.

"Good morning class. You may sit."

The students all returned to their seats. Krarshe sat down, a bit perplexed at this ritual. *It must be a school thing?* He thought uncertainly, realizing he'd likely never get an answer. His own supposition would have to suffice.

"Welcome, everyone, to the Remonnet Academy of Magic. As you all undoubtedly know, we have a reputation here at this school for producing the best mages in all of Remonnet. This class WILL be no exception," he said, as he paced back and forth, glaring at the class. "Failure to reach our expectations will result in punishment. Continued failure will result in expulsion." With this statement, he stopped and turned to the class. The lines around his clean-shaven mouth were deep, his eyes had a cruel sharpness to them, as though to stare through the students. Krarshe could feel the uneasiness in the room. "But," he continued, "if you manage to make it through the program, I assure you that you will bring honor to your families, and will be capable of serving the country as an exemplary mage." He returned to his pacing as he continued to explain the structure of the academy.

There were four other teachers who taught the more experienced students, specializing in different fields of magic. While senior students only had class every other day, alternating with self-study and research, the beginner students had class every day in the large classroom. There was a hands-on training area behind the building, undoubtedly the walled-in area Krarshe saw when he first came to the academy. Additionally, the students were each required to work in the store. By doing this, the school reasoned, the students would be exposed to the different magical implements and get to know full-fledged mages who frequented it. The students, unfortunately, were not compensated for the work. While there was usually a senior student in the store to assist, the main storefront would be operated by a beginner student on a rotation, commencing after one lunar cycle's worth of classes. It was up to the student to get information on missed lectures. To Krarshe, this seemed counter to the intent of the school, that being to learn, and he had to wonder if he somehow found his way into another merchant job rather than a magic academy.

Professor Owyn continued his long-winded speech, explaining class expectations and advancement to the senior classes and what those classes entailed before shifting to exaltation of the school and its long, proud history. After almost an hour of this, Krarshe's early morning began to catch up with him, and the speech began to become background noise for him, letting his attention turn to the window again. Twelve stones now, creeping almost up to thirteen. Krarshe tried in vain to stifle a yawn. He looked back at Owyn, but the teacher seemed to have not noticed. His proud lecture, or rather sermon, was becoming more intense. Looking over the class, half of the students seemed to be in awe, the other half bored. Not as bored as Krarshe felt, as he didn't notice anyone else taking up counting stones on the pavement outside as a pastime, but they appeared to be more or less disregarding what the teacher was saying. He saw one student at the far end of the room who seemed to be strangely rigid, almost as if she was trying to appear more attentive than she was.

Krarshe observed her for a minute, taking notice of her chestnut brown hair that hung loosely across her shoulders, before realizing who she was. It was the girl he met two days ago, the timid one who was working at the store. Krarshe studied her for a minute, the gears in his head beginning to turn, pulling him out of his sleepy stupor. *How was she running the store two days ago if she's a beginner student?*

"Hey, Tibault," Krarshe whispered, not taking his eyes off the girl. After getting no response, he looked over at Tibault. He was completely fixated on professor Owyn, mesmerized almost. *What a respectable, responsible student.* Krarshe jabbed him in the side a bit, prompting a grunt from Tibault.

"What?" Tibault whispered, slightly annoyed.

"Why would a student who has been here a while be in the beginner class?"

"... What?" Tibault looked even more annoyed now. "That's why you're distracting me?"

Krarshe just nodded, looking back forward, pretending to pay attention to Owyn.

"I'd assume they didn't pass the test to advance to the senior class."

"There's a test to advance?" Krarshe asked.

"Weren't you paying attention!?" Tibault harshly whispered.

Clearly, Krarshe had let his mind wander too early. He couldn't help it. He was tired, and this was dull. He came here to learn magic, not listen to some fanatical rant on how great the school was and how great a mage the teacher was.

Tibault turned his focus back to the teacher, and Krarshe to the sunlight in the courtyard again. He half paid attention to the lecture, if you could call it that, to make sure he didn't miss anything important. Thirteen stones.

* * *

After Krarshe had watched the sun cross every stone in the courtyard, the class finally took a break from the lecture for lunch. The morning was filled with only the half-mad ravings of a teacher so egotistical that Krarshe had to question why he

belittled himself by teaching students rather than heading the Council of Mages for the queen. Maybe it was to make himself feel even more superior by surrounding himself with beginners.

As the students filtered out of the classroom, Krarshe followed the flow of bodies and started to look for the girl from the other day. If she was already a student, she would probably know a lot about what to expect here. Definitely an asset, as Krarshe's merchant mind saw it.

"Hey, Karsh," Tibault's voice called out from behind him. "Where should we have lunch?"

You're coming with me? Krarshe thought. He sighed. "I'm not sure. But I wanted to go talk to one of the other students for a bit."

"We can invite them too. The more the merrier, right?"

I'm not getting rid of you, am I? Krarshe resigned himself to spending his break with Tibault. Tibault's good nature was evident, and something Krarshe was already beginning to appreciate, but was perhaps too energetic and spirited for him on an already draining day. He continued to look over the mass of students as they emptied out of the courtyard. When most of them had vacated the premises, Krarshe spotted the girl sitting alone on a stone bench at the far end of it near the gate. She had something wrapped in a cloth, which she was carefully opening on her lap.

Krarshe made his way across the sunny courtyard toward her. As he approached, she looked up at him, her hands halting before coming to rest delicately on top of the wrapping in her lap. Krarshe stopped just in front of her. As he studied her, he could see the confusion in her dark brown eyes. Krarshe felt his chest tighten as she looked up at him through her long bangs.

"Umm... Can... I help you with something?" she asked. Krarshe wondered how long he had been looking into her eyes before she snapped him from his trance.

"Sorry, I didn't mean to be so suspicious. I was just..." Krarshe trailed off. How was he going to breach this subject? If she had failed the promotion, it probably wasn't something she wanted to talk about. He had to be certain though. "Forgive me. You looked like someone I met in the school store not too long ago. I must be mistaken though. My apologies."

She looked down, her downcast eyes hidden by her chestnut bangs. "That... very well could have been me," she said barely above a whisper.

The girl sat there quietly, staring at the ground in unsettling silence. It seemed he had struck a sensitive subject, and Krarshe felt bad, but he had to push a little further. "But aren't you in the begi—"

"Yes. I know. I'm in the beginner class again." Her hands, shaking, turned into fists, crushing the wrapping in her lap. She looked up at Krarshe, her enchanting brown eyes welling with tears of indignation. "Do you think I'm a failure too?! That I'm some kind of idiot who can't pass even after three tries?!" Her voice was beginning to crack as her anger devolved into anguish. She looked to be on the verge of breaking into sobbing.

Her reaction took Krarshe completely by surprise. He expected her to be upset, but this was beyond his calculations. "Uhh, no, that's not what—"

"Just leave me alone!" she shouted at him. She stood up from the stone bench, the wrapping spilling out onto the ground, and deliberately pushed past Krarshe with a bit of a shove and headed toward the many-windowed building in the corner of the compound. Krarshe began to raise his hand as though to stop her, but changed his mind abruptly, letting it fall limply to his side. He was at a loss, unable to find the right thing to say. Maybe it was better he didn't say anything, given the brief exchange they just had. Krarshe looked at Tibault. He just looked back at Krarshe, disappointment and confusion written all over his face.

"That could have gone better," Krarshe muttered, mostly to himself.

"That was probably the worst thing you could have said." Tibault watched her as she ran. "You really should apologize," he said, looking back to Krarshe, his face more serious than Krarshe had yet seen.

"Yeah," Krarshe agreed.

"Aah!"

Krarshe and Tibault turned to look where the yelp came from. The girl had tripped over the uneven stones of the courtyard. She just laid on the ground, barely moving. Krarshe dashed over to her and squatted down. "Are you okay?"

Seeing her more closely, she appeared fine. Physically, that is. While on the cusp of crying, the trip had sent her over the edge into full bawling.

Krarshe wasn't sure how to handle this. In his years of travel, this was not a situation he was accustomed to. None of his mercantile expertise equipped him to console this girl. What was he supposed to do?

Left without any answers, he just did the only thing he could think of. He plopped down on the ground next to her. "I... I'm sorry. I didn't mean to bring up something painful. I'm sorry for being such an idiot." His head hung low. As unimaginative as his words seemed, he meant every word of it. It was never his intent to bring a girl to tears. He only wanted to gather information. His mistake was treating her like a commodity, and he was ashamed of himself. "Really... I'm sorry. Please. You can hate me all you want, but don't let an idiot like me stain that lovely face with tears."

"He's right. He's just a big idiot," Tibault joined in, having made his way over as well.

Krarshe heard her sniff. He looked up to see she had stopped crying, though she continued to hiccup slightly as she recovered.

"The biggest," Krarshe said, smiling at her.

She sniffed again, wiping her cheek and rubbing her eyes with the back of her hand. "Y-yeah," she managed to croak. She gave a slight smile back.

"I'm Tibault," Tibault said, proudly, pounding his chest as he struck as gallant a pose as he could muster. "Tibault Dumont."

Krarshe stood back up. He swallowed hard and said, "This biggest idiot's name is Krarshe." He reached out a hand to help her up. Hesitating slightly, she reached up and timidly took his hand. "Just Krarshe," he explained, as he pulled her to her feet. He was once again eye to eye with those dazzling brown eyes, still with a few tears caught in her long eyelashes.

She sniffed again. "I'm Bridgette. Bridgette Bulliere." She wiped the remaining tears from her lashes. "Everyone calls me 'Bri'."

Krarshe gave a low, exaggerated bow. "It is my greatest pleasure to make your acquaintance, Miss Bulliere." He looked up to see her smiling genuinely.

"You really are a huge idiot," Tibault teased before shoving Krarshe playfully.

Krarshe looked sharply at Tibault before smiling. The three of them stood quietly in the empty courtyard, the sun high in the sky. The morning chill had been replaced by the ever-growing heat of midday. In other words, lunch time. Krarshe looked back to where Bri had sat to eat. "Alas," Krarshe started, "while we may have saved this damsel from her grief, her poor lunch was not so lucky."

Bri and Tibault also looked back to the bench where she had been seated earlier. The wrapping had fallen apart in her hurry, spilling a half of bread and slices of preserved meat across the stone pavement.

"'Tis no problem at all!" Tibault proclaimed, following Krarshe's theatrics. "We'll simply have to invite her—nay, insist that she join us for lunch!"

"It's okay, he'll pay," Krarshe whispered to Bri.

"Wait, what?" Tibault exclaimed.

Krarshe and Bri both laughed. Krarshe started toward the gate, followed by Bri.

"No, I'm being serious. I'm paying?!" Tibault called out, chasing after the two.

* * *

"This is your fourth time through the beginner class?" Krarshe asked, tearing a piece from his loaf of bread.

Bri just nodded, looking at her stew. "My parents are livid. I had just gotten a pretty serious scolding from them the other day, and you bringing it up just..." She inhaled and released it forcefully. "I just couldn't handle it. I'm sorry for the undignified showing I made earlier."

"No, I was in the wrong. There's nothing you need apologize for," Krarshe assured her.

Bri sat quietly, stirring her stew for a moment, spooning out chunks of carrot before dropping them back into the stew with a soft plop. She released the spoon and picked up her loaf of bread, fingering it tenderly as she considered the best spot to tear from. She settled on a spot, but she just held it there. "Honestly," she started, "I decided to stay at the dormitory this time because I can't bring myself to face them right now. I'm... just... I'm so frustrated and angry with myself." She bit her lip, trying to maintain her composure before continuing, "I don't know what to do. I feel like such a failure..." She dropped her bread, nearly flinging her spoon from the bowl, and put her face in her hands.

"You're not a failure," Krarshe assured her.

"Yeah, I'm sure you've got it this time," Tibault said as he casually stuffed a bite of food into his mouth.

"I'm sure you're an excellent mage. Really, it's probably Professor Wild Brow's fault." He dipped his bread into his stew and quickly tossed it into his mouth before it could drip.

Tibault nearly choked on his stew as he sipped it.

"Professor... wild brow?" Bri asked, peeking out over her fingertips.

"Have you SEEN his eyebrows? I've been all over, and I haven't seen anything that crazy. The dwarves with their browbraids are close, but they still can't compare."

Tibault was coughing hard, trying to clear his lungs of the stew he had inhaled. Bri covered her mouth and turned away slightly to try to hide her amused smile.

"I can't be the only one who has thought this..." Krarshe said. "Right?"

After she had regained much of her composure, though a faint smile remained, Bri responded, "Well, yeah, I'm sure everyone noticed. It's hard to miss..." She almost whispered the last part. "Just, no one has ever actually come out and said it."

"I'm fine with being the first," Krarshe said, puffing his chest out proudly.

"Just don't be the first to say it to his face," Tibault choked out. "I somehow don't think he'd appreciate it."

Krarshe chuckled. "I'll try to contain myself."

"As... funny as it is," Bri said, again trying to keep herself composed, "if he heard about that, you'd probably be in serious trouble. He may be a professor at the academy, but he got that position by assignment from the Council of Mages. It doesn't matter who you are, you'd be in trouble getting on their bad side."

Krarshe nonchalantly tore another piece from his rapidly disappearing loaf of bread. "I'll keep that in mind. I promise."

"Why do I feel like you're not taking this seriously?" Tibault asked, seemingly recovered from nearly choking.

Krarshe put his hands up, defensively. "I swear. I honestly am not looking for trouble."

"Well, let's just hope people weren't listening to us," Bri said, glancing around the room.

Krarshe followed her gaze as it darted around. The tavern was busy as would be expected during midday. A few men sat at a table about halfway across the room. He watched as one of the two men tried, and failed miserably, to drink the stew he had from the bowl, the thick broth dribbling down his previously clean beard. A noble lady and gentleman sat just past them, talking about something inaudibly. Krarshe could only assume the man was flirting with the woman, based on his forward posture and her shy one.

Those, Krarshe reasoned, were too engrossed with their own affairs for it to matter. The other students that also came here, however, were a different story. He looked over the faces of his fellow students. There were seven or so, Krarshe guessed without trying to make it obvious that he was observing the cluster. They seemed perfectly oblivious to the goings-on around them, almost bumping into a waitress as she walked past them, laughing and joking amongst themselves. This was sufficient to allay any concerns he might have had, not that there were many.

As he returned to his food, a memory struck him. He looked at the cluster of students again. Among them happened to be the boy, Armand, who had run into him days ago. There was no mistaking his blond, wavy hair, defined jaw you'd expect on a gallant knight, and seemingly permanently smug and self-important expression.

Krarshe watched this gathering. It seemed Armand and the boys in the group were doing their own courting. He would say something, follow up with a somehow even more smug expression, and conclude with awes from the boys and girls. He'd occasionally follow up by flashing a smile, eliciting giggles from the girls at the table.

Krarshe rolled his eyes. *He should probably take some lessons from the noble in the corner. Might learn something.* Krarshe decided to stop watching. He didn't want to ruin his lunch.

"So," Krarshe began, "when will we actually be learning some actual magic?"

Bri looked up from her stew. She swallowed before responding. "Typically, after his introductory speech, we learn a beginner spell later that day."

"Ooh!" both Krarshe and Tibault said in unison.

Bri waved her hand dismissively. "Don't get too excited. It's really not that interesting. He'll teach you the spell, then we'll try it out in the practical room. Oh, that's the outdoor courtyard he mentioned. It's really just to gauge everyone's mana pool."

"Mana pool?" Krarshe asked. He had a bit of experience with magic, but wasn't taught it formally. Terms like this were a foreign concept to him.

"How much mana you have. It dictates how many and how powerful of spells you can cast. He'll explain it before teaching the spell." Bri took another spoon of her stew, fishing up a large chunk of potato, which she ate cheerfully. "I love stewed potatoes," she said with a smile, mouth still partially full of food. The potato seemed to lift her spirits more than anything Krarshe or Tibault had managed to say.

"I'm just glad to have some bread," Krarshe said, tearing off a piece. "It's so rare here. Expensive too. Far too many bean dishes."

"I mean, it's hard to get wheat, what with the war and all. It's not as though they can just ask Gagerith or Pretis for some," Tibault explained. "Just need to hope some merchants risk the trip."

Krarshe just smiled, remembering his merchant days. "Yeah, you'd have to be crazy to risk crossing the border into 'enemy lands'." Krarshe took a bite of his bread, savoring the taste and texture. "Good profit I'm sure, though."

Bri and Tibault both nodded in unison, their mouths too full to respond. Krarshe noticed the other students leaving, half of their food still on their plates.

Bri noticed it too. "We best get back. I'm guessing class will be starting up again shortly." She stuffed one more potato into her mouth and stood up. Tibault stood as well, brushing crumbs off his white jacket.

Krarshe, not one to leave food behind, slurped the rest of his stew down, following Tibault's example of nearly choking on a carrot that was all too willing to thrust itself down his throat. He stood up and took the rest of his bread with him. No way was he going to leave that unfinished.

As they were beginning to leave, Bri stopped. "T-thanks... for lunch... and everything," she stammered, not making eye contact.

"No—" Krarshe started.

"No problem," Tibault interjected forcefully, slamming the pile of coins on the table. Krarshe and Bri both smiled, and the three of them rushed for the academy gates.

CHAPTER 4

"There are two main components of spellcasting," Owyn said, pacing back and forth in front of the class, just as he did during his morning rant. "First is your mana pool. Mana is the key component that makes magic exist at all." He stopped, turning toward the class, and raised his hand in front of his chest, curling his fingers slightly as though he was holding a ball. "All creatures contain some amount of mana, and this amount is what we refer to as a 'mana pool', or 'mana reserves'. The quantity of mana any creature has at birth is dependent on species." His hand returned to its original position, clasping his other hand behind his back, as he returned to his pacing. "Humans like us have, what we have designated, an average mana pool, though it varies by individual more than other races. Other races, such as kitsune or elves," he said, looking directly at Krarshe, "have above average mana pools. Others, such as dwarves and orcs, have lower than average pools. Though, they leverage other methods to compensate, such as runeforging." He stopped and turned to face the class once again, his sharp facial features stern and serious. "Do not underestimate them just because they, by this school's opinion, use inferior magic techniques." He returned to pacing.

"Professor, a question," one of the students spoke up.

Professor Owyn turned to him and pointed. "Yes, you may ask."

"What races have the largest and smallest mana pools?"

Owyn smirked, almost as if he was proud to answer this specific question. Krarshe saw, across the room, Bri sigh and rest her cheek against her hand, exasperated. *It must be a common question,* Krarshe thought.

"Many of the animal-folk tend to have smaller mana pools. Kitsune are an anomaly, being closer to fae than animal-folk. But species like ratfolk are often found to have the smallest. The largest..." He turned and faced the large black stone wall in the front of the room. "The largest is more of a monster than a race." He turned to face the room. "Any guesses?"

The room was quiet. After a moment, a hand raised. Owyn pointed at them before they spoke.

"Some form of demon?"

Owyn shook his head. "Extraplanar beings are rare, and so their mana pools are unknown, but good try. Any other guesses?"

There was a long pause as the class mulled over the question. "A dragon?" came another answer from someone Krarshe couldn't see at the opposite side of the room.

Owyn clapped and pointed at the student. "Yes. Precisely. A dragon. Magical researchers have, at great cost and experimentation on dragonborn, managed to measure, or more accurately estimate, the mana pools of dragons. While the exact size is unknown, suffice it to say that it overshadows any other known race's by such a margin that it would be impossible to ever reach a mana pool of that size. And THAT is only at birth."

"What's a dragonborn?" asked one student.

Owyn looked at the student, almost glaring at him. "Dragonborn are abominations, tainted creatures born from both dragon and common-race parents." He started walking closer to the students, menacingly. "They may bear the appearance of their common-race parent, but they are monsters, just like a dragon. Their physical and magical power are immense. For this reason, they cannot be trusted, and such children are—" He stopped, choosing his words carefully. "They are... dealt with."

The class was completely silent, petrified by his theatrics.

He turned back and resumed his pacing. "Ahem. As I was saying... Where did I leave off? ... Ah, yes. Those astute students undoubtedly noticed the particular choice of words I made. 'At birth'. Mana pools, in fact, are not rigid. Much like a warrior can become stronger through physical exertion, so too can mages expand their mana reserves and become more powerful. The act of exhausting your mana pool will strengthen it, cause it to grow. And that—" he said, turning to the class again, "is why we will practice and drill spells until you can barely stand. While impossible to reach the level of a dragon, it's perfectly possible to reach that of the elves in one's lifetime."

The class murmured slightly. Krarshe still wasn't particularly interested in the minutiae, he just wanted to get to the actual spellcasting portion. He looked at Tibault, who was practically at the edge of his seat. He turned to see Bri, still looking dreadfully bored. It wasn't surprising, as this was her fourth time through the same rehearsed lecture.

"Now," Owen said, louder than before, instantly silencing the class. "The second important part of magic is the spellcast itself. The incantation you recite and the hand gestures you make, these will be what dictates the spell you cast. Magic itself works by releasing mana, which is then manipulated by whichever spell you cast. While one can cast spells that have no spellcast, these are often not very useful. These 'arcane spells', as they're called, have few, very niche, uses, and we will not focus on them in this class. If you wish to study them, you may do so in the senior classes." He stopped for a moment to clear his throat, stroking his long, receding black hair to make sure it was in perfect form. "The first spell, that we will practice reciting here, will be one without any somatic components, or hand gestures. It will be a spell to generate wind. When we have practiced sufficiently, we will go out to the outdoor training facility to do it with mana release and measure the size of each student's mana pool."

The class erupted into whispering again, only to be immediately silenced by Owyn coughing and clearing his throat.

"Now, the verbal component is very specific. It can be found in your spellbook as 'wind burst' if you need to review it later." He pulled out a small white stone and began striking and dragging it against the black stone wall at the front of the room, leaving behind white streaks with an ear-piercing screech. Krarshe had to cover his ears as Owyn drew out a long series of strange characters. When he finished, he put the white stone into a pocket in his coat and smacked the stone wall. "This is the spell, written out in its original language. I know it seems strange, but you will learn this language in time. Now, it reads:

Se Esfiru hinoras, suesoo—"

Krarshe's ears perked up. "Is that draconic?" he interjected.

Owyn stopped, and looked straight at Krarshe. Krarshe furrowed his brow. Had he said something weird? He looked around nervously, before his nervousness sank deeper into his heart. The entire class had turned to look at him, shock and astonishment on their faces. Tibault and Bri as well, eyes wide with surprise.

"Where did you hear this?" Owyn's voice said, low, chilling. His face told him he was less than amused by Krarshe's outburst.

Krarshe was cornered. He wasn't sure what to say. *I guess this isn't common knowledge here... Well, I used the excuse before, might as well again.* "Umm... My... My father. He... He used to be a travelling merchant. He heard it from a prominent mage who travelled with him for a while."

The class started whispering to each other at this explanation. Krarshe swallowed hard. Using this fictitious merchant father was becoming a common excuse. He might need to fabricate a full story for this fictional character if he didn't want to have inconsistencies in his tales.

After a very long moment of silence, scowling the whole time, Owyn spoke up. "Well, that is correct. Spells are cast in draconic," Owyn said. The murmuring of the students became a rumble of voices. Owyn cleared his throat a few times, but the chatter of the class wouldn't cease. He slammed his hand against the black stone wall with a thunderous clap. The chatter ceased at once. Owyn glared at the class before his eyes settled back on Krarshe.

"Is everything okay in here?" another heavy-set man, seemingly another teacher, whispered from the doorway.

Owyn just nodded silently, dismissing his fellow teacher. Owyn turned back to Krarshe again, his eyes felt as though they would pierce the young elf. "I do not know who this mage was, nor where he was from. BUT! In Remonnet, as I'm sure in many other countries that still follow Imperial doctrine, knowledge of spellcast origins is to be kept a secret from the masses." He looked across the classroom, scowling. "To continue with my answer to your BURNING question," he remarked, sarcastically, looking at Krarshe, "spells are indeed in draconic. For reasons unknown, draconic carries mana significantly better than any other language yet found. Spells in other languages do not carry the same potency. As such, we have resigned ourselves to using draconic, and have developed a written form to allow us to put it on paper." He breathed deeply before looking at the class again. "This WILL not be spoken of outside the academy. Do you understand?" As he finished looking over the class, he came to settle once more on Krarshe, lingering there.

Owyn turned back to the front of the room. Tibault leaned over to Krarshe. "What are you doing?" he whispered.

"It was just a question..." Krarshe replied. "I didn't realize it was secret."

"I mean, I didn't either..." Tibault admitted. "But, I'd probably just stay quiet the rest of class."

Krarshe nodded silently.

"Ehem. With that disruption out of the way, repeat after me: *Se Esfiru hinoras, suesoo shu zeraus dzam mea'anom. Sem te mem tsanchaasha hihiinjon, shu grunda meaa tsandum saran,dun suesoo tsinchan.*"

The class repeated it, or attempted to. Several of them appeared to stumble over the words and sounds, many of which Krarshe had never heard in the common tongue.

Owyn kept the class repeating the spell over and over for what felt like forever. Krarshe had grasped it immediately. While the sounds weren't present in the common tongue, they were in other languages he'd encountered while travelling. The spellcast came naturally to him. When everyone seemed to have grasped it, Owyn said, "Okay, that will do. Please follow me out to the practice area."

Owyn grabbed a book, quill, and inkwell from his desk in the corner of the room and headed toward the door. The class all stood up and followed the teacher out into the hallway and through a large stone door. Krarshe looked at the heavy door as he passed it. It must have been over a foot thick and had several scorch marks and chips taken out of it. He worried about the training to come.

The training area was surprisingly disorderly, with various pieces of equipment lining the walls, shielded from the center of the room by segments of walls. The segments were left separated from the far wall, Krarshe assumed to grant quick access to the storage area from the central section. The equipment being stored was all familiar. There were staves and wands, similar to those in the store the school ran, but they looked heavily used. A few of them were broken. There were also several pieces of metal armor scattered around on wooden stands, some of which had dents and scorch marks. In the center of the room sat a strange mechanism. It was a large wooden frame with a wooden arm attached vertically, anchored to the base of the frame. The end of the arm had a wide, flat piece of wood mounted to it. There was a long piece of wood with notches drawn on it that stretched back from where the arm sat, parallel with the ground. Krarshe guessed this was some sort of measuring device.

Owyn explained to the students how to release mana, and at what point in the spellcast to do so. Krarshe, not being a complete novice with magic, knew this already, so he was more interested in continuing to look around the room. From the inside, it felt a lot smaller than it seemed from outside. Maybe it was all the clutter and sectioning of the space.

"So, you will take aim at the measuring device with 'wind burst'. While the area of the spell is fairly large, do try not to miss or you won't be measured properly. Also, to ensure we get an accurate measurement of your full capacity, be sure to release as much mana as you can. Don't worry, you will be okay. Even if you pass out, we have an infirmary on campus."

A few of the students groaned, nervously.

"Miss Bulliere, would you like to demonstrate?" Owyn asked in a grandiose manner, smirking slightly. Krarshe heard some disdain in his voice.

Bri stepped forward, seemingly unfazed by the teacher's disparaging tone, as though she was accustomed to it. The whole scene bothered Krarshe, especially given the events during lunch break. Regardless, Bri took position a dozen paces in front of the device. She stood firm, extending her right hand, palm forward, toward the target. She began reciting the spell, generating a small breeze in the direction of the target. As she finished it, a gust of wind pushed the target on the device, the arm tilting back a dozen or so notches, nearly half way down the measuring beam.

"Hmm. Not bad," Owyn said flatly, writing down something in the book he carried with him. He smiled the same disgusting smirk he had just previously.

As he reset the target to its starting position, Owyn called another student, this time Armand. Armand repeated the same process as Bri had. The target moved slightly, maybe four or five notches.

"Oh, very good. Especially for a beginner," Owyn said, emphasizing the word 'beginner', writing another note in the book.

Armand smiled proudly. A few of the other boys cheered for him.

This continued for a while, the late afternoon sun creeping its way toward its resting place. Some of the students moved it slightly. Some not at all. Some couldn't say the spell correctly, no matter how many times Owyn tried to correct them. Those who got no results were always met with a sharp, critical remark from Owyn. Tibault managed to move it slightly, almost one notch. He walked to the back of the group to a distant wall, looking a bit dejected. He joined up next to Bri and sighed heavily.

"I didn't manage to move it at all my first time," she said, patting him on the back. "Armand is just abnormal."

Tibault just nodded quietly.

"Our esteemed Krarshe," Owyn called out, sarcastically. This was more sarcastic than Krarshe had ever been himself, quite a feat.

Krarshe stepped forward.

"Whenever you're ready," Owyn said. Caustically.

Did I do something to earn this venom he's aiming at me? It was just a simple question, so calm down Professor Eyebrow, Krarshe thought as he walked over into position before the large wooden contraption. *Let's see if I can leave him speechless.*

Krarshe stood, his right shoulder turned forward. He extended his right hand, palm out, aimed at the target. "*Se Esfiru hinoras, suesoo shu zeraus dzam mea'anom—*" Krarshe began to feel a breeze coming from behind him, "*Sem te mem tsanchaasha hihiinjon—*" The breeze intensified, more than even Bri had generated at the spell's conclusion. Krarshe noticed the crackling of electricity as small sparks began arcing down his forearm towards his hand and from his palm.

"Wait... Stop! Hold!" Owyn began to say, panicked.

He heard a few students behind him begin to mutter something, along with some gasps of confusion. He could barely hear any of them. The wind was roaring in his ears now.

Maybe I shouldn't release ALL of my mana? Yeah, let's hold back a bit.

"*Shu grunda meaa tsandum saran, dun suesoo tsinchan!*"

As Krarshe finished the spell, a massive torrent of wind blew past him, accompanied by a scattering of lightning. The blast of wind sent the device smashing into the far wall, sending a spider web of cracks radiating out from the impact. The stray bolts of lightning crashed randomly before him, blasting away portions of the stone walls and floor in front and to the sides. Krarshe could feel a comparatively smaller gust of wind from the two side storage areas, along with the sound of metal crashing and wood splitting, and the cries of surprise from his classmates behind him over the deafening wind and lightning.

After the wind died down and the dust settled, Krarshe looked at the target range. It was a mess. He looked to the storage areas, where several pieces of equipment had found their way out into the main space. He saw Professor Owyn on the ground, his coat pulled half over his head, struggling to pull it back down. Krarshe turned to look at his classmates. Everyone, except Bri, Tibault, and a few others who had chosen to wait by

the back wall, were on the ground, their uniforms disheveled. Those at the back wall stood, their arms covering their faces. Krarshe saw Bri and Tibault lower their arms, their hair was all over the place. Bri tried to comb the tangle of hair out from in front of her face. Both she and Tibault stood there in shock, stunned by what they had just witnessed.

Owyn scrambled to his feet, wrestling to get his coat off of his head with a series of popping and ripping sounds. He looked at the state of the training area in horror, and then looked at Krarshe. Krarshe noted how his eyebrows were the neatest they may have ever been, having been pulled in the same direction when Owyn had pulled his robe from his face. Aside from that, the ever reddening of the teacher's face told Krarshe he was probably furious.

"So... Uhh... How'd I do?"

CHAPTER 5

K rarshe picked up the armor stand and set it against the wall. He breathed deep and let it out with a sigh, looking at the results of his hours of work. "Finally done." He turned his gaze up to the sky in the training facility. It was night now and the waning crescent moon hung low in the sky while the second moon had yet to crest the horizon. A smattering of stars filled the clear sky, the luminous river seemingly ferrying the twin moons to the far horizon. Krarshe wiped the sweat from his forehead; the day's heat still hung in the air, and the stone walls still radiated with the warmth they had stored from the sun. A small torch was the only thing that lit the room, which did little more than what the night sky did on its own.

After the spell he had cast that afternoon, Owyn was beyond angry, as Krarshe had expected. The students were all dumbfounded, unsure of what had happened. None of them said anything to Krarshe, not even Tibault or Bri. Owyn had demanded an explanation, but Krarshe had none to give. He had cast the spell just as the rest of the class had.

Without an explanation, Owyn was forced to just chalk it up to being an elf, and told the class that Krarshe had demonstrated the difference in mana pool between a human and elf. The class accepted the explanation, as far as Krarshe could tell, but there still seemed to be some suspicion. Krarshe was assigned to stay behind and clean up the mess he had made, while the rest of the class was dismissed for the day. The few remaining students who didn't get an opportunity to cast the spell were told they would have to do it again another day.

As the class left, he could hear a few of them snickering and muttering something rude under their breaths. He thought a few were accusing him of casting a different spell. It was a fair accusation, having been a mixture of wind and lightning, except that they had heard him cast the spell. Every word was perfectly recited, Krarshe was sure of it. Why the spell came out the way it did made no sense. As for the force of the spell, Krarshe had thought he had held back. Quite a bit, he thought. Left without answers, he was forced to accept that it was just a fluke.

Krarshe sat down on the stone floor as he looked up at the sky. It was so serene, the night was quiet. Castle Ward didn't have anywhere near the noise that Feyfaire did at night. If nobles wanted to get rowdy, they went to Feyfaire. They wouldn't make a mess in their own yard. He sat there for a few minutes and listened to the sound of insects chirping. Occasionally there were faint voices from beyond the school's walls, but it was very rare, and never loud enough to discern what was said.

He felt isolated.

He looked over the facility again. While he cleaned it as best he could, some things were beyond repair. The measuring device they had used was in pieces, the wooden frame and components had shattered to splinters. The stone wall at the far side... Well, Krarshe couldn't do anything about that. It was a shallow crater where the device had slammed against it. A few shards of the wooden measuring device were still lodged in the fractured stone. The impact was apparently enough to shake the school itself, as it had shattered a couple windows, and the other teachers had come running out to see what had happened. The blame was set squarely upon his shoulders.

What really gnawed at him, though, was Tibault and Bri. Despite the rough start he had with both of them, he thought he was starting to make some real relationships, something he had never been able to do as a merchant. However, they didn't so much as make eye contact with him when they left. Krarshe wasn't sure why it bothered him so much, but it did. Did he feel lonely? That feeling of isolation... Maybe it wasn't just because of the quiet room he was in, alone at night.

Krarshe stood up. He had been alone before. In fact, he'd been alone for years. Travelling merchants rarely had friends, if you exclude their horse. He knew he would get over it. He walked to the scarred stone door and entered the school. He walked down the silent, dark hallway through to the store. He found the teacher that was left to wait for him to finish cleaning, one who taught one of the senior classes, and let him know he had finished cleaning and was heading home.

The old, gaunt man squinted at him through a small pair of glasses that sat upon the bridge of a large, bulbous nose and his long white mustache hanging from his lip down to nearly his belly. His white hair seemed to be in disarray, probably from the result of too many spells gone awry. "Ooh, yes, yes. I almost forgot that you were here. Heh heh," he said, his old, quiet voice said slowly. "Be safe out there, lad." He waved slower than he spoke, his hand rigid as if it was wooden. While Krarshe wasn't certain, he seemed like one of the nicer teachers at the school. After the incident that afternoon, he was the only teacher to not make a huge fuss over it. He just kind of laughed. It was a bit odd, to say the least, but Krarshe appreciated not receiving more animosity.

Out in the courtyard, Krarshe made his way toward the gate. The school grounds were sort of eerie with no one around, void of the hustle and bustle of the day. *What a first day THAT was,* Krarshe thought. He was tired, more than he would have expected.

"H-hey, K-kuhrash," a small voice said from around the corner of the store, struggling with his name.

"That's a new one," Krarshe commented before he even saw who it was. He didn't need to see, he recognized the soft voice.

"Oh, umm... S-sorry, I'm not very good at pronunciation. Probably why spells are hard for me," said Bri. "Karsh?"

Krarshe shrugged. "Close enough. Tibault can't pronounce it either. He's also wildly inconsistent. Maybe hold the last syllable more."

"So, Karshe?"

"That's workable," Krarshe joked. He turned to face her. She was wearing a dress, one of those shorter one-piece dresses that he had seen noble girls wearing during the Sirnus cycles. It was purple or blue, exactly which one was hard to tell in the dim light of the night sky. Her chestnut hair hung down, spilling over her shoulders. In all, it looked good on her, though he dare not say that out loud. "What are you doing out here?"

"I was just wondering what happened to you. I never saw you leave for the day. Were you in there this whole time?"

"I only just finished cleaning up," Krarshe responded, rubbing his shoulder as he rolled it. "Was pretty exhausting."

"I can imagine. That's real armor, after all," Bri said. She stood there, rubbing her arm as she looked around nervously. "Hey, about that spell..."

"I don't know," Krarshe said, cutting her off.

"I didn't even ask anything yet."

"You were about to ask why that happened," he retorted. "The teachers pressed me quite a bit about it. Simply put, I don't know what happened."

Bri shook her head, causing her bangs to sway back and forth. "I wasn't going to ask that."

"You don't think I cast a different spell too, do you?" Krarshe asked.

"Who said that?" She raised an eyebrow.

"I heard a few students muttering about it on their way out." Krarshe walked past Bri, over to a stone bench along the store's wall and sat down. "I know I cast the right spell."

Bri sat down next to him, tucking her short dress under her. She looked up at the sky. "I know you did, too." She paused for a moment and then looked at him. "I would know. I've cast it far too many times," she said with a smile.

"It showed. You were the best by far."

The smile faded from her face. "Yeah..."

Remembering Professor Owyn's snide remark, Krarshe turned toward her. "Ignore that dreg of a teacher. He's not worth wasting your thoughts on."

She laughed slightly. "I know... Thanks."

"Besides," Krarshe said, turning forward again and leaning back to stare at the stars. "He got what he deserved today when he ended up on his ass. And I helped him with his eyebrows."

Bri giggled. "You really did. Tibault and I talked about them after class."

The two sat on the stone bench, watching the moon and stars. The second moon was beginning to peek over the horizon before either spoke again.

"You know... Your hair seems to have a faint blue glow in this light."

Krarshe turned to see she was studying his head. "Must be the moonlight," he reasoned.

"Yeah, maybe."

They returned to pensive silence and watched the night sky.

Bri leaned forward to stare at the ground, avoiding looking at him as she broke the silence. "Karshe," she started, but then stopped. The way she sat and her hesitancy seemed to imply she was afraid to breach the subject on her mind. After a moment, though, she continued, "You're powerful, aren't you?"

Krarshe just continued to stare at the sky. This was a question he wasn't prepared for, nor did he know how to answer.

"I guess? I honestly don't know. I never thought of myself as such, but I've never had anyone to compare to."

"Really?"

Krarshe nodded. He sat quietly, trying to plan what he'd say next. Tragically, he was too tired to really think, and he just let them spill from his mouth. "Truth be told, this was not my first time using magic."

Bri turned suddenly to Krarshe.

"I mean, it's not like I did any major spells or anything," Krarshe said, frantically waving his hands in front of him defensively. "That was my first actual spell. Up to this point, I've never actually recited one."

The look on Bri's face clearly showed her disbelief.

"It's the truth. I swear it," Krarshe said, trying to convince her. He wasn't sure why he was being so forward about this. This isn't something he ever expected to talk about with anyone. Why did he trust her so much? Or maybe he was too tired to rein in his mouth.

She sighed and turned to face the sky again. "I guess I'll just have to take your word for it. It was a bit frightening, truthfully. But..." She stopped and sat there quietly, staring at the stars. "I wish I could get that powerful..." she said wistfully.

Krarshe looked at the sky, and then back to her. He could make out her brown eyes, shining with the stars, or maybe they were glistening with tears once more. He wished he could help her, but what could he do? He didn't understand this kind of spellcasting. Even his own spells went awry. There was nothing he could do to help.

"You'll get there. I know it," he said, the only token comfort he could offer.

Bri just sat there quietly. She closed her eyes and muttered something Krarshe couldn't make out.

"What?" he asked.

Bri stood up from the bench. "Nothing." She brushed the back of her dress where she had sat on it. "Are you living in the dorm?"

Krarshe shook his head.

"You should get going then. They'll be closing the gate soon, and they will think nothing of locking you in here."

"Really?"

Bri nodded. "And they won't let you stay in the dorm either. Not without paying at least."

Krarshe jumped up. "Yeah, I should leave then. I still have a long way to Feyfaire."

Bri raised her eyebrows in surprise. "You're staying in Feyfaire? That's a long way."

"Yeah, but it's a lot more affordable than anything in Castle Ward."

"Sounds like you have it hard. Well, I won't keep you." Bri turned toward the dorms. "See you tomorrow, Kaushe. Karshe?"

"Close enough," Krarshe said as he started toward the gate once again. "See you tomorrow, Bri."

* * *

The isolation continued the next day at school. It was different compared to yesterday, however. While he wasn't overtly ignored by the students as they came into the room, it felt like they were trying to keep their distance from him. They would stare at him and whisper to each other as he looked out the window, only to avert their gaze when he looked back at them. It was unsettling in a way that he hadn't experienced before.

"Mind if I sit here?"

Krarshe turned to see Bri, gesturing to the seat next to him. He shrugged. "I think Tibault has claimed that seat. So feel free."

Bri chuckled. "Well, hopefully he doesn't mind. I can just move if I have to."

Krarshe returned to staring out the window, counting the stones that were illuminated by the morning sun. This would become habit if he kept at it, he knew, but he didn't mind it. He could hear the whispering of the students start again. A bit more than it had before.

"They're such a nuisance," Krarshe muttered, still staring out at the world outside.

"Hmm?"

"Our classmates. It seems I'm the centerpiece of their gossip today."

Bri looked around the room, noticing all the stares and secretive whispering. "Seems like it. I wouldn't let it bother you, nobles just like to gossip. I always tried to brush it off as nothing."

"Oh? I'm surprised you've had to deal with this before."

"Pretty much started with my third go-around," she said quietly.

"Oh..." Krarshe shrunk back into his seat. "Sorry about that."

"Don't worry about it. I'm past the point of caring," she said.

"Didn't seem that way yesterday," Krarshe responded, hoping he didn't just make a huge mistake.

Bri punched him in the arm. "You think I'm too weak to recover from that? You don't know the pride of the Bulliere family!"

Krarshe rubbed his arm. Her punch had a surprising amount of strength behind it. "My apologies, my lady." They both exchanged smiles before Krarshe turned to the window again.

"What are you looking at?" she asked.

"Nothing."

"How can you look at nothing?"

"That's a good question, but too philosophical for this time of day. To be more specific, I'm watching the sun as it passes over the stone pavement."

"That... sounds painfully boring," Bri said with a straight face.

"No more boring than listening to Owyn," Krarshe replied, grinning back.

Behind Bri, Krarshe saw Tibault hurry into the room. "Hey! You took my seat!" Tibault said when he saw Bri sitting next to Krarshe.

"Told you," Krarshe said to Bri.

"Do you want it back? Would you really demand a lady surrender her seat?"

Krarshe turned to look at Tibault. His hair was back to its curly brown mess. He must have tried to make it look better for the first day, but given up on it today. The fight must not have been worth the trouble. Tibault pursed his lips, caught by Bri's trap.

Tibault sighed. "I'll just sit here," he said, defeated.

A wide smile spread across Bri's face. "Boys are too easy..."

"Settle down, and take your seats," Owyn's voice boomed. He came in swiftly, walking across the front and slammed a book down on his desk in the front left corner of the room.

"Oh boy, he's angry," Bri said, barely above a whisper.

"Yesterday?" Krarshe asked.

"Most likely." Bri turned to Krarshe. "What you did yesterday was probably a first for him. I know I haven't seen anything like it in my time here."

"You did damage the school," Tibault whispered, leaning over toward Krarshe, practically on top of Bri.

"No talking!" Owyn slammed his hand on the desk. Bri and Tibault sat upright and the entire class froze, still as statues.

Owyn smoothed his hair back, tightening the ponytail. He reached into his pocket and pulled out that white stone again and began to write. It was apparent that Owyn had no desire to go through formal greetings the way he did the first day.

"What is that he's writing with? I hadn't seen it up until yesterday," Krarshe whispered, leaning in toward Bri.

Bri turned to Krarshe, raising her eyebrows in surprise. "You haven't seen chalk before?" she whispered back.

Krarshe shook his head. "Is that what it's called?"

She nodded.

Guess there really is a lot I don't know about the world still, Krarshe thought, sitting upright again.

With the final stroke on the chalkboard, the chalk snapped in half, startling the class. It was probably more to do with the anger Owyn was displaying than the act of snapping chalk, Krarshe reasoned. The class was clearly on edge.

When Owyn turned back to the class, he had written out a series of characters. Each strange scribble paired with a character in the common tongue. "We'll be learning the writing system used in your books. With this, you'll be able to read a variety of spells. Be sure to take notes."

Notes? On what? Krarshe wondered. He then saw the other students had paper, ink, and quills on the tables in front of them. Tibault scrambled to get his materials out, laying a crumpled paper on the desk as he hurriedly tried to smooth it out ineffectively. Bri just sat there, watching the lecture.

"W-was I supposed to buy ink and paper?" Krarshe asked Bri.

Bri turned to Krarshe and then covered her face with her hand, exasperatedly. "Curse me, I knew I forgot to tell you something yesterday." She took the hand from her face and leaned in toward Krarshe. "After we left the training area, he told the class to bring them today."

"Oh, my, Krarshe. Are you UNPREPARED for class today?" Owyn asked, stepping toward Krarshe's table in a dramatic fashion. "Well, I guess you'll just have to watch and hope you can manage." He flashed a smirk as he turned back toward the board.

Krarshe couldn't believe it. He would have believed that Owyn had just forgotten to say anything to Krarshe, but that smile dismissed any possibility of that. This was intentional. This was spite. Was he really that upset about yesterday?

"Don't worry, I have all the notes for this class," Bri whispered to him. "I'll share them with you later."

"Thanks," Krarshe said. "The two of you are really saving my life here."

"What?" Bri asked, then turned to Tibault inquisitively.

"I, uhh, snatched the last spellbook in Feyfaire, so I offered to share it with him."

"Now I'm starting to suspect you're doing this on purpose, Karshe," Bri said as she shot a glance at him out of the corner of her eye, her head cocked to the side accusingly.

Krarshe just smiled.

The lecture proceeded for what felt like an eternity. The class feverishly scribbled the characters on their papers, trying to keep up with the lesson. Owyn snapped countless sticks of chalk as he wrote, almost as if he was deliberately trying to go too fast for the class to keep up. Krarshe heard a few students mutter curses as the faint sound of snapping quills or the clink of tipped ink wells could be made out over the screeching of the chalk. Poor Tibault was beginning to sweat as he tried to keep up, his penmanship becoming increasingly messy and illegible.

There were a slew of these strange characters. Several of them appeared to be sounds that matched multiple letters in the common tongue, some as many as four. *What is this convoluted alphabet?* Krarshe asked himself. *This doesn't even begin to make sense.*

As the sunlight reached the last and final stone in the courtyard, Owyn clapped. "And that's all of it." There were audible sighs and groans of relief as nearly everyone collapsed, heads resting in their arms on the tables. "We will take a break here for lunch, and then we will do another practical lesson with a new spell. I'm sure, this time, everyone will cast the correct spell," he said, enunciating every word as he turned to Krarshe. "You are all dismissed."

Bri reached one arm high above her head, gripping it with her other hand in a big stretch. "This lesson gets more boring each time I sit through it. Come on, Tibault, don't look so down," she said, giving him a slight shove. Tibault just groaned a response as he laid his head on his crossed forearms in front of him on the desk.

"So, where would you like to buy us lunch today, Tibault?" Krarshe joked.

"I'm not buying you anything," Tibault said, muffled by his arm. "Not after you two just sat there all lesson, carefree as could be."

Krarshe and Bri laughed. "Come on, I'll buy today," Krarshe said, standing up.

"I just want to lay here until I rot away, Teva taking me in her embrace," Tibault groaned.

"You'll like the afternoon lesson," Bri said, trying to encourage him, patting him on the back. She immediately pulled her hand away, looking disgustedly at her palm that was now coated with Tibault's sweat. She shook her hand a bit, and then wiped it on her uniform's skirt. "Though, I'm more concerned about it than I was last year..." She looked at Krarshe.

"I didn't do anything," Krarshe exclaimed.

"Yeah, except nearly destroy the school," said a voice from the other side of the room.

Krarshe and Bri looked in the direction of the voice; Tibault lifted his head. Armand was huddled with the group of boys he was at the tavern with yesterday. Their faces were twisted in contempt.

"I didn't do that," Krarshe said, repeating his defense.

"Yeah? Then who was it who wrecked the academy's equipment? Who was it that nearly injured everyone? Huh?" Armand blurted out.

Krashe knew that technically, his accusations were accurate, leaving him without a retort. Honestly, he just wanted to ignore Armand and not give him the attention he so desperately wanted. Seemed the wisest route.

"No one was 'nearly injured'," Tibault fired back before Krarshe could counter, attempting to back up his new friend. He was sitting upright, alert, as though his previous fatigue was just an act.

"This doesn't concern you, lesser noble shit," Armand said with a sneer.

Tibault clicked his tongue and looked away, at a loss for a comeback.

"I cast the same spell you all did," Krarshe stated.

"Yet, none of our spells were tainted with lightning." Armand wasn't letting up. The situation was only getting more heated. "You trying to show off, you fucking elf? Think you're better than us?!"

"Him being an elf has nothing to do with it! It WAS the same spell! I know it was!" Bri shouted at Armand, standing up aggressively.

Armand snickered. "Yeah, you ought to know. How many times have you been through that lesson? Seven? Eight?" His friends laughed. Krarshe wanted to just smack that smug expression off his perfect face.

Bri clenched her teeth, her fists tightening. Tears began to well up, though Krarshe was unsure if they were of anguish or anger.

Krarshe could read the situation. If he just continued to sit quietly, this would escalate. He wasn't looking for a fight, but he didn't want to let Armand get away with insulting his defenders either. He stood up, and walked over to Armand and his posse, each step coming down hard and deliberate enough to draw everyone's attention. The students who hadn't left yet all held their breath as they watched, anticipating a fight. Armand's friends cowered away as he approached. Armand stood there defiantly, but Krarshe could see his uneasiness.

He got face to face with his antagonizer. Krarshe could feel himself tensing, his own anger beginning to take over as he faced down his foe. He breathed deeply before suddenly backing off from Armand. "Let's go," Krarshe said to Bri and Tibault. "This *krun* isn't worth our time." He fired a smirk at Armand and turned to walk out of the room. Bri and Tibault hurried after him, exchanging disgusted looks at Armand as they passed. Armand's legs gave out and he flopped into his chair again as the class all released their collective breaths.

"Five curses on you, sprite," Krarshe heard Armand grumble, followed by a slam of his fist on the table.

* * *

Lunch passed uneventfully. Neither Krarshe nor his friends wanted to talk about what had transpired in the classroom. It wouldn't have changed anything, and bringing it up would just frustrate them further, so they all just ate together in silence. As they returned to the school grounds, Krarshe saw Armand through the window, already back in his seat. Or maybe having never left.

"Hey," Krarshe started, addressing his two new friends. They both stopped and looked at him. "I appreciate that you both stood up for me there b—"

"Of course we would," Bri said with a smile.

"Yeah," Tibault chirped. "He was being..."

"A jerk," Bri finished Tibault's statement.

"Not the word I would have picked, but yeah."

"Well, I appreciate it," Krarshe said finally. "But, you don't have to do that. I don't really know who your families are, or what family he's from, but if you're both nobles, I don't want you feeling like you need to defend me. I wouldn't want you tarnishing your family's reputation because of my actions."

Tibault and Bri just stood there quietly, surprised by his comment. "Listen," Bri began, but then stopped, seemingly still formulating her thoughts.

"You don't have to worry about me," Tibault said. "It's like he said, I'm a lesser noble. Can't be thought of any less than

90

that anyway. And I'm sure my family would be happy to hear I stood up for someone."

"There is honor in that," Bri agreed. The three were quiet again, standing out in the empty school courtyard, the hot Sirnusian sun bearing down on them. "Regardless, let us be the ones to decide how to hold ourselves, as nobles," Bri said with a smile.

Krarshe was at a loss for words. Even in such a short time, it felt the three of them were already closer than he had been with anyone since he struck out on his own. Finding this feeling was why he started this journey in the first place. He could feel himself choking up as he thought about it. He swallowed hard to try and regain his composure.

Krarshe raised his hands in resignation. "Okay, okay. I get it. I'll just do whatever I feel befits a commoner and leave you two to act on your own." He started toward the classroom entrance again.

Bri and Tibault just looked at each other and laughed slightly before hurrying to catch up to Krarshe. As they entered the room, the class hushed and just watched them. Armand was the lone exception, avoiding all eye contact and staring at the table he sat at. His handsome face was more appealing to look at when he was so visibly annoyed.

Not a minute later, Owyn came in. He immediately pulled out another stick of chalk and began striking the chalkboard. The class took the subtle hint and quietly hurried to their seats.

"For this afternoon, we'll be learning a light spell," he said as he finished writing out the spell, spinning around to face the class fast enough for his ponytail to sweep around from behind him to drape itself around his neck like a thin black scarf. His eyes were still filled with fury as they looked directly at Krarshe. "Normally," he started with emphasis, "we'd just cast this spell in this room. But, given the incident yesterday, I've deemed it safer to go out to the training area again. So, ahem. Repeat after me."

Owyn recited the spell, with the class following. The spell itself was significantly easier than the wind burst spell was, with fewer syllables and ones not particularly complex. After a few repetitions, the teacher clapped and led the class out to the training area once again.

"Wow, you did a good job," Tibault joked as he observed the training room, noting the stark difference between the mess Krarshe had made yesterday and how neat it was now.

"He was here until second moon, after all," Bri clarified.

"Quiet!" Owyn yelled at the two of them. Bri and Tibault jolted, and then looked down at the ground, embarrassed. "Now, simply hold your hand like this," he explained, holding his hand out, palm up, "and recite the spell." He recited the spell, and a glowing sphere appeared floating above his hand, about the size of his head. "The more mana you release, the brighter it will be. But, you do not need to exert a lot of effort for this exercise. Just creating the orb will suffice." He looked at Krarshe. Clearly, his words were directed at him. "You may all cast at once. And don't get confused with the other student's spellcasts. It's not unusual for multiple mages to be casting at the same time, so you must learn to focus on your own cast and not be distracted."

Krarshe walked over to the far corner of the facility, slightly behind the stone wall that separated the equipment from the main section. He figured if the spell went out of control again, it would be better to put a wall between him and the other students. He watched for a moment as the other students slowly began finishing their casts. Bri cast without hesitation, creating an orb nearly identical to the professor's. He didn't take any notice, instead focusing on the rest of the students. Tibault appeared to be struggling, before moving away from the other students. After less than a minute, most of the class managed to create an orb of light.

Guess it's my turn, eh? Krarshe thought to himself. *Let's see if I can release just a bit of mana this time. Though, it's only a light spell, so it should be fine.*

He held out his hand. Owyn immediately looked over at him, watching carefully. His wild eyebrows lowered, clearly focused. Krarshe breathed. "Just a bit," he said to himself.

He recited the short spell and an orb began to form above his palm. Almost as quickly as it began, the orb's light burst forth from it and overwhelmed the light from every other student's orbs. It even dwarfed the light from the sun. The light was so intense that not a single shadow could be seen. Krarshe heard Owyn start cursing and crying out about his eyes. He looked over to see everyone shielding their face from the light.

Well, I guess it's technically right? Krarshe thought. He stood there confidently, until the first bolt of electricity came arcing off of the orb and striking the ground between him and the rest of his class, causing the stone floor itself to shatter and erupt with a shower of debris, leaving behind a small crater. Before he could react, a second bolt of lightning struck the wall of the storage area, bouncing off the wall and crashing through some armor stands. Another fired off, crackling into the sky. A fourth struck the wall, causing more stone shards to explode from where he had just cracked the wall the day before.

Krarshe stopped his flow of mana as quickly as he could, cancelling the spell instantly. He looked at the class. As they lowered their arms, they beheld the smoking pits his lightning had left behind, their eyes going wide, jaws dropping. Professor Owyn, curled up in the fetal position, continued to clutch his eyes with his hands, shouting profanities, apparently blinded by the light of Krarshe's orb.

Krarshe made eye contact with Tibault, who just stood there, mouth agape. He turned to Bri, who was making a nervous, toothy smile at Krarshe, clearly concerned by what she saw but not wanting to alarm him. As with the day prior, the senior teachers came rushing out a moment later. They looked at the destruction for a moment before running over to Owyn. The older teacher from last night just looked around the area, nodding slowly as he stroked his long mustache. He seemed to just be marvelling at all the damage Krarshe had caused, not a hint of concern or malice showed on his face.

The other teachers helped Owyn to his feet, and guided him out of the room. One stopped and addressed the class. "You're all dismissed for today." He turned to look at Krarshe. "You, please wait here until we return." He then grabbed the elderly teacher, still lost in his own thoughts, and pulled him out of the room.

As the students began to filter out, Krarshe was able to make out some snide remarks. He caught a passing glare from Armand as he left the room. Krarshe knew this was only proving that smug kid's point and he hated it. Bri and Tibault came over to him.

"Whoa," Tibault said, as he walked past the crater in the middle of the floor, looking at it more closely. "This was way worse than yesterday."

"Yeah," Bri agreed.

"I... I tried to hold back," Krarshe stated.

"That's holding back!?" Tibault exclaimed, pointing at the nearly demolished far wall.

Krarshe shrugged.

"That's two spells that have somehow gone awry," Bri noted. "I've never even heard of this before."

"I don't think the teachers have either," remarked Tibault.

"Why do you think they're having me stay behind?"

Bri shrugged, shaking her head. "I haven't the slightest clue. Can't be good though."

Krarshe sighed. "Well, what's the worst that can happen?" he asked cheerfully, trying to stay optimistic.

"Reported to the Council of Mages," Tibault answered seriously.

"Don't even joke," Bri reprimanded him. Tibault gave a shrug, his face twisted in concern. "Hopefully that's not the case. That would be disastrous."

"I guess I'll find out soon enough." Krarshe looked at the damage he caused. The craters were beyond his ability to deal with. He looked at the storage area. Only a few pieces of armor looked damaged. They appeared to have blackened, deformed in a few spots. Two breastplates had fallen over, welded together. "Glad I decided to do it over here though," he said pensively. "It could have killed someone if this wall wasn't here."

"I mean..." Bri started, looking at the crater in the middle of the room, but stopped herself. She didn't need to say it, it was clear what she was thinking.

"You two should get going. I'll be fine," Krarshe said. "Even if I get kicked out, or something worse, I'll be sure to find a way to tell you guys."

"Right," they both said quietly, their eyes lowering.

"Well, good luck," Bri said as she turned to leave.

"Yeah, best of luck," Tibault echoed, following her.

Krarshe watched them leave. It was like he had been in almost this exact position just a night ago. Sitting alone in the training room, listening to the deafening silence. There were some midday flies buzzing around his head this time, though. He sat there, watching the sun march its way across the sky and swatting at flies, awaiting his sentence.

* * *

For the next hour, Krarshe was alone with his thoughts. He meandered around the training room, first picking up the equipment he damaged, or the ones that could still stand. Once that was done, he kicked chunks of stone around absent-mindedly before thinking to put them back from where they had escaped, or as best as he could. After that, though, he was out of ideas for constructive things he could do to pass the time, so he spent the remainder just sitting on the ground, staring at the sky.

Finally, one of the professors returned and beckoned for him to follow. Krarshe obediently, meekly, followed the balding, heavy-set gentleman through the dimly lit hallways of the school. As he passed the other classrooms, he noticed that they were empty. Perhaps the senior classes had also been dismissed. Eventually, they arrived at his classroom where the other four teachers, including Owyn, were waiting. Owyn's eyes appeared to have recovered, though they looked quite wet, likely a result of whatever treatment they had given him. The teacher who had led Krarshe in closed the door as they entered and joined the other teachers.

"So, Krarshe, was it?" asked the hefty teacher.

Krarshe nodded.

"That name, very curious..." he said, more to the other teachers than to Krarshe. "Well. We've been informed by Professor Owyn about the two recent mishaps in the training room. For whatever reason, it is clear the spells you are casting are not acting normally. You don't happen to be carrying any enchanted items that would result in this, correct?"

Krarshe shook his head. "Nothing, sir."

"No... curses on you? Nor your family?"

Krarshe furrowed his brow. "Not to my knowledge, not through tale nor sensation."

"Sensation?" asked the long-mustached teacher.

"From what I know of them," Krarshe explained, "curses tend to affect mana differently from spells. And if you were cursed, you could feel it in your own mana." Krarshe paused. The expression on the teacher's faces, both as they looked at him and at each other, implied this was new information to them. He may have just triggered a trap. "At least, that's what I heard," he added.

"From whom, might I ask?" another of the teachers asked. His thick, bushy beard hid his mouth. If his breath from his question hadn't blown on his beard, Krarshe wouldn't have known who had asked the question.

"A mage that my father knew. During his time travelling as a merchant."

The unknown teacher nodded slowly, hand on his chin thoughtfully, as he watched Krarshe closely. "And sensing mana?"

Krarshe knew he couldn't pin this on his fictional father's mage friend again. So he tried another tactic. "It's something taught to everyone where I'm from," he said. "A small country, north of Armia," he added quickly before they could ask.

"I see... I wasn't aware this was part of elven upbringing, though I wouldn't be surprised..." The look on the teacher's face told Krarshe that this was sufficient convincing. The other teachers seemed content with that explanation as well, save for Owyn who was still scowling at him.

The teachers huddled together and talked amongst themselves. Krarshe watched their expressions as best he could. He could make out inquisitive glances, disapproving looks, and angry glares; the glares were exclusively from Owyn. Krarshe looked past them to the windows. There were still some students mulling about and socializing in the courtyard, free from their classes for the day. He didn't recognize any of them, so he guessed they were mostly senior students.

After a moment, the teachers turned back to Krarshe. After clearing his throat, causing the fat folds of his neck to jiggle, the heavy-set teacher spoke up again. "With the cause still being a mystery to us, the fact remains that twice now your spells have gone out of control. Endangering your class is grounds for expulsion."

Krarshe anticipated this. He had already prepared himself mentally, and had begun thinking of new adventures he could go on. As he was about to ask if he could reclaim some of his tuition money, the heavy teacher spoke again.

"However, Professor Landry has requested that you stay," he said, gesturing to the long-mustached one in traditional mage robes. Professor Landry gave a small bow and smile, which Krarshe reciprocated, slightly confused. "He wishes to conduct tests with you, to see if he can understand this anomaly."

So, I'll basically be used for experimentation. That... may be worse than expulsion, Krarshe thought.

The teacher continued. "As you have paid your tuition, you are still allowed to access the classroom lectures, if you so desire, when Professor Landry is busy with his class. Additionally, as he has other duties after midday break, your afternoon practical sessions will be spent in the store we run here instead."

So, not only am I a test subject, but I'll be a merchant. Again. Krarshe stifled a sigh. Best not to let them know what he thought of his punishment. He looked over at Owyn. He was looking away, looking as grumpy as he had when Krarshe walked in. *Is he POUTING? Is he a child?*

"Do you have any questions?" the teacher asked, finishing his explanation.

Krarshe shook his head again. "No, sir."

"We should just expel him!" Owyn finally cried out. "He tried to blind me! This was a deliberate attack!"

"That is not clearly known," said the fifth teacher, spoken as softly as his gentle, pale features would have led you to believe. "Besides, this anomalous behavior must be studied. On that, I agree with Landry."

"As do I," said the heavy teacher. "An unknown like this could bring us much attention. Letting it leave would be a mistake."

'It'? I'm an 'it' now?

"But!" Owyn contested.

"This debate is over, Owyn," Professor Landry said sharply, a side of the old man Krarshe hadn't seen in his brief encounters with him. At this, Owyn backed down, unable to challenge the old man. Krarshe figured there must be some form of seniority taking place here. "Krarshe, please go seek out Cyril in the store and tell him I requested he show you around the store and explain what to do. I have a class tomorrow, so I will see you two days from now. You are dismissed," Landry said with a kind, old smile.

Krarshe bowed, and left. After the door shut, he could hear Owyn start complaining again. *I guess this punishment isn't all bad,* he thought with a smile. *Funny, though. I wanted to move on from a merchant, but here I am again.* He sighed, and headed to the store to find this Cyril so he could reluctantly restart his merchant life.

CHAPTER 6

Krarshe sat there as he had the past few mornings, staring out the window into the barren stone courtyard, watching the students flock to the classroom, counting stones as they were illuminated by the morning sun. Per usual, none of the students who entered spoke with him. He was happy with that, though. Peace and quiet worked just fine for him, though he was concerned he might fall asleep with boredom. He wasn't sure why he insisted on arriving so early, though it likely had to do with this moment of quiet that he had grown so accustomed to. He realized he should have slept later today, however, as he was restless last night, but it was too late for that. He'd just have to deal with it.

"Karshe!" Tibault called out as he entered the classroom, shattering Krarshe's tranquil morning. His pronunciation had changed; maybe Bri had corrected him. "I honestly didn't expect to see you here today. What happened?"

Krarshe sleepily turned to him, doing his best to hold up his heavy eyelids. "I'm going to be studied."

Tibault stood there, waiting for a follow up explanation, but Krarshe just turned back to the window. Through it, he saw Bri, turning the corner by the store with her head down. As she approached, she looked up and made eye contact with Krarshe. He could see her gloomy expression change as she hurried into the building.

"Is... that it?" Tibault asked, still waiting for Krarshe to go into more detail.

"Karshe!" Bri yelled as she entered the room, nearly identical to how Tibault had just done. "What happened?!" she asked as she ran over.

I knew this would happen, Krarshe thought. He turned to face both of them. "As I told Tibault, I'll be studied." Krarshe waited for the confusion to set into Bri as well, for no reason other than his own twisted enjoyment, watching them both get anxious. "Professor Landry thought my case was strange, so he wants to study my spellcasting. He has a class today, so I'm allowed to come to class while he's busy. But, from now on, I guess I'll only attend class every other day."

"That's... not what I expected to happen," Bri admitted.

"I thought you were certainly going to be expelled, at the very least," Tibault stated.

"I am, however, not allowed to attend the practical lessons in the afternoon," Krarshe added. "I'll have to work in the store instead."

"Already? How do they expect you to run it?" Bri asked. "I've worked in there a lot, and there's still items I don't know."

Krarshe thought back to the first day he saw her in the store. Maybe this ignorance was the cause of her nervousness back then. "A senior student or teacher will always be present while I'm there. For a while, at least."

"Just try not to be more bored than you seem in class," Bri laughed. "Trust me, time seems to slow to a crawl in there."

"I'm sure I'll find a way to entertain myself," Krarshe said with a smile, his blue eyes shone mischievously.

"If you break anything, or play with what you shouldn't be touching, you might just get expelled this time," Tibault warned.

Just as Krarshe was about to reassure him, Owyn stormed into the room. His usually neat black hair was in disarray, though still well-groomed compared to his eyebrows. *He must still be angry,* Krarshe thought. As the class got to their seats, Krarshe heard a whisper from beside him.

"I'm glad you're still here," Bri said quietly.

"Me too," Tibault agreed.

Krarshe just smiled quietly as they bowed to the teacher. The lesson continued as if nothing had changed. Krarshe paid attention for the start of it. It seemed to be an introduction to somatic components to casting; the introductory example involved a few small hand gestures and was performed simultaneously with the wind burst they had learned the first day. Apparently, it augmented the spell, be it for controlling the direction or power of the spell, or to be used in conjunction with group casting. After the first thirty minutes or so of explanation, it started to become redundant. It was clear that specific uses for each gesture would be dependent on which spell it was. Krarshe's vision was starting to blur with sleepiness as he struggled against the weight of his eyelids. As the lecture turned into a lesson on the history of somatic casting, Krarshe again shifted his gaze to the courtyard. He could feel his consciousness slipping. For the rest of the class, he fought the pleasant sensation of resting his eyes, though he was uncertain how successful he was. He'd have to ask Bri and Tibault if he missed anything later.

* * *

The morning class seemed to end in an instant, evidence that Krarshe had eventually lost to his tiredness at some point. While the morning lecture was dull, the latter half of his day in the store was significantly worse. Krarshe was told to not interact with any of the customers, not that there were many, and a senior student would handle everything. The student in charge today didn't even give his name, so Krarshe would just refer to him as 'supervisor'. Occasionally, a customer would wander in and the supervisor would engage them almost immediately. Krarshe listened a bit to the interactions, but it was usually pretty basic. The customer would say they were looking for something, the student would bring them over to a product. Monetary exchanges were also handled by this supervisor. Krarshe did nothing but sit and watch quietly, which got increasingly more difficult with each hour that passed as the continuing battle with his drowsiness was a losing affair. On more than one occasion, he thought about sneaking off to the back room and taking a real nap.

The only unique interaction all day was with an elf woman who Krarshe overheard was not looking for anything today but just inspecting the goods they sold. She was probably the only thing that shook up the monotony of the afternoon, this attractive blonde elf slowly making her way around the store. Curiously, the supervising student was also meandering around the room at the same time. At first, Krarshe wasn't sure what he was doing, but it became apparent after a minute that he was indeed watching her while trying to keep some distance in an attempt to be less conspicuous. Watching this chase through the maze of shelving was some much needed entertainment for Krarshe.

As the day dragged on, he was able to see the students leaving for the day. Tibault and Bri stopped to wave at him through the window as they left for the day, but all it did was make Krarshe wish he could leave. The store had to be manned until closing, his supervisor had explained, so they would be there until the sun set. As such, his friends' farewell was more annoying than encouraging.

With no customers and being on the final stretch of this incredibly long day, Krarshe wandered the store, looking at the products. The staves that lined the side wall appeared dull and uninteresting at first, but upon closer inspection were actually more than just durable sticks. They had some symbols carved into them, different from the symbols used in class for spellcasting. Krarshe guessed they were some kind of rune, though that seemed to contradict Owyn's opinion of dwarven runeforging. The wands were much the same, with small symbols carved into them. Krarshe was left to wonder how they managed to write so small without any mistakes. Most of the armor also contained symbols written on the inside, but not all of them. He was fairly certain that everything in the store was magic in nature, so he wasn't sure what to make of those pieces without markings.

"Those are imbued with magic during forging," said a soft, elderly voice. Krarshe turned to see Professor Landry standing behind the counter, watching as Krarshe inspected the goods. "It's a newer technique compared to inscription. Admittedly, I don't know the exact process for it, but the magic is part of the metal itself."

Landry walked around to the armor stands and looked over one of the breastplates, almost as if he was trying to understand the imbuement process himself. After a second, he picked up a gauntlet unsteadily instead, and showed the inside to Krarshe.

"You see," he said, gesturing to the inscription on the inside, "this armor's enchantment only holds while this inscription remains. If it's damaged, the enchantment won't work anymore. Not a good thing in the middle of battle." His long white mustache twitched as his mouth curled into a smile, the wrinkles around his eyes deepening. He set the armor back on its stand and walked back to the counter. "You're free to go now, Krarshe. I'll close up here. I'll see you tomorrow in the training range."

"Thank you, sir. I'll see you tomorrow morning," Krarshe said hurriedly, excited to finally be able to get out of that store.

"Take care, and make sure you get plenty of rest. I have a lot of things I want to test," the professor said, laughing his slow, weary laugh.

* * *

Krarshe sat at his table in The Easy Lute, eagerly awaiting his dinner. He had remembered last night that he never got to enjoy the fish he wanted his first day here. This time, though, he managed to get it, and he was unquestionably excited for it. Valerie, the waitress teaching Na'kika, had recommended the seared fillet with herbs and greens, and he had taken her up on the recommendation. In high spirits in anticipation of the fish, despite the drag of a day he had to that point, he ventured to chat with Valerie after placing his order. In addition to her name, he learned that the bard that spent so much time at this inn was Henry, the future son-in-law of the owner. They weren't picky about the musical selection, and not restricted to lutes, but this was Henry's preferred instrument. Occasionally there would be other bards who would fill in, but Henry was the regular musician, and most people came to hear him. Or to laugh at his expense, as he did tend to stumble more than most. It apparently was all in good fun, though, and he'd usually laugh along with them.

Before long, Na'kika brought out his fish and set it down in front of him. "Thank you, Na'kika," Krarshe said to her. She smiled back at him and turned to return to the kitchen. "You know," Krarshe started, stopping her abruptly, "does Henry know any other songs?"

Na'kika just tilted her head to the side, questioning him.

"I mean, he plays The Five Curses a lot. I think I hear it at least a few times every dinner these last few days. Honestly, I don't know how much more I can hear about the Wanderer, or the Snatcher stealing children in the night," Krarshe joked, smiling. "How many times a night do you tend to hear him recite it?"

Na'kika looked away and put her finger to her lips pensively. She then held up ten fingers, then closed them and opened them again. After a pause and another thoughtful glance, she repeated the gesture.

"That's... a lot. You have my condolences," he said.

She smiled, and then shook her head. Na'kika gestured to herself and then waved her hand with confident dismissal, before smiling an even bigger smile than before.

Krarshe laughed. "I see, I see. My concerns were unwarranted. Also, isn't this song a bit too... cheerful? I mean, it seems a pretty somber topic to have such a happy tune, doesn't it?"

Na'kika nodded her head up and down. She turned her palms up and changed her head shaking to a side-to-side motion, agreeing to Krarshe's confusion. She then began to gesture as though she held a lute and began to play it slowly before once more nodding at Krarshe expectantly.

"Yeah, I agree. It'd make much more sense."

Her smile kept growing. This was the first time Krarshe had seen her so animated in the few days he spent at the inn. Her tail whipped and curled excitedly, her slit cat eyes clear as she focused on Krarshe. She seemed much happier than usual.

"Maybe I should recommend something to him. Mmm... Actually, I don't know many songs. I'd be in trouble if he asked for lyrics," Krarshe laughed.

Na'kika couldn't resist giggling, as she tried to hide it with her empty tray. That was the first sound he'd ever heard her make.

"Oyy! Na'kika! Got 'nother plate!" called the chef, coming out from around the corner of the kitchen.

Na'kika waved an acknowledgement before turning to Krarshe and bowing, her tail still waving around wildly. She then turned and dashed to the kitchen.

"That was nice of you."

"Valerie, you weren't watching that whole time, were you?" Krarshe asked as he turned around.

"But of course! I'm mentoring her, after all." She stood a dozen or so paces behind him, carrying a tray of empty mugs. "I don't get to see her that happy usually."

"From just a conversation?"

"Yeah. She doesn't get to communicate with people that often. And she hasn't had any real conversations with customers, even brief ones like yours, since starting here." She picked up a few more empty mugs from a nearby table and put them on her tray. "Most of the time, they ignore her, or don't know how to interact with her. Truthfully, I think it just makes her more self-conscious of her inability to speak when they're cautious around her," Valerie said, twirling to the other side of Krarshe's table to make way for a customer, her dark brown hair fluttering around before landing on her shoulder.

"It honestly didn't feel like much. I'd do more if I could."

"Doing this much is more than you realize. Being understood for a change makes a world of difference. I hope you have more conversations with her. I'm sure it'd make her happy too. And I'll ask Henry to work on some new songs," she said, flashing a smile as she started toward the kitchen.

Krarshe sat there quietly for a minute. "A simple conversation is enough to bring her happiness, huh? I hope I can do better than that," Krarshe said to himself as he dug into his much-awaited fish dinner.

Chapter 7

"Okay, now for this next one..." Professor Landry said, marking his book with his quill. He sat in the back of the training area, behind a wooden barricade he had his students erect following their first experiment session. The wood was heavy and thick, and had clay plastered on the front of it to inhibit any stray bolts of lightning that happened to come his way, though it was beginning to wear and crack under the constant barrage of the last half-cycle since the experiments had begun. "Looks like the last element is fire. Can you recite this? *Ingriru, hias dzam do'e, se me hinoras. Mem krandza hindoo sem te, dun hias.* Aim it toward the sky like you have been."

Krarshe stood in the middle of the training area. The space was a mess, with shattered stone strewn about the room. Krarshe was covered in the dust from the impacts, so much so that you couldn't tell his hair was blond. He waved his hand in front of his face, trying to clear the dust, and sucked in a breath of dusty air and recited the spell, while raising his hand straight up over his head. As the spell finished, a large column of fire burst forth from his hand into the sky, well above the stone walls of the enclosure. As with every other spell he had cast that morning, and in the past thirty days since the start of these experiments, electricity accompanied the spell, spilling out from his palm and striking the ground and walls around him. After a couple seconds, he ended the spell and the flame died out.

"Hmm... I see, I see," said the old teacher, scribbling a few more notes in his book. "Not only were both elements there again, but the volume of the spell was beyond expectation as well."

"Was it? What spell was it?" Krarshe asked. He had an idea already, but figured he'd ask.

"A simple flame spell. Like this." Landry stuck his hand out from behind his barricade and recited the spell. A small flame, small enough to fit into his palm, came forth. "It's typically used as an alternative to flint to start a fire, or light a lamp. So yes, I'd say the volume of your spell was irregular." Landry closed his hand, extinguishing the flame, and slowly stepped out from the barricade. "How are you feeling this time?"

"Fine."

"Hmm. No signs of fatigue again..." Landry scribbled something else into his book.

Krarshe sat there, dusting himself off. The sheer amount of debris that shook free from his hair depressed him. He knew he'd be cleaning it out for at least a quarter-cycle. Looking at the professor, he noticed some dust had snuck under the barricade where he was sitting, and the ends of his long mustache must have been in the blast zone; the tips of his exceedingly long mustache were covered in dust like his shoes.

"It appears to almost be time for lunch break to end, so we'll need to make room for the junior class." Landry stopped and looked around the room. 'Chaos' wouldn't have done justice to the mess Krarshe made. "Actually," he paused, bringing his hand to his mouth pensively, "I don't know why I didn't have you try this first. You must exhaust all possibilities, not just focus on irregularities." He turned and hurried behind the barricade again, as quick as his old body would carry him.

Krarshe stared at the barricade hiding the teacher for a moment. *I figured cleaning up a bit would have been the logical next step, but okay,* Krarshe thought, kicking a few pieces of stone to the side of the room.

"Try this spell!" Landry called from his hiding spot. "*Se Esfiru hinoras, suesoo shu zeraus dzam mea'anom. Grunda sem te, mem krandza zonya, sem tsaru mrom, dun zerais.*"

Krarshe raised an eyebrow, but then shrugged and raised his hand. "*Se Esfiru hinoras, suesoo shu zeraus dzam mea'anom. Grunda sem te, mem krandza zonya, sem tsaru mrom, dun zerais!*"

A bolt of lightning came from his palm the instant his spell finished, streaking into the blue sky. Krarshe stared at the sky in wonder. The spell wasn't particularly interesting itself, a simple bolt of lightning. But that wasn't the important part. It was that there were no stray bolts. A singular bolt, clean of any distortions.

"Aha!" Landry cried out, jumping out from behind his wood and clay barricade, betraying his feeble behavior to this point. "That was exactly right! Fool I was for not trying it first! But... Oh, the conjectures that stem from this discovery!" The elderly man hopped around excitedly, no sign of the fragile old mage Krarshe knew.

Krarshe was equally excited. Maybe not as outwardly excited as Landry was, dancing around like a maniac, but this was reassuring. He decided it best to just stay silent and watch the professor have his moment of jubilation. He then heard some murmuring coming from the heavy door. "Umm, Professor. I think the junior class—"

"One more!" Landry interrupted. "Just once more. I need to see this with more mana put into it, see if that affects the outcome. With that, we'll be able to call it a day."

Krarshe sighed. He didn't really want to risk showing these experiments to his classmates, especially with how they had reacted to any of his prior spells. He knew how much mana he was letting slip out, and there was no way to know what would happen if he released more. Scaring his classmates more seemed the worst possible route. Though, could they really be considered classmates if he'll never be in class that much going forward? He assumed the position again.

"Professor Landry, it's time for my class—" Owyn said, entering the room. "What happened in here?!"

"Shh! Watch this!" Landry said, hushing Owyn. He wasn't behind his barricade anymore. He, Owyn, and several students stood by the door, watching Krarshe.

Great, now I have an audience.

Krarshe recited the spell again, feeling the mana circulating through his body, coursing down his extended arm. *Only a bit more mana. I don't want to risk anything,* he thought. As he finished the spell, an enormous bolt of lighting exploded from his hand, the clap of thunder shook the training room with enough force to knock over the armor stands. The force of the spell almost buckled his knees. Krarshe could feel the lingering static of electricity around his arm afterwards, along with some slight numbness.

"See? See? Aha! This is glorious!" Landry shouted excitedly.

Krarshe turned to see Landry hopping around again. More funny, however, was the look on Owyn's and the other students' faces: pure astonishment. And their hair. Their hair stood at attention, charged with electricity. Krarshe just stood there before his stunned class, in the center of the broken and damaged room, smiling nervously.

* * *

Krarshe sat behind the store counter, tapping his fingers rhythmically. Landry had dismissed Krarshe that afternoon as he danced off with his research data. Owyn didn't say anything as Krarshe had walked past, still staring up at the sky. His eyebrows had been even more disheveled with the static electricity that was filling the air. Apparently Armand had been one of the ones watching. Like Owyn, he was gawking at the sky, his hair on end. Actually, all of the students who had witnessed it had pretty much the same response. Or lack thereof. It wasn't until he got through the door that he encountered something different. While some looked frightened after the building shook, and others astonished as they watched Krarshe, all of them were whispering to each other. Tibault and Bri, however, didn't say anything as he walked past. Both just looked at him nervously.

That's what bothered him the most. Not the class' reaction to him, but the reactions of the two he considered his friends. They had been astonished by his spells before, and that was perfectly reasonable. But this time was different. They actually seemed frightened. The silence as he walked past, the lack of reaction when he smiled at them. It all gnawed at him. Maybe he should have spoken first. Maybe he should have said something, anything, so he could understand what they were thinking. Maybe he should have done a lot of things, but it was all moot now. After fretting over it for a couple hours, he was more nervous than he was at the time, and knew that breaching the subject would be next to impossible. His stomach was in knots thinking about it. Now, being largely alone in the store with nothing but his swirling thoughts to entertain him, it made the whole situation worse and the knots tighten.

It was almost the end of the day, and there hadn't been a single customer the whole time. The senior student in charge spent most of his time in the back room doing who-knows-what. Despite his uneasiness, his stomach growled ferociously. Since he was delayed because of Professor Landry, he wasn't allowed to get food before going to the store.

I'm not even technically supposed to be here. And there's another student. I don't understand why I couldn't quickly get something to eat, Krarshe thought, still gripping his stomach. The alternating feeling of knots and hunger were making him nauseous.

The click and creak of the door opening pulled Krarshe's attention away from his stomach. He immediately recognized the customer as the blonde elf woman from the day before. As her eyes met his, she addressed him.

"Good afternoon, I've returned to make a purchase." Her voice was soothing, but harbored a hidden confidence to it that was almost unnoticeable.

"A customer?" the senior student asked, immediately poking his head out from the back room. When he saw the elegant customer, the chubby student plodded his way out to the store floor, nearly pushing Krarshe out of the way. He brushed his hair back with his hand and cleared his throat. "How my I help you?"

Real smooth... Krarshe thought, rolling his eyes. *Isn't she a bit old for you, kid?* He wasn't sure how old she was, as judging an elf's age was difficult even for those with a better eye for age than he was, but he would have guessed her to be a couple hundred years old. Her youthful appearance was misleading, but the mature way she held herself was indicative of someone with ample life experience.

"Actually, it is for my daughter," the lady said. She stepped aside and guided a girl in.

Krarshe froze as his heart skipped a beat. The daughter was stunningly beautiful. She couldn't have been much older than Krarshe, judging by her appearance in the short, red summer dress she wore. Her long, straight blonde hair hung down just past her shoulders, a single braid traced the right side of her face. The features of her face were delicate and fair, her pale skin shone radiantly, the perfect combination with her shining golden hair. She stepped into the store elegantly, her green, glistening eyes surveying the room as she entered.

The senior student appeared just as enamored as Krarshe was, as he began stuttering. Krarshe could see him begin to sweat as he tried to say something. The mother stood there

watching the perspiring young man for a moment, creases in her forehead showing her concern. She turned to Krarshe, who still held a strong facade, and called to him. "Perhaps you could help us?"

It took him a moment for it to register what she had asked before Krarshe snapped out of this enthrallment. "Y-yes, of course!" he said, stumbling around the counter, knocking a book off the edge of it. He clumsily picked it up and put it back on the counter and ran over to them. As he approached, he caught the eye of the young elf girl, who promptly turned her attention to the shelf of goods next to her, tucking the braid behind her ear.

"I-I-I've g-g-got this!" the senior student stuttered, but the customer and her daughter had already left him behind. He was left there, standing dejectedly. It was a sad sight to see, but Krarshe's focus was elsewhere.

"What can I do for you both?" Krarshe asked, mustering all of his fortitude to not overtly stare at the daughter. His eyes weren't in complete control as he continued to shoot quick glances at her.

"I'm looking for a staff for my daughter. Preferably one that is durable, and has no spells affixed to it."

Krarshe turned to look at the daughter fully. She almost seemed to be hiding behind her mother, not wanting to look at Krarshe directly. He caught her eyes doing as his had done just a moment ago, flicking from him to random points in the room. Krarshe felt a twinge of tightness in his chest again.

That's when the realization struck him: he still didn't really know what was in the store. How would he know what kind of staff they were looking for? They all looked like sticks to him. He began to panic as he looked around the room at the shelves.

He looked at the daughter again. As before, she averted her gaze. He breathed deeply, not wanting to embarrass himself in front of this cute girl.

"Hmm... You appear to be a discerning customer," Krarshe mused, as he looked at the mother. His merchant's knowledge told him that she probably knew far more than he did on this matter, remembering how she had looked around the store the day before. "The staves are this way."

He guided the two over to the side wall where the staves were leaning. He hoped that his judgment wasn't wrong. "Is she training to be a mage?" he prodded, hoping for more information.

"Yes. She's just beginning her training."

"Oh? That's wonderful! Who will she be training under?" Krarshe didn't actually know of any mages other than his teachers, so he wouldn't know who they were even if she was to mention someone well-known. He hoped it wouldn't matter.

"I will be in charge of her training," said the mother, smiling slightly. "I wouldn't dream of leaving something this important to anyone else."

Krarshe stopped and looked at her. She just smiled back at him and continued past him toward the staves. *She's a mage? And she teaches??* The daughter walked past him and he made brief eye contact. Her green eyes held his for only a moment before she looked away and hurried past him to where her mother was inspecting a staff. Krarshe could only stand there and look at them. *I wonder how skilled she is.*

"If you need anything else, please let me know," Krarshe finally said.

"Thank you very much, young man," said the mother, looking up from the staff in her hands only long enough to nod a bow to him. Her daughter turned fully to Krarshe and nervously bowed to him. Krarshe could only watch as her hair flipped over her head in a deep bow, still reeling from her beauty. Once he snapped out of the trance again, he returned the bow.

Krarshe walked back to the counter, still sneaking glimpses of the young woman between the store shelves. He couldn't keep his eyes off her. This was a new experience for him. *Could this be charm magic?* He wondered. *They could be looking for a better price.*

When they looked like they had chosen one and made for the counter, Krarshe looked away, not wanting them to know he had been watching the whole time. He noticed the senior student still over by the door. He was looking at the floor, pacing a bit back and forth, muttering to himself.

"We'll go with this one," the mother said, placing a staff on the counter, seemingly identical to the rest to Krarshe's untrained eye. The daughter was still half hiding behind her mother, sneaking glances at Krarshe.

"... How much will that be?" the mother asked.

Krarshe blushed, realizing he had probably been staring at the daughter while the mother was waiting for a response. He wasn't even sure how long she had been standing there. "Umm... That... That'll be one and a half gold roses," he managed to say. Truthfully, not only was he embarrassed at his own misstep, but he had no idea what the staff cost. One and a half seemed reasonable to him, though probably significantly cheaper than it really was according to the school.

"Oh my, so cheap?" the mother asked, fishing out a coin purse. "I would have guessed it would be nearly ten."

Are they that expensive?! If that were the case, this could be bad for him. That's too big to be called a discount. He felt a sinking feeling in the pit of his stomach, but the deed was done. He'd just have to deal with it later.

The elf woman placed the money on the counter. "I'll have to visit this store again," she said, tightening the drawstrings of the purse and tucking it away. "The prices are fantastic. And the service was perfect, not pushy at all. Right, Lycia?" She turned toward her daughter, exposing her from her hiding spot.

Lycia looked toward the floor and nodded slightly. Krarshe could have sworn he saw her face redden a bit. He felt his own face growing warmer.

"Well, we best be going then," said the mother, smirking at her daughter. "Thank you again, young man."

"R-right. You're welcome." Krarshe wasn't sure how he managed to say that without stumbling too badly. Lycia bowed quickly again to Krarshe and hurried after her mother. Krarshe watched her golden hair swinging behind her as she tried to catch up.

"G-g-g-good e-e-evening!" stammered the senior student, who hurried to stand beside the door as they left. With his stuttering, they had left the store by the time he managed to get it all out.

Both the senior student and Krarshe watched Lycia as the two elven women walked through the gates and off the school grounds. That was the first time Krarshe experienced that feeling when he saw her. He wasn't sure what to do about it, but he didn't hate it. In fact, he secretly hoped they would come back again.

CHAPTER 8

K rarshe awoke from his fitful sleep again. His bed sheets were damp with sweat, thanks to the heat of Sirnus. And humid. Disgustingly so, given the time of day; the sun had yet to crest the horizon. He tossed and turned for a bit before finally tossing them off onto the floor. He splayed out on the bed and stared at the ceiling, having given up on trying to fall asleep for the fourth time.

"What should I do?" Krarshe pondered. After the last spell he cast yesterday, he really didn't want to deal with his classmates' gossiping, especially with this being the third time he'd done something abnormal. More than that, though, was Tibault and Bri. He was fine with their astonishment after his first two spells, but this time was different. More uneasy, more fearful. That was probably the last thing he wanted them to feel. His thoughts raced back to a memory from before he set out on this journey. "Simply fear you..." Krarshe muttered, echoing the words his father said before he left. "Nothing simple about it." He was prepared for people to fear him, he just wasn't ready for people he'd started to build a relationship with, for his friends, to abandon him so quickly. Was their relationship so fragile to shatter from a single event? A single spell? Krarshe hoped not, but he couldn't dismiss this gnawing apprehension.

Complicating his emotions was his run-in with the girl Lycia. He couldn't pin exactly what this feeling was, but she was occupying his mind more than one would expect from the short meeting. Every time her bashful look came to his mind, a nervous excitement overtook him.

Krarshe's thoughts were a whirlwind of concern and confusion, his emotions rapidly alternating between gloom and a strange, gleeful delight. Krarshe rolled over to face the lone window in his room. The sky was dark, stars covered by clouds of an oncoming rainstorm. "How appropriate," he commented to himself.

As the time passed slowly, the sky was beginning to brighten, turning the clouds from the darkest black to a bland gray. He wiggled himself to the edge of the bed, tossed his feet over the side, and sat up. *It may be best to just skip class today and not see them,* he thought. *At least until I figure out what to say.*

Krarshe stood up and walked over to the sack he had and pulled out the outfit he bought for himself when he was an old man. Looking at them now, they did seem fairly shabby, but it didn't matter much. He threw them on and made his way out of The Easy Lute.

The streets of Feyfaire were quiet this early in the morning. It was actually a bit spooky, considering the commotion that usually filled them normally. With Feyfaire so desolate, and the other districts likely the same, he decided to head toward South Bank. Normally, it wasn't the safest place, but his shabby clothes would likely work in his favor this time. Additionally, any unsavory people had likely given up on finding targets by this time and scattered to the shadows as the number of city guards rose with the sun.

The shift from Feyfaire to South Bank was anything but subtle. It was as though two distinct cities had been placed next to each other by the hands of the gods, a divide between the bright, cheerful pavement of the trade district and the dark, melancholic stone of the impoverished port district. The shoddy buildings on South Bank's side of the street were in stark contrast to the well-kept buildings of Feyfaire on the opposing side. The further into the district one went, the worse it got. Broken crates and debris from crumbling buildings littered the alleyways, along with barrels of fish scraps so rancid that even the stray cats avoided them. Krarshe hurried through the heart of the district, not wanting to linger in this squalor.

By the time he cut through the heart of South Bank to the Silver River, it was dawn. A few people began mulling about as they prepared for their day. Krarshe found a secluded spot with a good view of the wharf, hopped up onto the low stone wall that guarded the street from the bank of the river, and sat down. This was the main dock for fishermen in Remonnet and he could see it was already busy, bustling with boats of night fishermen unloading their catch. Further down river, the dregs hauled up catches of their own, dragging the decaying matter which got caught in the wharf up from the riverbed and hauling it out of the city. The goings-on here was likely the only activity at this time, and the best distraction he'd find from his thoughts.

The stench of fish was overwhelming, even from this distance. He couldn't imagine what it smelled like on the wharf itself. At least this fish was fresh. He looked across the river to the residential sector of Stormbridge. Despite being just across the river, the buildings there were in much better condition than those in South Bank. He wasn't sure if it was just newer, or if the city had just invested more in Stormbridge. It was guarded from attacks by a branch of the Silver River which had split from the main river a bit upstream, granting it safety and thus a better place to invest in. The split apparently appeared not long after the start of the war, likely man-made, and has served as a deterrent to attacks from the north ever since. Or so Krarshe had been told, with no way to verify the claim. Regardless of the reason for this, only one thought filled his mind: did it smell of fish on the far shore too?

After watching the boats come and go for nearly an hour, Krarshe heard his stomach growl. He hadn't yet eaten breakfast, and the reprieve from his troubled thoughts had given his stomach a chance to complain. He had gotten what he was hoping for, a reprieve. Looking once more over the river, he got up and hopped off the wall. As he turned the corner, he bumped into a big burly man, his black beard covering his ridiculously broad chest.

"Ach! Woochit kid! Fookin' li'l shit. Ahh, muy heead," he grumbled, wincing and grabbing his large, oily forehead. Krarshe could smell the booze on his breath, somehow overcoming the stench of fish. "Snatch'r take yeh, fookin' brat!" He stumbled past Krarshe and continued on.

Krarshe watched the man staggering slightly for a bit. His clothes were pretty dirty, stained with unknown substances. They were tattered in places, worn down from excessive use. It wasn't just the buildings that were run down here. South Bank was unquestionably the most dangerous district in Remonnet, mostly occupied by poor fishermen and the desperate. You could easily find your purse missing. Or worse, disappear into a back alley, taken by some thugs and sold into slavery. It wasn't unusual for parents in other districts to use South Bank as a scare tactic for misbehaving children, not that they'd ever let them actually come here. But, it was also probably the best place if you wanted to vanish from public knowledge intentionally, too.

Krarshe shifted uneasily, thinking about some of the goings-on here. Turning his attention from it, he figured he should probably leave South Bank to find food, to avoid any incidents. Even in the relative safety of the day, it was dangerous, and he wasn't looking for any trouble. Being careful to not run into anyone else, he made his way back to Feyfaire.

* * *

Krarshe sat down heavily at the table in The Easy Lute. He had spent most of that morning wandering around Feyfaire, checking out the wares of various street merchants, though it felt more like he was walking around for the sake of keeping himself busy. In the afternoon, he went to the school store in hopes of the girl Lycia showing up again, but he was not so lucky. Not a single customer showed up, and he ran out of things to keep himself distracted within the first hour. He was exhausted, physically and mentally. He just sat at the table and waited for a waitress.

The bard, Henry, was joined by another person, a slightly chubby woman with blond hair which hung down in several tight curls. She was adjusting the collar of his loose-fitting shirt with a serious face, though Henry just smiled back at her. After she finished, she walked back behind the counter. Henry sat there adjusting his lute strings methodically, his hands well-practiced. The woman eventually came back out with a small ring of wood with some kind of material stretched over it. She tapped it a few times, making a dull thumping sound.

Henry and the woman talked for a moment before turning to face the room. She started with a beat against her instrument rhythmically, followed shortly after by Henry. The two began to sing a song Krarshe didn't recognize, but it was a quick, cheerful tempo. The woman's higher pitched voice mixed harmoniously with Henry's lower, smoother tone. Before Krarshe knew it, some of the more inebriated customers began trying to sing along to it, albeit poorly. The whole room seemed to be filled with a jolly atmosphere. Krarshe groaned. He wasn't in the mood for this.

As he stared at the table, trying to stew in his frustrations, he felt a tap on his shoulder. He turned to see Na'kika, standing

125

with a tray and a friendly smile. She gestured to Henry and the woman and raised her eyebrows questioningly.

"They're quite good," Krarshe forced himself to smile back, not wanting to bring the catfolk girl into his dilemma. "Who is she?"

Na'kika pointed toward the back room and then put her hand out to her side, around waist height, as though she was indicating one's height.

"I'm not sure I follow..." Krarshe said, face contorted in confusion.

Na'kika scratched her head for a bit, before smoothing out her short orange-red hair and trying again. She again pointed to the back room and then crossed her hands in front of her, palms open and faced up. She then began turning back and forth slowly while looking down at her empty arms.

"Umm..."

Na'kika furrowed her brow and pursed her lips, clearly getting frustrated. She breathed deeply and started gesturing again. This time, she pointed at Henry and the woman, and then clasped her hands together, fingers laced. She brought her tail over and wrapped it around her clasped hands loosely. She once again, more insistently, raised her eyebrows at Krarshe.

Krarshe had no idea what she was trying to say. "I'm sorry, I still don't know what you're trying to say."

"Ugh. She's trying to say that she's the innkeeper's daughter and Henry's betrothed. Even I could see what she was trying to say," said Valerie from behind Krarshe, startling him.

"Seriously, are you always behind me?"

Valerie just laughed, evading his question. "Do you really not get any of those gestures? Cradling a baby? Marriage entwining ceremony?"

"Honestly, those are... Well, that's not how things are done where I'm from..." Krarshe admitted.

Valerie and Na'kika both just gawked at Krarshe in surprise. "Really? Not even holding a newborn?" Valerie asked, bewildered. Na'kika gestured what Krarshe could only assume was the same astonished question.

"It's... Just differences... I... I don't know how else to explain it."

Na'kika made a sympathetic face and then petted Krarshe's blond hair gently.

"You poor boy," Valerie soothed. "I don't know where you're from, but that... I just can't even fathom..."

Krarshe looked up at Na'kika. She just kept petting his head with a smile on her face. Krarshe couldn't compete with her, and his face cracked into a heartfelt smile. She really is a kind girl.

"I'm fine, Na'kika. Thank you," Krarshe said, stopping her hand.

Her smile widened, revealing her enlarged canine teeth. She gestured to the kitchen and then to his table.

"If there's any fish stew, I'll have that," Krarshe said.

Na'kika nodded once and hurried to the kitchen.

"I hope you appreciate the new song too, just for you," Valerie quipped with a grin.

"Yeah, she's really good. Thank you," Krarshe said, watching Henry and his betrothed.

"No, don't thank me. Na'kika was the one who suggested bringing in Giselle."

Krarshe turned back to Valerie. "Really?"

"I swear on Teva's name."

Krarshe was surprised. His talk with Na'kika last time was intended as just a friendly chat, but she took it seriously.

"Giselle is also a musician, but she's got real experience unlike Henry. So again, you should thank her later. Oh, I have to get back to work," she said, scurrying off to a customer waving his empty mug. "Enjoy."

Krarshe sat alone at his table, once again accompanied only by his thoughts. But now, he had another thing on his mind.

This catfolk girl was making her situation weigh on him even more. She really didn't deserve what happened to her, and it frustrated him. More and more, he was seeing her as a friend, and he wanted to do what he could. *Friends...* Krarshe thought. "Ugh, well, there's that issue again..." Krarshe muttered, remembering the events at school the day before. He shook his head forcefully, trying to dismiss his thoughts. He focused on Henry and Giselle and tried to let their merry music distract him, with middling success.

CHAPTER 9

Krarshe coughed forcefully as the dust began to settle in the training room. After nearly a full lunar cycle and a half of these experiments, the training room was in shambles. No matter what was done to each spell, the results were the same. Whether somatic components were added, or the spell was altered in some way, it always caused aberrant lightning, and it had wreaked havoc on the stone walls; the one exception was with lightning spells, which behaved normally aside from its unusual intensity. Landry had instructed Krarshe to move the armor and other equipment into the hallway prior to beginning each day, but the room itself was not so fortunate.

"Okay," coughed Landry from behind his barricade, now worn down and beginning to crumble, despite the attempts to dampen the lightning's impact. "That will be enough for today. Please return the equipment to its spot." He got up and dusted himself off.

Krarshe sighed and made his way across the uneven ground, spotted with holes and blackened stones. This had been the majority of his school experience: moving the heavy equipment out into the hallway, destroying the room with a few more steps than the previous day, and then moving the equipment back again. He hadn't attended any lectures since that lightning spell demonstration, spending his time wandering Remonnet and seeing different parts of the city he'd never been to before. It had been fascinating seeing the farms outside of Stormbridge, as well as seeing some of the smithies in the industrial quarter. But, no matter where he went, his thoughts were with him, and they kept him from the classroom. He still went to the store in the afternoons, hoping to see that girl again more than because of the school's mandate, but fate was not so kind.

Krarshe set down the final armor stand, clanging as it hit the floor. He stood up and arched his back for a minute. While not immensely heavy, they were still quite bulky and there were a lot of them. He brushed his hair to try and get the dirt and dust out of it as he said his goodbye to Professor Landry, who silently kept his focus on the book he regularly took notes in. Krarshe quickly but quietly made his way down the hall toward the school store, not wanting to draw attention from the classrooms still in session, particularly his own.

Upon his arrival, he greeted the senior student in charge of the store, who, similarly to Landry, didn't respond and just sat in the back room with his nose in the book he had. Krarshe plopped himself down on a stool behind the counter and just laid his head on his crossed forearms.

His days were feeling longer than usual. Learning magic wasn't proceeding as he'd first hoped. *Maybe I should just leave,* he thought to himself, scribbling on the counter with the dust on his finger. He couldn't really learn much about the items in the store either, as every senior student appeared disinterested with explaining anything. He couldn't even get them to explain what the prices were for the different products. He was expected to just sit there and watch the store.

As he sat there whittling away his time, he heard the door open. Krarshe turned to the back room to see if the supervising student had noticed, but it appeared he had not. Krarshe slowly pulled himself to his feet and walked out from the counter. He headed toward the front of the store, looking for the customer to see if there was something in particular they were looking for. As he turned the corner around the shelf of mage robes, he saw the shimmer of golden hair, his breath catching in his throat.

He had showed up to the store, day after day, hoping. But here, on this day, as he was questioning why he bothered to continue trekking all the way from Feyfaire, there she stood. Lycia. The braided strand of hair was once again tucked behind her pointed ear as she looked around the left wall of the store.

Krarshe hid himself behind the shelf and furiously rubbed his head, kicking dust into the air and all over the store's goods. He patted himself down and turned the corner again to see she wasn't there. He hurried down the rows of shelves before catching sight of her again, looking at some glass phials. Krarshe was about to approach her, but froze. He remembered he still had the same problem the first time she visited the store: he didn't know anything about the store's merchandise. He'd probably look like an idiot if he pathetically attempted to help her. Resigning himself to worthlessness, he decided to just return to the counter and keep an eye on her, in case she ever actually needed his meager assistance.

As she set down the phial, Krarshe noticed her peek in his direction out of the corner of her eye. She turned and went down another aisle of goods.

Krarshe stood behind the counter and perused the ledger on it, trying to make it look like he was doing something, anything, while being attentive to the customer. She wandered around the store, looking at each shelf. Occasionally, she'd stop and inspect an item more closely before setting it back upon the shelf. This went on for a considerable amount of time.

I feel like she's been down every aisle now. What could she be looking for? Krarshe had seen her wandering endlessly. *Does she need help?*

As he paid closer attention, he noticed her peeking at him while holding a book. It was so subtle that he hadn't realized it when he was feigning being busy. As she continued to wander, another trend became evident: all of the goods she would inspect were within vision of the counter. She never passed near the counter, even traversing a longer route to avoid it, but each spot she stopped was visible from where Krarshe stood.

... I have to be imagining things. Maybe she's hoping I'll come help her, he thought. He decided to just ask her, overcoming his fear of looking stupid.

He walked down an aisle and came up behind Lycia. She held a wand in her hand, but she wasn't looking at it. Instead, she had completely turned her attention to the now vacant counter. Krarshe swallowed hard before saying, "Is there anything I can help you with?"

She jumped and spun around. Her golden blonde hair fluttered in front of Krarshe as she turned, shining with the light that shone in from the window. Her green eyes glistened, wide with surprise. He had to turn away slightly to keep his composure.

She shied away slightly. "Oh. Umm... I... Umm...... I was just..." she stuttered, looked up at him bashfully. Then, her bashfulness melted away, leaving behind a look of confusion. "W-what... happened to you?"

Krarshe wasn't prepared for that question. Not in the least. "What... What do you mean?" he asked, feeling his cheeks and ears warm.

"You're all dirty. Aren't those uniforms normally black? And I feel the last time I saw you, your hair was blond," she said with a smile.

"Oh, just... Well, you know... Training?" Krarshe said, unsure of himself. He laughed a bit, trying to dissolve the awkwardness, but it just made it more pronounced. After the longest moment of embarrassment Krarshe had ever endured, he decided escaping the topic was his only option. "Was... there anything I could help you with?"

"Huh?" The shock on Lycia's fair face was clear as day. "Oh, umm..." She fumbled around, putting the wand back on the rack, nearly knocking the rest of them onto the floor. Krarshe watched as she clumsily attempted to stop the whole rack from clattering to the ground, amused and assured that he wasn't the only awkward one in this conversation. After she managed to get the wands under control and back on the wall, she laughed slightly as her face flushed. She traced the braid behind her ear with her delicate hand, trying to give the air of composure. Krarshe was smiling plainly, but the tightness in his chest was bothering him. "S-sorry about that. I, uhh, was looking... for..." She looked around frantically before grabbing a spell scroll off the shelf behind Krarshe. "This!"

Krarshe raised an eyebrow. "Just that?"

Lycia nodded. "Yes."

"Is that the right spell?"

"Uhh..." She opened it and looked at it quickly. "Yeah!"

Krarshe was much more comfortable not being the one on the back foot. Watching the golden-haired elf girl red as flame and flustered as he was a minute ago was very entertaining, though the tightness in his chest was just getting worse. He wasn't sure why, but he wanted to tease her a bit. "Which spell is it?"

Lycia froze. Krarshe didn't think it was possible, but her face reddened even more, spreading the rose color to her ears. She shakily opened the scroll and looked at it again. She mumbled something that Krarshe couldn't make out.

"What was that?" he asked.

She stood there silent, just holding the scroll open in front of her face. After a moment, she closed it suddenly, crumpling the paper, and exclaimed, "I-I-it's the right one, okay?! I'm sure!" Her green eyes stared straight at Krarshe, filled with anger, but her face just said she was embarrassed beyond belief.

Krarshe just smiled. He was enjoying the teasing, but he knew when it was enough. "Oh, that's good. Because, honestly, I have no idea what spell that is... I can't read spells yet." The sudden change on Lycia's face when she realized he was teasing her made Krarshe laugh.

"A- A- Y- Y- You..." Lycia stumbled with her words. Her anger and embarrassment wouldn't let her formulate a sentence.

Krarshe was laughing so hard he began to cry. When he finally could control his breathing again, he said, "Okay, okay. I'm sorry." Lycia's pouting face said she was still angry at him. "How about a discount? Since I was so rude to you."

He saw her expression soften slightly. "... How big of a discount?" she asked before pouting again, though it seemed more forced now.

"Hmm..." Krarshe said as he led them back to the counter. "That'll be forty silver roses."

She raised an eyebrow. "This store really is inexpensive. Is that before or after the discount you promised me?"

"Honestly, I'm not sure," he said, leaving Lycia puzzled. He leaned in and whispered, "I'm not sure what that goes for. Don't tell anyone."

Lycia, still puzzled, just nodded slowly. "Okay... Well, I suppose I'll forgive you. Just don't get in trouble," she said quietly, pulling out the rose-emblazoned silver coins.

"I'm sure it'll be fine." Krarshe laughed. He took the coins she offered. "Thank you for your purchase," he said with a wide merchant's smile.

She bowed, and turned to leave, much to Krarshe's disappointment. After a few steps, she stopped and turned to face him again. "Umm... M-my name's... Ellycia. Though, 'Lycia' is fine." She blushed as she said it, re-securing the braid behind her ear nervously.

Seeing her blush made Krarshe's face redden as well. He averted his gaze and said, "M-my name's Krarshe. Though, people call me all sorts of different things."

She smiled shyly. "N-nice to meet you," she said with a bow.

"L-likewise," Krarshe responded, reciprocating the bow.

The two stood there quietly for a moment. "Well... I must get home. Goodbye, K-, Karsh-, Karshe?"

"Again, all kinds of things," he laughed. "Safe journeys, Lycia."

She bowed again, and hurried out of the store.

"Youth, huh?" came a voice from the back room.

Krarshe turned to see the long, still dusty mustache of Professor Landry. Exactly how wide his smile was was impossible to tell after it disappeared behind the mustache. Krarshe just blushed more.

"Don't worry, Krarshe. I'm sure she'll be back," he said, turning back into the back room.

Krarshe turned back to face the entrance, still embarrassed. But even so, Landry didn't seem like a bad person. Better than Owyn, at least. Perhaps he misjudged the teachers, letting his poor opinion of Owyn color his assessment. Krarshe turned his attention to the window. Lycia was nearly to the front gate by now. *I hope he's right...*

* * *

The Easy Lute was busier than usual. The addition of Giselle to the live music drew a lot more people to the inn, though Krarshe wasn't sure if this was due to her reputation around the district or simply because the pairing of her and Henry together was significantly better than Henry ever was alone. Unfortunately, some of the new customers were more rowdy than the regulars, as if Giselle attracted some of the worst people in Feyfaire, like the Wanderer to the warmth of a campfire. Generally, the staff seemed to be able to keep order, so the inn's dining room was just more noisy without the brawling you'd see elsewhere.

Krarshe noticed one of the more burly, leather-clad customers trying to get touchy with Valerie, but she was not tolerating it. She smacked away his hand and scolded him, standing firm with one hand on her hip and the other waving a finger at him, though what exactly she said was drowned out in the noise of the inn. For all of her tempting, Krarshe had learned she was not one to play games. Her sexy appearance was a weapon, and she wielded it as a professional. Her seduction was a trap from which any ensnared man couldn't escape.

A plate of bean curds and a half of a loaf of hard bread were placed on the table in front of Krarshe. "Thank you, Na'kika," Krarshe said, turning to her. She smiled in reply. She had been his waitress every day for nearly a half-cycle. He wasn't sure if it was coincidence or if it was the will of Valerie or Na'kika herself requesting it. He didn't mind it, however. In fact, he kind of enjoyed talking to her. Seeing the joy such simple conversations gave her helped lift his spirits, especially since the incident in the training room.

Na'kika pointed to Krarshe and made a gesture, tracing her smile with the same finger she had pointed with. She then raised her hands questioningly.

"Yeah, I guess. Something good happened today, so that's probably why I seem more cheerful."

She waved behind her and pointed to him, then to a frown, and once again concluded with a questioning pose.

"I—" Krarshe stopped. "I don't know. It's complicated."

She put her tray down on the table and sat in the other vacant chair at his table. She gestured for him to continue.

She was becoming very forward, Krarshe noticed. "Just... Something happened at the academy I attend. Something I did. And it seemed to frighten the friends I had. So I've been avoiding them since then. That's probably why I've seemed bothered."

Na'kika furrowed her brow, her orange, white-tipped ears pulled back. Krarshe didn't need her to gesture, it was clear she was displeased with him. Despite that, she went on a voiceless tirade, her hands gesturing faster than he could keep up with.

"Whoa, whoa. Slow down. I can't understand you."

She pointed at him, then tapped the side of her head. Then she turned her hand into a fist with the thumb out, pointed down, and shook her head disappointedly.

"I'm stupid?"

Na'kika nodded. She then gestured questioningly, pointed out the door, tapped the side of her head again and finished by pointing at him. Her head tilted inquisitively.

Krarshe tried to think of what she could be saying. After a few seconds, she started gesturing again. She pointed at him, and then recoiled in fear, her ears back. She then returned to her normal seated position and shook her head side to side.

"Oh. I mean, I'm sure they think that. I didn't ask them directly, no, but the look on their faces—"

Na'kika put a hand up in front of Krarshe's face, stopping his explanation, and shook her head again. She took his hand, clasping it with both hands, and looked straight into his eyes. Her amber-colored cat eyes locked on his brilliant blue eyes, more serious than he'd seen before. After a minute of their eyes locked on each other, she just shook her head side to side slowly. She then lowered his hand back to the table and gave him a big smile, her head tilted slightly in a reassuring gesture.

Krarshe, hesitating for a moment, eventually smiled back at her. "Yeah. I guess I shouldn't assume their feelings, huh?"

She nodded, still smiling. She stood up and picked up her tray. Before leaving, she pat his head and left. Her tail was more active, indicating her mood than her casual step let on. Krarshe knew she was right, and that he needed to talk to Bri and Tibault directly. But it had been nearly a full cycle. Breaching this topic with them now would be a challenge.

CHAPTER 10

Krarshe made his way through the quiet stone courtyard of the school toward the entrance. He found it drew less attention if he snuck into the training area before anyone else showed up, so he had been arriving before the morning fog cleared. As he made his way across the barren stone pavement, he felt someone grab the back of his jacket collar and pull him back.

"This is when you've been getting here!? Curses, you made this difficult. I had to wake up WAY earlier than I would have liked," said a voice he recognized.

Still being held by his jacket, he managed to turn around slightly to see Bri standing there. She didn't look happy. Rather, she looked tired, based on the bags under her eyes and drained face. "Oh. H-hey Bri..." Krarshe said sheepishly, giving a small wave.

"Don't 'hey' me, you dreg. What, in Teva's name, have you been doing!?"

She's definitely upset. "W-what do you mean?" Krarshe let out a nervous chuckle.

"You know damn well what I mean!" She released Krarshe's clothes. "You haven't been to class in nearly a cycle! You sneak onto the grounds every morning at this unholy hour, and then sneak into the store every damned afternoon! You don't think Tibault and I see you in there every day!?"

Krarshe just stood there, his eyes lowered to stare at the stone pavement gloomily. He had no answer that wouldn't just make her more upset.

"Karshe. No. Kr- Krashe. Shit." She breathed deeply before trying again, enunciating each syllable slowly, carefully. "Kr-a-r-she."

Krarshe looked up. She still looked very angry, but he was kind of happy she managed to say his name right, even if it was laboriously.

"Krarshe," she said again, more smoothly. "Why have you been avoiding us?"

Krarshe averted his gaze. Remembering his conversation with Na'kika the day prior, he realized how ridiculous his reasoning would sound were he to say it aloud. "I don't know..."

Bri grabbed him by the collar of his robe again and yanked him toward her, staring right at him but a foot from his face. "Answer me." Her large brown eyes were bloodshot from sleepiness, but full of rage. Going roundabout with non-answers wasn't going to work.

"It's just..." he started, under his breath. He had never been engaged like this, and wasn't sure how to handle it. It was such a departure from the Bri he knew to that point, and that put him even more off-balance. He decided to just be candid with her, she deserved that at least. "I saw how you both looked after that day. I figured you both wouldn't want to talk to me. Too afraid to—"

Bri yanked his robe again, forcing him to turn and face her. "That?! Maddener rob you, for all your idiocy!" She shoved him backwards. Krarshe tripped over a stone jutting from the pavement and fell backwards, landing hard on the mist-dampened stones. "I can't believe you..."

Krarshe recovered, pushing himself up onto an outstretched arm. "Bri, I—"

"Kar—" she caught herself. "Kr-arshe. Are we friends?"

"I mean, I think—"

"Are we friends?" she interrupted, asking more insistently.

Krarshe looked down. "Y-yes..." he stammered, quietly.

He looked up to see Bri smiling softly now. "Yes. We are friends." She reached out a hand. "Why would we be afraid of you?"

Krarshe took her hand as she pulled him to his feet. "I mean, the force of that spell—"

"Was incredible," she interjected. "Krarshe, we knew you were powerful. Maybe not that powerful... But that's no reason to be afraid of a friend. It's not like you turned the spell on us."

"I guess not..."

"Besides, the look on professor Owyn's face was amazing," Bri laughed. "He basically stood there staring at the sky the rest of the day."

The thought of Owyn's face frozen in awe, hair standing on end, brought a smile to Krarshe's face. "Yeah, I wish I could have enjoyed it longer."

Bri and Krarshe both laughed.

After they settled down, Bri turned to Krarshe. "If we feared anything, it would be that you'd be leaving the class already..."

"What do you mean? Why would I leave?" Krarshe asked.

"Are you serious? Perhaps the Maddener already took your wits..." Bri said, covering her face with her palm, shaking her head disappointingly. "Krarshe," she started, more serious than she had been but a moment ago, "that level of power gets noticed. I can all but guarantee you that your name is already circulating amongst the Council of Mages." Bri turned and took a few steps away from Krarshe before stopping and looking up toward the sky, clasping her hands together behind her. "If they took notice of you, they could have you pulled from the school and into the mage corps, sent to the front lines of the war. It could very easily be the last time we saw you... We were actually worried that might have happened..." She paused for a moment before turning back to him. "Well, before we saw you sitting in the store trying to balance a wand on your nose," she said with a smile.

"Uhh... I don't want to talk about that... I was really, reaaally bored," Krarshe explained, his face reddening slightly.

Bri laughed for a bit before going quiet again. She made her way slowly across the stones of the courtyard, keeping a fixed distance from him, eyes fixated on the ground. She stopped after a few paces and turned slightly to look at him. "Krarshe, will you come back to class? Tibault and I both wish you'd come back." She paused before adding, "If for nothing else than to joke about how weird Owyn's eyebrows are." Bri gave the biggest smile Krarshe had ever seen as the sun spilled out over the horizon behind her, bathing her in the morning light.

Na'kika was right. I was being foolish. Apparently, I still don't understand people well. Krarshe smiled. "Nothing would make me happier."

* * *

Krarshe walked back to The Easy Lute that night, a slight spring in his step. He felt a lot better after talking with Bri and Tibault, who stopped into the store after classes had concluded. Bri had explained what had transpired that morning when she cornered him. Tibault, like Bri, just harped on Krarshe's stupidity and complete lack of ability to judge people. "A friendship is not so shallow," he had said. The three of them had caught up for a bit before Owyn, the teacher assigned with closing the shop that day, had come in and told them to leave. Krarshe was actually looking forward to going to class the next day.

As he approached the inn, he noticed that it was past the point of crowded tonight, with a throng of people clustered outside the entrance. There might not even be a table available. Krarshe pushed his way through, having to squeeze himself between two men who smelled like stale sweat and stumbled into the dining hall.

Sure enough, a lot of people had congregated in the inn. Looking toward Henry's usual spot, there was a third person now, a dwarf, playing a golden harp. He wasn't sure who it was, but he seemed to be an acquaintance of Giselle's, based on how well he played off her beat. Or, maybe he was just an experienced bard. Either way, the three of them were drawing a very big crowd, which was great for the inn's business, but was disheartening for Krarshe's stomach.

"Probably no fish stew left," he muttered.

"Oh, Karshe!" Valerie yelled, cutting through the crowd while trying to balance a tray over her head. "Over here! We—" she paused as she squeezed between two customers, "have a table over in the back for you."

"Quite a crowd tonight," Krarshe said in a quiet yell, trying to be audible.

"Yeah. A friend of Giselle was in town, and she managed to get him to come play," she said, looking toward the dwarf. Despite his thick fingers, he plucked the strings of the harp swiftly, never missing a note. "It's great, but this is exhausting. I hope Na'kika's all right."

"On her own tonight?"

"Yeah," Valerie said, tightening the ribbon that held her dark brown hair up in a ponytail. "I made sure to put her closer to the kitchen. It's the section you're in," she said with a smirk.

So it was her call to have Na'kika serve me every day, Krarshe thought. "Okay, so in the corner by the kitchen?"

"Yeah, you'll see it. Sorry that it's kind of a makeshift table, but at least you can sit somewhere. We like to make sure that, no matter how busy, we accommodate those who are staying here long-term. Good luck getting there though." Valerie laughed as she lifted the tray over her head again and plunged into the sea of customers.

Krarshe stood there, watching the mob of people, trying to find an opening. When it was clear that there wouldn't be one, Krarshe dove in as Valerie had, pushing his way through. The whole place reeked of booze and sweat. The clinking of bottles and clomping of mugs was nonstop. A few people were cheering, others were jeering, and a few were arguing, though all of it was indecipherable through the din of the rest. Eventually, as he made his way further back, he managed to claw his way out into a less crowded area in the back corner. Looking around, it was apparent that the entrance and near the musicians was where the throng was thickest. In the back, it was still busy, but you could at least walk around.

Krarshe stopped for a minute, taking a breath of fresher air while he looked around for his table. He spotted Na'kika carrying a tray of food. When she saw Krarshe, she smiled and pointed her tail toward a crate and a small stool in the back corner. "Makeshift indeed," Krarshe noted.

He made his way over to it and sat down. Na'kika came over almost immediately and leaned in close, trying to hear his order over the noise.

"I'm not picky today, so whatever the chef has available," Krarshe said into the white-tipped ear. He didn't want to stress out the chef if he could avoid it.

Na'kika nodded and dashed toward the kitchen.

Krarshe sat and listened to the music. It somehow managed to ring out over the clamor of the crowd. It was good. Very good. He couldn't make out the lyrics, something about some heroic captain or something. He was never keen on songs like this, not knowing the tale took away from his enjoyment. Despite this, the tune was quite exhilarating and the instruments all harmonized perfectly. He could understand why so many customers came to hear them, the three together were way better than just Henry alone.

He was snapped out of his reverie by a loud, obnoxious laugh from the customer at a nearby table. It was the large man from the day before, the one who had made a pass at Valerie. The man had to be an adventurer, just based on his leather armor and his sheer size. The muscles of his arms were as defined as his square, stubbled jaw. His hair appeared to be slicked back, but it could have just been incredibly greasy. Adventurers didn't seem to prioritize cleanliness. At least, from Krarshe's limited experience with them. The man gulped down his ale, slammed it down on the table, and laughed with the other men at his table.

Krarshe just leaned on his makeshift table and rested his head on his hand. He closed his eyes and listened to the music, trying his best to cut through the noise. Despite how loud the room was, gradually the melody was gently shepherding him to sleep. That is, until he heard the crash of mugs and bottles.

He awoke with a jolt and looked around the room. He saw a bunch of mugs and bottles on the ground at the table with the adventurers. The brawny one was gripping Na'kika by the wrists as she struggled as he and the rest of the adventurers were laughing. Na'kika's ears were back and tail rigid. She was clearly struggling, twisting and pulling in an attempt to free herself of his grasp.

Krarshe looked around, but there were no other staff in sight. Valerie was lost in the sea of patrons, and wasn't here to put them in their place again. Seeing Na'kika fight in vain against the adventurer, Krarshe knew he had to help her. He stood up and immediately hurried over to them. As he approached, the assailant's friends looked at Krarshe. He could feel his heart begin to race, his palms began to sweat with nervousness, but he couldn't just let them do this to her. Standing before them, he swallowed and said, "R-release her."

The man holding Na'kika stopped laughing and looked over at Krarshe, still firmly grasping the catfolk girl as she continued to struggle. His face was a bit flushed, and his breath stank almost as bad as the whole crowd combined. *How many drinks has he had?* He looked Krarshe up and down appraisingly, before laughing again, along with his party of friends. "We're jus' havin' shum fun, *hic* right boys?" They all laughed even harder.

Krarshe looked at Na'kika, who was looking at him, panicked, and pleading with her eyes. The man yanked her again, pulling her focus back to the struggle.

More firmly, Krarshe spoke again. "She doesn't like that. Please stop."

"If she don't like it, she could jus' ssshay sho," he laughed, slurring his words. "Go a-head. All you hafta say is 'shtop'."

Na'kika's flailing continued, trying to pull away from him. The men laughed again.

Krarshe continued to stand there, his vibrant blue eyes glaring straight at the man. Eventually, the adventurer stopped laughing and turned to look Krarshe straight in the eye. "Look, kid. Gedda fuck outta here 'fore we hurt you. You're ruinin' mah fun, get it?"

His friends stood up from their chairs. Krarshe's gaze shifted for a moment. He noticed in his periphery that one of the men was sliding to the side. He was going to be surrounded. It was four versus one. Not good odds. Krarshe wasn't looking for a fight. In his years since setting out from home, he had never once fought anyone. The adventurers, however, undoubtedly had plenty of experience. Even one-on-one, he didn't stand a chance. The truth was clear: this wouldn't be a fight, it would be a slaughter. He looked at Na'kika; her face was filled with desperation, her chin quivering. He felt a pang of guilt hit him as he looked into her eyes, but he was out of options.

Gritting his teeth, he turned back toward his table. He heard the men start laughing again and the clatter of chairs as they all sat back down. Krarshe took one step before stopping.

Why had he taken this form? Wasn't he frustrated at being unable to do anything? As an old man, he couldn't help anyone. He always ran. But Na'kika was a friend. He hadn't realized it until now, but it was true. Their friendship was only built upon simple conversations, and they were no longer just merchant and customer. Seeing Na'kika in trouble, seeing her begging for help, the odds weren't important. Not now.

Krarshe felt anger welling up within him. His fingers curled into a fist. His weight shifted. In one swift motion, he spun around, sending his clenched fist flying, catching the adventurer squarely in the jaw. Krarshe could feel the crunching of bones, though he wasn't sure whose.

The man tumbled back off the chair and onto the floor. Na'kika managed to wrench herself free as her assailant toppled. She stood there, surprised to see the man on the ground. She turned to Krarshe with the same shocked expression. The adventurer's friends reacted the same way, taken aback by seeing their friend flung to the ground by this scrawny elf boy. Nearby members of the mob quieted and turned to watch.

Krarshe stood over the adventurer splayed out on the ground. He could feel his hand begin to throb, but he didn't care. "I said, leave her alone, *krun*."

After a triumphant moment, Krarshe felt something hard impact him on the side of the head, catching him just off his cheekbone and sending a jolt of pain through his head and eye as he tumbled to the wooden floor. As he looked up, he saw one of the other adventurers standing over him. The other two quickly joined their friend and proceeded to kick and stomp on him. Krarshe curled himself into a ball, protecting his head with his arms, as he felt each leather boot come down on him hard. One kick managed to catch him in the gut, knocking the wind out of him. Another stomp came crashing down just behind the guard of his elbow, a sharp pain shooting through his side.

"Hey! Hey!"

"Hold him!"

"Argh!"

Eventually the beating stopped. Krarshe looked up from behind the shield he made with his arm. He could see a few of the other customers had jumped in and were pulling the adventurers off of him. He hadn't initially realized it, but the music had stopped, and the entire mob was watching the fight.

"Five curses! Get them out of here!"

Krarshe turned to see the innkeeper had come out from the back and was barking orders to the people holding back the adventurers. The crowd parted and made way for the men dragging the adventurers out as they twisted and squirmed, trying to get free from the mob's grasp. The man Krarshe had punched was walking out on his own. He turned to look back at Krarshe with a sneer and spit some blood in his direction. He made his way out, being shoved and jostled by the crowd as he did.

Krarshe felt a gentle hand on his back and helped pull him up into a seated position. He winced in pain as he turned to see Na'kika kneeling beside him, her face twisted with concern, tears welling up in her amber eyes.

Krarshe breathed deeply, trying to regain composure, but he felt the sharp pain in his side again, causing him to cough. *No blood, luckily,* he thought, inspecting the hand he coughed into. "I'm okay," he choked out to Na'kika. It must not have been very convincing as a tear streamed down her cheek.

"Karshe! Curses, what happened?!" Valerie came running from the throng of patrons.

He took a labored breath again, making sure to not breathe too deeply this time. "Just some assholes... I took care of them," he said, forcing a smile.

Na'kika took his hand and looked directly into his eyes. She then rubbed her cheek against the back of his hand a few times, letting it rest there for a bit.

"Seems she's thankful," Valerie said with a smile. "I don't know what happened, but it seems you helped her out." She looked around at the overturned table and chairs and the drops of blood on the ground. "You have my thanks too."

The innkeeper came out with a small pail and cloth. As he looked toward the innkeeper, Krarshe realized that his right eye was beginning to swell, obstructing his vision a bit. He heard the sloshing of the pail as it was set down next to Na'kika. A moment later, he felt a cold, wet sensation touching his cheek. It stung for a second, but quickly changed to a soothing coolness. He could feel Na'kika still supporting him.

Valerie chuckled. "Seems someone's attached. Well, I'll just leave you two alone then," she said, grinning devilishly. She turned back toward the mass of onlookers, still watching and murmuring to themselves. "Okay, okay, go back to your business, everyone. Nothing to see here," she said, dispersing the crowd that had gathered to watch the fight.

Krarshe just sat there, Na'kika tending to his injuries. It had hurt immensely, and he'd most certainly have to take it easy for a while. But, as he rested in Na'kika's embrace, sensing what he could only describe as purring, he didn't regret it for a second.

CHAPTER 11

K rarshe awoke, blinded by the sun that had crept in through his window. He stretched slightly before the pain in his ribs gave him a sharp reminder of the previous day's beating. He wasn't sure what time it was exactly, but the light that shone into his room made it clear that it must have been close to midday. Sleep had been hard to attain, but he had decided to make the most of it when he finally fell asleep. School could wait.

He tried to slide carefully to the edge of his bed, but still incurred the wrath of his injuries. He stood up and walked over to a pail of water that had been left for him, cupped his hands and scooped some out. It was lukewarm, but that was fine. Closing his eyes, he lowered his face into his cupped hands. He winced as his right eye breached the surface of the water but held there for a few seconds, his wound stinging while his face was submerged. He lowered his hands and tried to blink away the water. Even blinking hurt.

As he breathed deeply, he realized he was still in pretty bad shape. The innkeeper had called in a doctor to look Krarshe over after the fight, a form of thanks for stepping in to protect his staff. Krarshe had some serious bruising on the right side of his face, where he had been blindsided by the adventurer's fist, but there was no permanent damage to his eye. The few cracked ribs had luckily not punctured anything internally. To his own embarrassment, the crack he heard and pain in his hand when he punched the adventurer was apparently his own knuckles breaking. Evidently, this body was pretty fragile, something he'd have to keep in mind in the future.

With the diagnosis, the doctor wrapped some bandages around his torso, which Krarshe found did little to help, as well as setting the bones in his fingers. The doctor said his eye would heal on its own, and the rest would just take time and care. Valerie and the innkeeper seemed relieved by the diagnosis; Na'kika seemed too enthralled with tending to him to have much of a reaction, but she seemed happy. To Krarshe, it just meant he'd be hindered for the foreseeable future.

After clothing himself carefully, he made his way down to the dining hall. Krarshe didn't realize how much his torso was involved with walking until now, each step sending a jolt of pain through his ribs. The stairs were even worse. By the time he reached the bottom, he was bracing the wall as though it was the only thing keeping him upright.

When he reached the last few steps, he saw Na'kika tending to a customer. Once she saw him, she immediately placed her tray down on the customer's table and rushed over to help him down the last few steps. It didn't help much with the pain, but he appreciated the gesture. He just wondered if it was okay for her to abandon her customer. As the customer looked back and watched the catfolk and elf cling to each other, Krarshe could see his displeasure at being abandoned by his waitress mid-order.

Na'kika helped Krarshe over to the nearest table and helped him sit down. As he got situated, Krarshe noticed that Valerie had stepped in to help Na'kika's customer. She met Krarshe's gaze and just smiled. After he was set in a bearable position, Na'kika gestured her common request.

"Anything soft is good. Maybe if they have a soup of some sort. I'm not sure I could chew much right now," Krarshe answered. *Curses, even talking hurts. Is that doctor sure my eye's okay?*

Na'kika nodded and hurried into the kitchen.

"If you think she was doting before, you've not met a devoted catfolk," said Valerie, stopping at his table after taking the other customer's order.

"I just hope she doesn't forget to do her job. I wouldn't want her to get into any trouble because of me."

Valerie smirked. "I fully expect it. I'll just make sure to help. But, try not to spend too much extra time in the dining hall flirting with her, okay?"

Krarshe leered at Valerie, unamused at her jab. "I won't."

"Yeah, yeah. Sure, sure. Whatever you say," she said with a dismissive wave, still smirking as she returned to the kitchen.

Maddener accursed, what is she talking about? Krarshe pondered. *Where did that idea even come from?*

Not a few seconds after Valerie disappeared into the kitchen, Na'kika came out with a bowl and spoon and set it down on the table in front of Krarshe. This was significantly faster than he had expected.

"Thanks, Na'kika," Krarshe said.

Na'kika smiled. As Krarshe picked up his spoon, he noticed she hadn't moved. She was just standing there, fingers interlaced behind her back, her white-tipped orange tail twitched and waved around excitedly behind her.

"Umm..." Krarshe started, looking around awkwardly. "Is... Is there something you need from me?"

Na'kika just shook her head no. She still continued to stand there, watching him eat.

"I-I'm fine, Na'kika. I can manage this on my own."

No change.

"If I need something, I'll let you know."

There was no reaction from the catfolk. She just watched him, almost with anticipation.

This act was starting to unnerve Krarshe. He looked toward the kitchen and saw Valerie watching, her hand up to her mouth to stifle a giggle. *So THIS is what she meant...* He tried to subtly gesture a question to Valerie, trying to figure out what he's supposed to do. She responded by rubbing the top of her own head with her hand and then pointing to Na'kika.

Krarshe felt a nervous lump form in his throat. This seemed very strange to him, and far too bold. He shakily reached up and pet Na'kika's head. As he did, she lowered her head slightly to meet his hand. "Thank you very much," Krarshe said, still finding the whole ritual very unnatural for him, but she seemed even happier than before, her tail was flailing more vigorously. As he took his hand away, she caught it and rubbed her cheek against the back of his hand, purring.

Krarshe's pulse was racing. This was way more intimate than he was comfortable with. He looked toward Valerie. She was turning away slightly, her whole body curling up as she tried to contain her laughter. He was certain he heard a few snorts escape as she did it.

I hope this isn't going to be a normal occurrence... he thought, looking back at Na'kika. Finally, she released his hand and took a step back. With a smile big enough to reveal her fanged teeth, she bowed deeply and returned to the kitchen. *If it is, I'm not sure I'll be able to handle this.* He returned to his steamy soup as he quietly contemplated what to do about this overly affectionate catfolk.

* * *

Krarshe stopped to catch his breath on Stormbridge, looking out over the Silver River as the late-Sirnus sun glinted off its

156

surface. His right eye still stung slightly, and the pain in his ribs were made worse by all the walking he had done that day. Every apothecary he could find in the city was sold out of healing potions and salves, the ongoing war making such things very scarce; he wondered how the adventurers were managing without them. The church in Castle Ward, the one that served the vast majority of the city, was demanding a large sum of gold for healing miracles from their clerics.

Krarshe had just about given up on receiving any healing when he heard someone mention the small chapel outside the gates of Stormbridge, in Ironpole. With nothing to lose, he had headed toward the small subdistrict. He had never been to Ironpole, but knew it was where most of the farming agriculture for Remonnet took place. The fact that they had a chapel was news to him. Now, he just hoped it wasn't false information, after having nearly killed himself walking all over the city.

As he was about to continue his trek, he saw a horse-drawn cart coming from Feyfaire. Judging by the look of the man, it was likely he was a farmer and his cart looked as though he had just finished his delivery. Krarshe didn't wait and waved down the man.

"There somethin' I can do fer ya?" the man asked, bringing his cart to a stop. "Bless ya, lad. What happ'ned ta yer eye?"

Krarshe hadn't gotten to look at it at this point, but apparently it was out of place enough to garner a reaction. "Oh, it's a long story... I was just wondering, are you from Ironpole?"

"That I am."

"Is there a chapel there?"

"That there is," the weary-eyed, tanned man said with a smile. "Ya headin' there fer healin'?"

Krarshe smiled sheepishly. "I was hoping to, yes." He must have looked pretty rough for this man to guess his intent.

"Care fer a ride then? I can bring ya."

"Oh, no, I'm fine. I don't want to impose."

"Nonsense! Ya look tired. 'sides, I'd like the comp'ny. Ol' Marie here's nice 'n' all, but she ain't much fer conversation, ya know?" the farmer said, smiling.

Krarshe couldn't help but chuckle. He remembered his days of travelling, and the long, one-sided conversations he had held with his horse. "All too well. Then, I appreciate your generosity," Krarshe said, pulling himself up onto the cart. He winced as he did it, and sat down gently.

"Ooh, ya okay there, lad?"

Krarshe relaxed into the seat. "Yeah. Let's just say it's not just my eye," he replied, holding up his broken hand and rubbing his cracked ribs tenderly.

"If ya don't mind me askin', what happ'ned?"

"Guess I've got time for that long story."

The two smiled as the farmer snapped the reins, driving the horse onward. Krarshe recounted the tale of his gallantry and frailty as he watched the city pass by. The cart made the trip much faster, though he had to be careful of his ribs with each bump in the road.

After the story concluded, the man said, "Lad, that was the right thing ta do." He placed his calloused hand on Krarshe's shoulder. "I hope ya get yer healin', Teva willin'."

"Teva?" Krarshe had heard the word multiple times, but still wasn't sure what it meant.

The farmer turned fully to Krarshe, dumbfounded. "Ya goin' ta the chapel, but don't know the name of the goddess it's fer? Lad..." he said, shaking his head, disbelieving.

Krarshe looked off to the side of the road, realizing how audacious this must have seemed. The gate was just ahead of them, much less busy than the merchant's entrance in Feyfaire. "I'm sorry, I'm actually not from around here."

"Don't ya worry, lad. I'm sure Teva'll forgive ya. She IS the goddess of fergiveness, after all."

"Goddess of forgiveness?"

The farmer nodded, once more watching the road in front of him. "And of justice and agriculture. We in Ironpole hold her in highest regard of the whole pantheon, ya know? Chief deity fer all of Remonnet, since the previous queen."

Krarshe felt like he insulted not only this kind farmer, but everyone in Remonnet. He shrunk back in his seat as they passed under the large stone gateway. "I'm sorry, I didn't realize."

"Lad, there be nothin' wrong with not knowin' somethin'." He turned to Krarshe with a smile, the sun bathing him in light as they passed through the gate. "It's how we learn. A whole lifetime of not knowin' is how ya become wise."

Krarshe just smiled. He looked off into the distance and his eyes widened. The fields of Ironpole were vast, covering every inch to either side of the road. He had seen farmlands before in his travel, but the perfectly symmetric rows upon rows of crops were still something marvelous to see.

The rest of the journey was more subdued. The farmer told Krarshe how a few of the fields in parts of Ironpole flooded every year, so the land was naturally fertile. In other parts, however, they used fish scraps to fertilize their fields, benefitting from the strong fishing industry in Remonnet. He went on and on about all the crops they raised, and how it was the best in all of Armia because of this fertilization. Listening to him explain every little detail about how they managed the fields, Krarshe knew this man was a lifelong farmer, and proud of it.

Finally, they approached a clearing in the fields, with a small building positioned right next to the road. "Well, lad. Ya were great comp'ny, but here's where we part ways." He brought the cart to a stop in front of the chapel.

"Thank you so much for the ride. Now that I know how far it was, I'm not sure I would have been able to make it here at all, let alone before the sun went down."

"Ya're very welcome. If ya see me again, don't be 'fraid ta say hello."

Krarshe climbed down carefully. "Of course. Oh, and for your trouble," he said, as he pulled out his coin pouch.

The man held up a hand. "No, no. I won't be takin' any payment. 'round here, we like ta help those 'n need. Ya just take care of yerself." He paused for a second. "Use it ta buy that sweet girl somethin'," he said with a wink.

Not this again... "You're too kind. I'll remember your kindness and pay you back somehow. My name is Krarshe," Krarshe said with a nod, unable to bow in his current state.

"Name's Alban. Be well, Karsh. May Teva bless ya." He cracked the reins once more, and the cart started with a jolt. Krarshe stood there for a minute and watched as Alban and his cart bounced down the uneven dirt road. It seemed as though the road got more rough past this point. Rubbing his ribs tenderly, he thanked whatever deity it was who spared him.

Now at his destination, Krarshe turned to look at the chapel. Compared to the church in Castle Ward, it was barely distinguishable from a woodsman's shack. It was small, with a simple, weather-worn wooden door for an entrance. The windows were small, and lacked any of the colors or decorative features that the other church had. If Alban hadn't brought him there, Krarshe would have assumed this was just used for storage by the surrounding farmers.

As he approached the door, he could see a small metal ring with seven barbs stemming from it. He recognized it from the Castle Ward church, as well as other churches he'd seen during his travels. While it was usually much larger and affixed to the top of the churches, this smaller one affixed to the door marked this building as a place of worship for followers of the pantheon. Despite what Alban had said, there was nothing distinguishing it as having Teva as its chief deity.

Krarshe gave a sharp knock on the old wooden door with his uninjured left hand and waited for a minute. He stood outside, watching the sun slowly lowering in the sky. One of the twin moons was leading just ahead of the sun, signalling the final half-cycle before the harvest season. *How strange time is,* he mused, thinking about how he had started this new life nearly a cycle and a half ago, at the start of Sirnus. He'd had so many different experiences these past hundred or so days that it dwarfed his years as a travelling merchant in his mind.

Krarshe snapped out of his reverie, realizing he'd probably been mulling this over for too long waiting for a response. He tried the handle of the door, which swung open with a creak. *I can just apologize later.* He stepped into the quiet room, trying to not break the silence. There was no one around. Just rows upon rows of benches. Backed benches. *Why doesn't the classroom have BACKED benches?* In the front of the room, at the end of the center aisle, stood a wooden pedestal. There was a pair of red curtains which hung along the front wall, bordering either side of a large, wooden version of the symbol signifying the pantheon. The whole room was very simple. And clean. Surprisingly clean, in fact, considering how dusty the road was.

Krarshe cleared his throat, causing a small twinge of pain in his ribs. "Excuse me. Is anyone here?"

"Ah! Just a moment," called an unseen voice. A moment later, a man stepped out from behind the red curtain on the left, startling Krarshe. He had assumed it was just decoration hung on the wall, but apparently it served as a door. "How my I help you?" the middle-aged man asked gently. His voice was soft and gentle, a perfect match for his features.

"I'm looking for the head priest," Krarshe said. After a short pause, he added, "To request healing."

The priest raised an eyebrow. "Well, I guess you could call me the head priest, being the only cleric serving here," he said with a smile. "I thought healing might be what you sought." He tapped his cheek, just below his right eye. The black eye was apparently Krarshe's most distinguished feature that day.

"How much will it be?"

"We don't charge for healing. I would never think of taking money for the generosity of our most holy, Teva. If you desire to give back, though, we do take donations to help maintain our meager chapel," he explained, gesturing to a small copper collection dish on the floor next to the entrance.

Krarshe was shocked by this response. He had figured it would be cheaper, but not free. This was a significant difference from the church in Castle Ward.

"I can't, however, guarantee healing."

This was another shock. Krarshe wasn't sure he understood.

His confusion must have been written on his face, as the priest added, "It depends on how Teva judges you. Clerical blessings and miracles are a gift from the gods and goddesses. As such, it depends on them."

"How will I know how they'll judge?"

"No one can know for certain. Though, clerics are often trained to understand how each god will view an act."

Krarshe still didn't understand. This was completely different from magic. The idea of a spell not working because some being deemed it unworthy was completely illogical to him.

"Perhaps it's best to explain how you got injured. I cannot speak for other gods or goddesses, but I do understand a bit of how Teva thinks, and I can guess at how she would judge you." The priest's voice was calm, unperturbed by needing to repeatedly explain. Krarshe couldn't see any hint of dismissiveness, only eagerness to help.

"I... got injured... in a bar fight..." Each word out of his mouth made Krarshe sound undeserving of healing.

The priest stared at Krarshe for a moment. "I... I'm sorry, but I don't think you would be judged favorably. Teva is the goddess of justice, so I believe she'd wish for you to learn a lesson from your injuries."

"Would it change anything if it was for a good cause?" Krarshe was hoping he could get any kind of healing at this point.

"Such as?"

"Well..." Krarshe proceeded to explain the events of the night prior. How he had hurt himself trying to protect someone. How the offenders had beat him. Hopefully, it would be viewed as justice.

At the end of the tale, the priest said, "That certainly is a different circumstance. However, I suspect Teva would still expect you to live with the decision you made, as you still harmed another." Krarshe could feel his hope dissipating. "Although, she is also the goddess of forgiveness. Perhaps she would give you some small gift." The priest smiled. "For a good deed."

"Then, I leave it in Teva's hands."

"Very well. Please kneel before me."

Krarshe knelt down in front of the priest, easing himself down with the back of a bench.

"O your holiness, Teva, our goddess of Justice and Forgiveness, I beseech thee." The priest held out his hand before Krarshe's forehead. "Take this man, and search his soul. Grant him your judgment, your gift, if thou judge him worthy of your blessing." Krarshe could feel a warmth envelop him. The dim room seemed brighter too. "May you aid him in healing, if you deem him deserving, if you deem him just, if you deem him worthy of forgiveness..."

Krarshe closed his eyes and listened to the priest's prayer, laced with a strange soothing he hadn't experienced before. The priest's voice began to soften, almost sounding distant. Before he realized it, he found himself devoid of any sensation; not the pain he was experiencing, not the sounds of the priest's voice, not even the heat from the fading season. It was complete serenity.

So you're the one he picked? From this expanse of serenity, a thought came to Krarshe, and he was certain it wasn't his own. *I guess I can see why.*

Umm... What's going on here? Krarshe thought.

It's fine, don't worry. Hmm... I guess I can at least help a little bit. Not too much though, or you won't learn anything from your recklessness.

Am I seriously having a conversation with the voice in my head? In all his years, this was a first for Krarshe. He couldn't understand what this intrusive voice was. Perhaps he had gone insane.

Oops, time's up. We'll be able to talk more later when you two meet. Oh, and when he gives you that amulet, make sure you don't lose it, okay?

Krarshe felt his senses, and pain, return to him. A sudden feeling of warmth and tingling engulfing his body. The sharp pain of his injuries began to lessen, though he wasn't sure if the warmth was just distracting him.

After an unknowable amount of time, the priest placed his hand on Krarshe's shoulder. "How do you feel?"

Krarshe opened his eyes. How long had he been kneeling there? It felt like an eternity. And what was that voice in his head? "Umm..."

"Seems she didn't judge you worthy of healing, I'm afraid," the priest said with a pitiful smile, tapping his cheekbone again.

Krarshe stood up. The pain in his ribs remained, but the sharpness was dulled. He moved the fingers in his right hand carefully. It still hurt, but less than it did earlier. "Actually, the pain seems better. Still hurts, but unquestionably better than when I first arrived," Krarshe said with a smile.

"Hmm. Perhaps she didn't want you to forget this lesson, but sympathized with your plight."

Krarshe froze for a second before nodding. The priest's assessment aligned awfully closely to what that voice in his head said. Frighteningly so. Still, Krarshe decided it was probably best to not mention the strange dialogue he had with some nameless voice, and tried to dismiss his concern and confusion about the whole thing. "I appreciate her judgment." *Healing quickly works fine for me. Certainly better than recuperating for a whole cycle.*

The priest smiled. "I am overjoyed for your blessing. May Teva continue to be kind and understanding. Praise be to Teva." He pressed his palms together over his bowed head solemnly.

Krarshe mimicked the gesture of prayer. "Thank you," he said.

"Again, I'm just a servant for our holiness, Teva. May you take care, young man."

As Krarshe turned to leave, he stopped. *I must be going crazy, but I guess it's better to err on the side of caution.* "Do you... have an amulet to give me?"

The priest, who had begun to return to the room behind the curtain, stopped and turned back to Krarshe. "Pardon?"

"Oh, no. Sorry. I'm just not familiar with the customs of the church of Teva. I apologize." The priest bowed a goodbye again as Krarshe turned to leave once more. *Well, I feel like a fool, falling for my own fantasy.* Krarshe shook his head, disappointed in himself. As he made his way out the door, he dropped a couple copper Roses in the donation pan.

CHAPTER 12

The tavern streets of Feyfaire were at the height of their rowdiness by the time Krarshe had returned from Ironpole. He did his best to avoid the busier streets, not having the energy to evade a brawl if one erupted outside a tavern. The ruckus of drinkers was all a vague din as he staggered through the uneven pavement, exhausted from his day's travels. Despite his usual appetite, he just wanted to get back to the Easy Lute and sleep.

"Finally..." he muttered to himself as he neared his inn. He noticed it seemed quieter than it had been in some time. *Must be even later than I realized.*

As he nearly stumbled through the doorway, he was met immediately by Na'kika's smiling face. "Oh, hi Na'kika. I won't be need—"

She cut him off, grabbing him by the arm and dragging him to an empty table right in front of the usual musicians, completely ignoring him. She pulled out a chair and gestured to it.

"N-no, really. I just—"

"C'mon, lad. She's been-a waitin' fer yeh," the dwarf harpist said.

Krarshe looked back at Na'kika, still smiling widely and gesturing to the chair. He sighed. "Okay."

He sat down, nearly collapsing into the chair as his legs gave out, now given true reprieve from his journey. Na'kika pulled a neighboring chair up next to him and sat down, shoulder to shoulder. Witnessing this, Krarshe looked around, confused.

"She requested the rest of the night off. It's fine," Valerie said, passing by with a tray of mugs.

She's always quick with the follow-up, isn't she?

The dwarf cleared his throat, and strummed his harp quickly, getting everyone's attention. "Enjoy this one, lad," he said, giving Krarshe a sideways look and smiling. "There be tales of gods beatin' back the demons, of heroes slayin' fiercest of dragons, of boys bein' made inta great generals. But—" he strummed his harp again, "there be but ONE of emperors..." A couple of patrons behind Krarshe whistled and cheered excitedly. "An' so, as thanks, ta the lad 'ere, an' thanks ta mah great friends 'ere at The Easy Lute, I present ta yeh... straight from the halls of nobles an' royalty... *A Farewell ta Lords*!" he said, with incredible bravado and a final thrum of his harp strings, and was met with more applause and cheering.

Oh boy... What is happening here... Krarshe sighed. He looked over to Na'kika. She was clapping as enthusiastically as anyone in the audience. Krarshe looked behind him and noticed only a few patrons. This performance seemed a bit excessive for this number of people. "Na'kika," Krarshe whispered in her ear. "What's going on?"

She gestured to the musicians, as they began to somewhat clumsily establish the rhythm, and then gestured to Krarshe. After pausing for a moment, she clarified again by pointing to his black eye.

"Burmir already said it, right?" Valerie asked, startling Krarshe. She placed a bowl of fish stew in front of him. "It's as thanks."

Krarshe looked down at the stew. He could smell the savory aroma. It dawned on him how often he must order fish dishes that she was able to bring it out without asking his order. "But I didn't do anything."

"Tell that to her," she said, pointing to Na'kika.

Na'kika smiled enough to show her fangs, tail whipping around cheerfully. This might have been the happiest he'd ever seen her.

Their attention was pulled back by the deep, booming voice of Burmir, the harpist. Over the next hour or two, the audience listened to the tale of Armia's first emperor, Eduzin Arubas. The multi-part hymn told of how this mage-emperor came from the seas to the east, wearing his unique crown of Sagesteel, his immense magic brought the wild tribes and warring kingdoms of Armia to heel. It told of how his governance led the land into a time of great prosperity, how his might protected the empire from foreign invasion and monsters, and how his compassion unified the empire and earned him the love of his people.

Periodically, Giselle or Henry would interrupt the hymn and sing about a related story pertaining to the part of the tale Burmir was telling. Initially, Krarshe thought this was out of line, but after the third time it happened, he realized this was part of the performance. Whenever they would interject, he noticed Burmir would flex his fingers a bit and take a drink from a mug beside him. It was an opportunity to give him a break without disrupting the performance.

The story continued, telling of his exciting battle against the dark elves of the Black Swallow Hills to the southeast, bringing the patrons to the edge of their seat with anticipation. The audience laughed as Henry told of how Eduzin accidentally created the lake *Hiadza Mazu'e*, and they cried when Giselle sang of how grieved he was when he lost his teacher. The musical notes and tones of their voices told Krarshe far in advance of the story what kind of emotion the scene would evoke.

As the song wound down, the music slowed and Burmir's singing became more sullen. The room grew silent as he sang of the first emperor's sudden death, and the immense loss the empire experienced with his passing. The hymn concluded with saying farewell, and how there will never be a lord that can rival him until he awakens from his eternal slumber.

After striking a dour tune on his harp, the three musicians put down their instruments and bowed to the crowd. Slowly, the small audience began to clap. Krarshe noticed the staff had come out from the kitchen to partake of the performance and were joining in the applause. Krarshe began to gently clap as well, not wanting to reinjure his hand.

Though he wished he could have gone to bed, the hymn was a marvel, beyond anything he had encountered in his travels. But, as great as it was, Krarshe was uneasy. His actions the night before weren't with the intent of reward. And, really, he had only been beaten, causing trouble for the whole inn. He didn't feel deserving of this.

"Thank you all for persevering through this long, long performance," the innkeeper said, coming out in front of the small stage. "We appreciate you all staying for our farewell performance for Burmir."

"And our 'thank you' for our resident hero!" Valerie added from the back of the room. Several staff members laughed as Krarshe could feel his face redden.

"Ha-ha! Yes, indeed! I bid you all a pleasant rest of your stay!" the innkeeper concluded, bowing to the customers.

Looks like the performance is over. I didn't realize the harpist was leaving... Well. At least I can go to bed now. Krarshe began to get up, but was promptly yanked back into his seat by Na'kika. She shook her head and held up her index finger.

Slowly, the patrons of the inn made their way to the stairs and left the dining hall. The innkeeper walked over to the front door, shuttered the windows, locked the door, and returned to the kitchen.

Valerie pulled up a chair and sat next to Krarshe. "So, what'd you think?"

"It was quite a performance. And fairly educational," Krarshe said.

"For as much truth as it had," commented Henry, also dragging a chair to Krarshe's table.

"I don't know. I think every story has at least a kernel of truth," Giselle said, following Henry's example and bringing a chair over.

Wait, what's happening here? Why is everyone coming to MY table? "Umm... Well, I should head to bed..."

"What?! Nonsense!" Burmir exclaimed, clomping his mug on the table as he plopped onto the stool he had brought over from the stage. "Ye'll be-a drinkin' with us t'night, lad!"

"Wait, what?" Krarshe went to stand up in protest, but was held down by Na'kika, clutching his upper arm tightly with a wide, toothy grin.

"I can't let the man who saved one of my staff leave without his reward, now can I?" the innkeeper said, slamming a rather large jug of liquid on the center of the now-crowded table and pulling up a chair to sit next to Burmir.

"Ooh! What's that? Don't seem like the usual ale yeh typically drink around 'ere!"

"It's a rum I got off some traveller some time back," the innkeeper explained. "Traded it to me for a week's stay when he found his way into Remonnet without a copper rose to his name! Hahaha!"

"Yeh are quite the haggler, William! This must be least a golden rose!"

"I doubt it. Maybe fetch fifty silvers."

"Are yeh daft? Rum's been harder ta find than mead! And I should know! Haahaa," Burmir laughed, slapping the round table hard enough to almost knock it over.

"Can we stop talking about how much tonight would have cost and just get to drinking?" Valerie interrupted.

"Indeed!" said a man Krarshe didn't recognize. He set down a bunch of mugs for everyone. He pulled up a chair backwards to the table and sat on it, chest leaning against the back of the chair. "Name's Julien. How was the stew?" he asked, reaching out an open hand toward Krarshe.

Krarshe shook his hand carefully. "Fantastic, as always. I assume you're the chef."

"For the last eleven years." He smiled. He stroked the edges of his goatee with his forefinger and thumb. "You don't look like the type who'd put a big, burly adventurer on his ass."

"Uhh. Yeah, I'm not usually the type to do something like that..."

"Hear that, Na'kika? Only for you," Valerie joked.

Na'kika blushed and turned away, playing with her ear, clearly flustered.

"Oh Val, don't tease the poor girl," Giselle scolded.

"Least not before we all get some drinks in us! Haahaa!" Burmir laughed.

"Agreed!" William said, popping the top off the large jug and pouring the golden-brown liquor into the mugs on the table. He picked up the mug in front of him and raised it. "To Burmir's outstanding performances, and to Karsh's bravery!" he shouted.

Everyone grabbed their mug and followed suit, raising them. Krarshe awkwardly raised his slowly. Once William drank from his mug, everyone else did the same. Krarshe took a short sip, not sure what to expect. To his surprise, it was sweet. Much sweeter than the ale he'd grown accustomed to.

"Ahh! Goes down easy, eh? Haahaa!" Burmir slammed his empty mug on the table and leaned in toward Krarshe. "Now. Where's our little 'hero' from? Ain't seen a long-ears since... Oh, at least since I settled in Remonnet."

"I'm from the north. Outside of Armia." This line was beginning to feel very rehearsed.

"Foreigner, eh? Can't say I know much 'bout places past Dher Molduhr."

"It's a pretty small country. I'd be surprised if anyone knew of it."

"Don't know 'bout that! William, you were an adventurin' type. You been north-a Armia?"

"You were an adventurer?" asked Valerie. "Never would have guessed."

"That's ancient history," said William dismissively.

"Hey!" exclaimed Giselle. "Mind your words!"

"Did I strike a sore point?" asked Valerie.

"Ah, no, no. Giselle 'ere's the reason William quit. Back when his wife got pregnant with the lass 'ere."

"There was more than just that," William interjected, rubbing his brow. "I don't really want to get into it."

"That's a first. You usually like regaling us with stories of your former glory," commented Giselle sharply, a hint of annoyance lingering in her voice.

"Yeah, like the time you single-handedly fought off those dire wolves, saving those farmers," said Henry.

"Or the time yeh beat those thieves."

"Or when you slew that dragon!"

"I never did that, Julien."

"I know. Just wanted to add something exciting," Julien laughed.

The whole table laughed along with Julien as they continued to drink their rum. For the next hour, everyone continued to drink and talk, telling stories or asking questions of Krarshe or Burmir. Aside from the occasional question, Krarshe sat there quietly, sipping his rum. He generally didn't like being the center of attention, and it made him nervous. As the night progressed, the alcohol began to affect everyone more and more. People were beginning to slur their words. Henry and Giselle were slowly pulling their chairs away from the table a bit,

making more room for cuddling and flirting. Julien did as Krarshe had wished he could, leaving the table before the rum affected his mind.

"And THAT," William said as he wobbled a bit, attempting to point a finger at his fellow drinkers, "ish hhhow you... gotta fight *burp* dire wolves." He laid his head against the table. Krarshe watched him, wondering if he'd pick his head up again. After a moment, he could hear quiet, muffled snoring.

"... What was he even talking about? You can't start your story with a statement like that and then fall asleep," Krarshe said.

"Lad, it don't matter. Let 'im think he's a great storyteller." Burmir took another drink before pouring more rum into his mug. "Yer holdin' yer liquor well, lad. Yeh part dwarf? Haahaa!" He patted Krarshe heavily on the shoulder, sending a shock of pain through his ribs.

"No, I'm just a careful drinker," he said, sipping his rum again.

"Aww. That's no fun, lad! 'ere, drink!" Burmir poured more rum into Krarshe's mug, causing it to overflow onto the table a bit. "Oops! Well... The rum might be affectin' me a tad bit. Haahaa."

"So, a harpist. Didn't expect a dwarf to be fond of such an instrument," Krarshe said, sipping the rum from the rim of his mug so it wouldn't spill more.

"Ah? Harps be the pride an' joy of Dher Molduhr! All the instruments we make, actually! Yeh never see a dwarf carryin' such a sad instrument as that one Giselle uses. What's it called... Oy, Giselle! Wha's that thin' yeh play?"

Both Krarshe and Burmir turned to where Giselle sat, but neither she nor Henry were still at the table. When they left, Krarshe had no idea.

"Ah. Not import'nt. *burp* Fact is, lad, we dwarves love our instruments. All them humans talk 'bout is our weapons, but ask a dwarf, a well-crafted harp is a true treasure."

"Dwwwwarffffen weaponsssssare, mmmmmmm, reeeeeelly guuuud!" William shouted, startling everyone left at the table. After his outburst, he promptly fell asleep on the table again.

"Heh, this lightweight. Shockin' from a former adventurer, eh lad? Ahh... I'll be-a missin' this place. Always liked quiet taverns or inns more 'n them noble halls."

"Really?"

"Aye. Bunch-a frilly collars, they are. Just sittin' there, quietly appreciatin' the music. Real dull." Burmir took a drink of his rum, some of it trickling down the sides of his bushy beard. "Ahh! Well... They're good fer good coin, at least, eh? Haahaa!" He took another drink. "These taverns, though. The crowd cheers. They'll stomp an' clap along with-a tune. They sing along, or try ta. Fer a musician, fer a performer, nothin's better 'n that. I's the energy. Remin's me-a home..." Burmir went silent for a moment, eyeing his rum, then quietly added, "What I wouldn't do fer some mead 'bout now."

Krarshe watched him quietly. His eyebrow braids were short, hanging down just to his cheek bones. The few dwarves he'd met in his travels would regularly have them down at least mid-chest by his age, so it struck him as odd.

As Krarshe was about to inquire about his brow braids, Burmir spoke up again, cheerful once more. "So, lad. What's yer homeland like?"

"Hmm?"

"Yeh said yer from north-a Armia. Wha's it like?"

"Oh... Umm... Pretty quiet, I guess." Krarshe sipped delicately from his mug. The flavor of the rum was starting to grow on him, and he noticed the pain in his ribs and cheek had vanished.

"Wha's that suppos-ta mean? Haahaa! Yeh live in a forest, I reckon?"

"No, it—Well, I guess it is fairly forested. But it's in the mountains."

"Elves livin' in mountains, eh? Never thought I'd see the day."

"You're mountain folk?" Valerie jumped into the conversation. It was clear the alcohol was beginning to affect her. "Never would-a guesshed."

Krarshe laughed. "I know, it's a bit odd." His mind drifted back to home. The memory was still vivid, as though the past few years away had been but a day. "It's beautiful, though. The sight of the sun setting between the distant mountains, casting their shadows over the forested valley below. During the flowering season, the smells from the blooms below are carried upon the wind. And the harvest season, the valley is painted red and gold." He sighed.

"Shounds lovely, I'd love ta shee it. Right, Na'kika?"

Na'kika stopped drinking for a moment to nod vigorously. When she stopped, she blinked a few times, head wobbling slightly. She gripped the table in an attempt to stabilize herself.

"Don't drink too fassht. Jusss learn from me," said Valerie, gesturing to herself boldly as she, too, wobbled slightly. Krarshe and Burmir exchanged glances and laughed.

Another hour of drinking, or what Krarshe thought was another hour, and even he and Burmir were also beginning to be affected by the rum. Krarshe was having a hard time keeping track of what the dwarf was discussing, but he couldn't tell if that was because of his own drunkenness or Burmir's. It was apparent that Na'kika was being drastically affected, continuously rubbing her head on Krarshe's shoulder.

"The mountinshhh of Dehrrr... Dehr Moldr. They're reeeeeally lovely thish timea yearrr, you knoooow? Yeh sssshud shee 'em, lad!"

Krarshe just nodded. His head was beginning to swim.
hic

Krarshe heard a hiccup to his side. He turned to see Na'kika sitting hunched forward against the table. Her lips wrapped themselves around the edge of her mug as she sipped at the bronze liquid without the assistance of her hands. Her eyes were intently fixed on the rum. She hiccuped again, bumping the mug and spilling some rum onto the table. It dribbled down toward William, soaking into the sleeve of his shirt.

"Lookshh like-a weeeeee lassssssh 'ere'sa haffin' trouble holdin' 'er rum."

She turned slightly to look at Burmir and Krarshe without lifting her face from the mug. Her face reddened as she pulled down on her ears with her hands, as if it'd hide her face.

"Shooo cute." Krarshe didn't initially realize that he had let his thoughts slip. He straightened up and looked at his mug. "D-did... I... just say that aloud? I think... I had too much to drink."

"Haahaa! Naw, lad. Drink sshome more!" Burmir said, pouring him more rum.

How much rum is in that jug?! Krarshe wondered with a flash of clarity.

"Issh not fair! O'ly payin' 'ttention ta Na'ki*hic*kika!" Valerie said, throwing an arm around Krarshe. "Look 'ere, Kaarsssssssh." She looked straight at his face, struggling to keep her head steady.

After a minute or so passed, Valerie continued. "Why'sh it I can't find myshelf a nishe man? Why can't I... find a good 'un? I'm pretty... right Kaaaarshhh??"

"Y-yeahh." Krarshe was beginning to struggle to formulate his thoughts.

"Exxxxxactly! But only assssshhhholes try ta... Try ta......... Aaand anotthhher thing! ... Why're you sho q-quiet, Kaa... Karr......." Valerie stared at him blankly for a few seconds, wobbling as she tried to wrap her muddled mind around the pronunciation of his name. "Kash!" she finally exclaimed, pointing an uneasy finger at the young elf. "Why you... why you sho quiet? Kash. Kassh... You... You are... a nisshe pershon. You know that? You know that, Kaa- Karsh?"

"You're nice too, Val. Youuu'll find shomeone."

"You're sho nisshe... Karsh. Here!" Valerie thrust her mug in front of him. "You can... have dish. Ash a pre-... Pre-... A giffft."

Krarshe looked down at the mug. The rum sloshed around as Valerie wobbled, struggling to stay steady. "Thanksh."

"We're friendsh! That... ish what friendsh do." She swayed a bit before falling against Krarshe shoulder. "Mmm... You shmell nissshe. Mmm..." She rested against Krarshe for a minute before jolting upright. "Ah! Yer shhoooo shneaky, Karssh! Hmm... But maaaay*hic*be." She studied Krarshe up and down, then leaned against his shoulder again and whispered in his ear. "You wanna play adult shhings...?"

Krarshe recoiled in surprise as Valerie sat back in her chair again, giggling. She took another large drink from her mug, the one she had just offered to him. Krarshe watched as she guzzled large amounts of rum, her throat twitching with each gulp. His gaze slowly drifted to her dark brown hair resting on her shoulder. From there, it shifted uncontrollably to her breasts, the tantalizing cleavage on full display as she drank. The coupling of this sight and the words she had given to his ears only, aided by the alcohol, gave rise to a sudden urge within him. The strength of this compulsion was unsettling.

I—Wow, this loss of... control. I hafta be careful of liquor. I can't even... think clearly. Krarshe struggled to regain control of his mind and body.

"Hee hee! Shee! I aaaam pretty!" Valerie said, smiling coquettishly. "Buuut nope!" She pulled away from Krarshe, covering up her exposed upper chest. "I shee yer claimed aalready. Heeheehee."

"... Huh?" Krarshe asked. He could feel someone clinging to his waist, and something laying on his lap. He looked down to see Na'kika draped across his thighs, arms wrapped around him, sleeping quietly.

"Lemme play *burp* shometing!" Burmir hollered, grabbing his harp again, distracting Krarshe from his lustful urges. "Now......... Lemme sheee..." He plucked one harp string. Then another. And another. He began plucking them in a sequence, unevenly and scattered. Krarshe couldn't tell if he was trying to play a song or just plucking random strings. Burmir continued to pluck aimlessly, as the stray notes mixed with William's snoring and Valerie's drunken clapping and cheering.

Krarshe found himself beginning to clap, no longer in control of his body. Without another option, he gave in, going along with the jovial atmosphere, enjoying camaraderie like he had never before experienced. As his mind slipped further from conscious thought, the revelry carried on into the comforting, welcoming night.

CHAPTER 13

Krarshe yawned as he sat in his usual spot by the window again, looking out over the school courtyard. He spent the whole day yesterday resting to heal, to catch up on sleep from the night before, and to nurse the headache he had awoken with. He wished he could have taken another day to recover, but he figured Bri would have his head if he did. He already knew he was in for a scolding when he told her about the fight.

While getting into a fight in a bar, with a foe many times bigger and stronger than himself, was bad enough, he would struggle to explain why he had spent a whole night drinking. Heavily. To the point where he couldn't even remember how he had gotten to his bed. Truth be told, most of the night was a blur, with only a few memories flickering to the forefront of his mind when he thought about it. The only thing he could remember clearly was how close he felt to the staff of The Easy Lute. It felt like he had a second home, his first since setting out alone a few years ago. Regardless, telling Bri any of this part of the tale was out of the question. She wouldn't sympathize with him if he said that he'd skipped another day because he had slept until midday, awoke with a pounding headache, and his ribs hurt too much to move.

Krarshe shifted positions as he stared out at the courtyard and felt the sting of his injury next to his eye. *Ugh, how am I supposed to leisurely stare out the window, ignoring half of what Owyn says, if I can't lean on my right cheek?* Krarshe thought, delicately rubbing his sore cheekbone. He was healing quicker than expected, but he was still tender all over.

"There you are!" Bri yelled from the door to the classroom. Storming up to him, she continued, "After we talked, I THOUGHT you'd be back in class. Where were—Charmer scarring, what happened to your eye?!"

"I'll explain in a moment," Krarshe said flatly.

"What?"

"Karshe!" Tibault shouted as he entered the classroom. "Where have you—What in the world happened to your eye?!"

I knew that was coming... "Sorry I wasn't here a couple days ago, Bri, Tibault. I... uhh... got into a bar fight."

"Oh by the grace of..." Bri said, rubbing her brow.

"How'd you do that?!" Tibault asked.

"It's a long story. We can discuss at lunch." Krarshe sighed, looking at his two friends. "Sorry for being such an idiot, but I'm back," he said with a smile.

"Good to have you back, Krarshe."

"Hey! When did you learn to say his name? HOW did you learn to say it? I still can't get the sound right."

"More practice than I'd like to admit..."

"I appreciate the effort," Krarshe said with a laugh.

Owyn entered the room, more cheerfully than Krarshe had ever seen him. Upon noticing Krarshe sitting in his usual spot, any joy he had vanished, his smile melting away to a sneer. "Just when I thought I was rid of you..." he muttered, dropping all pretense of courtesy. What little there was to begin with.

"Happy to see you too, Professor." Krarshe smirked.

Owyn rolled his eyes and proceeded to his desk. After going through the formality of greeting the class, he pulled out a shard of chalk and began the day's lesson.

* * *

Krarshe sat behind the store counter, thrumming his fingers on its old wooden surface. While he was glad to see his friends again, this part of his day remained boring beyond reason.

Based on what Bri and Tibault were saying, he hadn't actually missed much. The lectures covered a few other basic spells, many of which Krarshe had already cast during his experiments with Professor Landry. Without Krarshe's disruptions, the afternoon sessions returned to what they were apparently supposed to be: the students casting the same spell over and over for hours, trying to perfect the recitation and build their mana pool. It became apparent that, despite having missed so many classes, he was significantly ahead of the rest of the class, simply from the experiments he had undergone.

Krarshe sighed. *What did I spend all this money for? To be studied, sit in a store alone, and spend my class time relearning the same spells I cast nearly a cycle ago?* He thought for a moment. *I guess I get to make jokes about Owyn with my friends too... Potentially worth the money.* He chuckled to himself. The laughter made his still-sore ribs hurt a bit.

The store's door swung open and Krarshe caught a flutter of gold. He felt a rush of futile hope overcome him. *She couldn't be here again, could she? I just saw her a couple days ago.* He leaned a bit to get a better look down the aisle, bearing the pain in his ribs, and felt his heart leap into his throat. Lycia was there, looking over the contents of the shelf. As she tucked her single braid behind her ear, she glanced toward the counter, only to look away quickly when her eyes met Krarshe's.

Krarshe swallowed hard and got up from the counter. He wasn't expecting her to visit again so soon, but he wasn't going to let this opportunity pass. Taking the next aisle, he came up behind her and cleared his throat. "Anything I can help you with?" His heart was pounding, but he stood his ground, maintaining his merchant's smile.

Lycia wasn't startled nearly as much as she was the other day, but she clearly didn't expect him to come up behind her. "Oh! U-umm... N-no, I'm just browsing," she said in her usual timid tone. Her green eyes met Krarshe's again. "What happened to your eye?"

"My eye? Oh. Oh! Right, my eye... I... Umm..." Krarshe didn't want to admit he was beaten half to death by a bunch of drunk adventurers, but didn't want to look like an idiot, claiming to have walked into something. *Nothing wrong with just omitting a bit, right?* "I got into... a fight."

"A fight?"

"With an adventurer."

Lycia raised an eyebrow. The gesture set Krarshe's heart aflutter.

"Y-yeah," he croaked before coughing again. "Yeah. He was pretty big. But I like to think I walked away the victor."

Lycia giggled, again setting his heart off. "Do you now?"

"Do you think I'd lose?" He tapped his fist against his chest boldly. "Ouch!"

Lycia giggled again, trying to cover her mouth. "If you say so."

His bravado was clearly transparent, so he decided to change subjects. "How goes your training?"

"Oh... It's... It's going smoothly. How is... umm... yours?" Lycia paused for a moment. "You ARE a student here... right? You seem to be in the store quite often. I feel like you were here in the store the last time I... umm... came here, too."

"Every day, actually. Well, aside from the last couple of days because, well..." Krarshe gestured to his eye.

"Is that... normal?"

"I think so. Wouldn't you take some time to recover from an injury?"

"Not that," she said with a smile. "Running the store."

"Ah. No, not really. I'm—Well, I'm an anomaly in that regard, I suppose."

"That's unfortunate."

"It's actually not that bad. You could say I'm ahead of the class. All of the spells they're casting now are ones I cast almost a cycle ago."

"Wait, you're already casting spells? That's pretty incredible. I'm still learning mana control." Lycia's usual timidness seemed to vanish in an instant.

"Mana control?"

"You know. Projecting your mana, controlling the amount released, having it take different forms. The bas...ics..." Lycia trailed off as she noticed the blank look on Krarshe's face. "Did... you not do that first?"

Krarshe shook his head slowly before answering, "N-no. This is the first I'm hearing of it, actually. We learned how to release our mana, and then went to spells immediately."

"Is this what Mom meant...?" Lycia muttered to herself.

"What do you mean?"

"Oh! No, nothing. Forget you heard me say anything," she said, waving her hands frantically.

"Hey! What are you doing talking to a customer?" the supervising student demanded, coming out from behind the counter, startling both Krarshe and Lycia.

"You're not supposed to talk to customers...?" Lycia whispered to Krarshe.

"Umm... I'm not going to answer that..."

"What are you even doing in this store then?"

Krarshe shrugged. "Staying out of trouble?"

"Get back behind the counter! Leave customers to me." The student eyed Lycia. "Is there anything I can help you with?" he asked with sickeningly fake cordiality.

"Oh, no, no. Everything's been taken care of." Lycia turned and made two steps toward the door before stopping. "Umm...

U-until we... meet again, Karshe..." she said, timid once more, before continuing to leave.

Krarshe waved an unseen goodbye and just stood there, watching as she left. *Meet again? Wait, why did she even come here? He thought for a moment. Was it... to see me?*

"Tch!" The other student clicked his tongue and returned to the back of the store, leaving Krarshe standing in the aisle alone.

Krarshe could feel a smile spreading across his face, his heart racing even faster than when Lycia was present. *Meet again...* The words echoed in his mind as he continued to think about her parting words. As he dwelled on what she said, his smile began to fade. *Mana control? Is that something we should have learned? What did her mother say to her?*

Krarshe turned and slowly walked back to the counter, mulling over their discussion. He couldn't tell what it was, but something felt amiss. Next time she came, he knew he'd have to press her on it. He wanted to know. He must know.

CHAPTER 14

"Good, good! Now hold it..." Professor Landry called out from behind the safety of his improved barricade. It had been reinforced with magic this time to be significantly more sturdy, but it was still showing signs of damage wrought by Krarshe's spells.

Krarshe held the flaming sphere over his head. The ball of fire encompassed most of the room, charring the tops of the dilapidated walls and expanding into the open sky above the training room. Krarshe focused as best he could, trying to maintain it. Before long, bolts of electricity began arcing along the sphere's surface.

"No! No! Focus!"

Krarshe tried to focus on the mana flowing through him, but it didn't help. The lightning grew more prominent, causing the great fireball to quiver and shake, losing its perfect form.

"Argh! It's breaking down! Stop the cast!"

Lightning collided with the already-damaged walls and floor, showering the room in debris. Krarshe ended the spell as quickly as he could. "No good, I guess," he sighed. This was the first day casting spells since his fight, having healed in just under a quarter-cycle thanks to Teva's blessing. He was hoping something might have changed, but it was futile. Lightning was the only element he had demonstrated any semblance of control over, everything else backfired.

"Hmm." Landry scribbled something down in his notebook and stood up. "You are quite the mystery. I thought we had stabilized it for a moment. The chaotic nature of your magic is…"

"Annoying?"

"Fascinating." Landry's mustache twitched in a smile.

Krarshe rubbed his hair, kicking loose some of the dust caught in his blond hair. "Not sure that's the word I'd use."

"Mysteries like this are what mages live for!"

Landry stood up and dusted off the bottom of his robes. Krarshe was honestly surprised the old man was still interested in these experiments. The results had been the same every day. With a few days until the end of Sirnus and the start of harvest season, he would have expected Landry's initial excitement to have waned by now.

"Professor?"

"Hmm?"

"Could you explain—Do you know, what is mana control?"

"You mean the act of releasing mana?"

Krarshe shook his head. "No. I mean, yes, but is there more to it than that?" Lycia's words had been bouncing around in his mind since they had last spoken a quarter-cycle ago, and he hadn't seen her in those fifteen days to ask for clarification. Having spent every other day with Professor Landry, Krarshe figured they had built enough of a rapport that he could be forthright about this.

Professor Landry leaned against his barricade and stroked his long mustache pensively. "I do recall reading about such techniques. Many years ago, in fact."

"What was it?"

"It's been a while, but I think it was the theory that one could control their own mana through will. That it was possible to control its structure and how it behaved through practice alone."

"That sounds incredible."

"It is. But it's largely a theory now."

"But, why? Why wouldn't it be used now?" Krarshe pressed the old teacher.

"Well, because it's extremely difficult. This was back during the height of the empire, when there were many fewer mages. Most people couldn't use magic, so it alone granted you noble status. The time they had to practice and the skill of mages at the time are not like they are today."

"So spellcasting became the common way to use it?"

Landry nodded. "This allowed for there to be more mages. Especially useful in times of war."

"Hmm..." Krarshe thought about Lycia's training. If she was learning mana control, what kind of teacher was her mother?

"It was said," Landry started, "that exceptionally gifted mages could cast spells through control of their mana alone."

"Only mana control?" Krarshe asked.

"Yes. No spellcast at all."

"That's... Can ANYONE do that?"

Landry shrugged. "I know of no one gifted enough to do that. You'd have to be as powerful as the first emperor was. Or so the stories go."

"Ehem!"

Both Krarshe and Landry were startled by a man clearing his throat. They turned to see Professor Owyn standing at the door, impatiently tapping his finger as he crossed his arms.

"Oh, it seems we've run over again." Landry laughed, clearly knowing that they had run late. It was all too common and it clearly annoyed Owyn, a fact that Krarshe derived twisted pleasure from. Since returning to class, Owyn had not hid his disdain for Krarshe. It made reciprocating the feeling very easy.

"My apologies, Professor," Krarshe said with an exaggerated bow.

"Yes, yes. Just leave. You can put the equipment back later, we won't need it today."

Again, Krarshe bowed and left for the store. *Mana control... Is Lycia actually learning that? I hope she's here again today.*

* * *

Krarshe rested his chin on his palm as he waited for Na'kika to bring out his food. Unfortunately, Lycia hadn't shown up at the store so he was left to speculate and theorize alone. *Maybe this mana control could help my spellcasting...* He hummed absent-mindedly to Henry's lute, the cheerful tune burrowing into his ears, undoubtedly to be stuck in his head as he tried to sleep later.

The Easy Lute was quieter since Burmir left. It took only a day or so for word to spread, thus returning the inn's occupancy to what it was when Krarshe first came. Furthermore, Henry had been on his own the last two nights. Giselle apparently had some business elsewhere, but Krarshe didn't want to be rude by pressing for details. With just Henry playing, the dining hall had only a few patrons, and Krarshe welcomed the quiet meal. It also helped that he didn't have to worry if they had fish left on any given night now.

The placid dining hall helped him get his thoughts in order. As he had walked through the busy streets of Feyfaire, he wondered if it would be better to leave the academy. Not for the reason he'd previously toyed with, but to pursue a new teacher. A better teacher. One who, rather than study him, would help him cast spells. Lycia's mother seemed to be a gifted mage, especially if she was teaching her daughter to control her mana. Maybe there was something to it, something that would stabilize his own spells. But his new struggle was the fact that he'd just reunited with his friends. The whole ordeal had made him painfully aware of how important his relationship with them was. It might have been better to have left before talking with them again.

A plate of grilled fish plopped down in front of him. "Thanks, Na'kika." He reached up and pet her head, which she accepted gratefully as she lowered her head to meet his hand. It had become a bit of a ritual for the two of them, one that took Krarshe some getting used to. It was awkward at first, but seeing how happy it made her, he forced himself to get over his embarrassment.

When she had enough attention, she stood up fully and gave a slight bow before turning to the kitchen. She seemed happy. Or at least, happier than when he'd first come to the inn. Krarshe wasn't familiar with catfolk, but he knew Na'kika well by this point, and her body language spoke volumes. There was a spring in her step, and her tail was always speaking to her joy.

Another thought entered his mind. "Oh, Na'kika. A moment, if you would."

Na'kika stopped and returned to Krarshe's side, swiftly enough to make him question if she was eager to come back. She tilted her head inquisitively.

"I was just curious... So, you know how I mentioned I was attending the academy here in Remonnet, yes?"

Na'kika nodded.

"What would you think if... I left the academy?"

Na'kika cocked her head to the side and raised her hands in a questioning gesture.

"I'm starting to think I won't be able to learn what I need to learn from the academy. There was another teacher I had in mind."

She pursed her lips and looked off to the side, carefully considering her response. After a moment, Na'kika shrugged and nodded in agreement.

Krarshe paused for a second before bringing up the next point. He wasn't sure if she had considered this when she responded, but he was afraid to tell her. He could anticipate her response. "You... do know that would mean I'd probably be leaving Remonnet... right?"

Na'kika's amber eyes opened wide, her tail stood up straight. She dropped her wooden tray and grabbed hold of his arm, hugging it against her chest. She began furiously shaking her head side to side, her orange-red hair brushing up against his robed arm.

Krarshe knew this would happen, just based on her behavior of late. He noticed Henry had stopped playing and was watching the scene, as had the few customers in the dining hall. Krarshe could feel his face redden with embarrassment. He looked down at Na'kika, who continued to cling to him, pressing her face into his arm.

Well, this could be a problem. "Na'kika, Na'kika, relax. I haven't gone anywhere yet." Krarshe put his hand gently upon her head.

She shook her head again. The fur of her ear tickled his palm. It was the first time he'd ever touched her ears, as she was usually very protective of them.

"What's going on?" Valerie asked, hurrying over to the table. She gestured Henry to go back to his playing, which he did without hesitation. Before long, the customers returned to their meals and Henry's music.

"I was just telling her I was..." Krarshe stopped and looked down at the troubled catfolk girl. Whispering, he said, "I was thinking of leaving Remonnet."

Valerie gave him a disapproving look and shook her head. She turned to Na'kika, still clinging to Krarshe's arm, and crouched down to put her arm around her. "Na'kika. It's okay. He's not going anywhere." Valerie looked at Krarshe. "Right?"

With just a look, he could read what she was thinking. "Right. Na'kika, I changed my mind. I'm not going anywhere." He again pet her on the head.

Slowly, she loosened her grip on his arm and looked up at him. Her eyes glistened with moisture, on the verge of tears.

"I wouldn't just disappear on you, Na'kika," Krarshe said, continuing to pet her head.

Na'kika sniffed and further relinquished his arm. She gave a hesitant smile, forcing a tear free from her eye and trickling down her cheek. She grabbed a hold of his hand and rubbed her face against it, smearing the tear across her face.

"There, now. You just return to the kitchen and take a moment to calm down, okay?" Valerie instructed.

Na'kika nodded and stood up. She staggered to the kitchen, bumping into tables and chairs as she went.

"Now, you," Valerie said, turning toward Krarshe. "Not that it's any business of mine, but why would you be leaving?"

"To find a new teacher. The academy isn't teaching me what I thought it would."

Valerie sighed. "Well, that IS a fair reason." She put a finger to her lip pensively as she turned to the kitchen. She stood there quietly, playing with her bottom lip as she stared idly, lost in thought. "I wish I could protect her, but there's not a lot I can do in this situation. Your business is your own, and it'd be unreasonable to demand you stay just for her."

Krarshe looked toward the kitchen as well. "It's not my intention to hurt her, especially with what she's gone through. But I may have no choice. I wasn't expecting her to get so attached to me."

"This is beyond what I expected as well. It was a good laugh, sure, but I didn't expect it to become this big of an issue."

"A laugh, huh?"

"Of course. You two were so cute together." Valerie giggled.

Krarshe rolled his eyes. "Well, we at least have time to figure it out. I haven't decided whether to leave or not yet anyway."

"I pray you decide to stay. For her sake."

"That would certainly be the easiest solution. The question of whether that's the correct one... That remains to be seen."

Valerie sighed again. "Well, enjoy your meal. I'm going to go check on her."

"Thanks," Krarshe said as she left. *For more than just your sentiment,* he thought. *Ugh. I wonder if it was a mistake to get so close with her.* He stopped and shook his head in disappointment. *No, I don't regret it. But this certainly adds another layer of difficulty to this decision.* He sighed, looking down at his grilled fish. He suddenly wasn't that hungry. *Wisdom, guide me.*

CHAPTER 15

Krarshe wiped the sweat from his brow as he slotted another book onto the shelf. The humidity was suffocating in the small office, and it wasn't even midday yet. Professor Landry wrote in a book, seemingly unaffected by the humidity. Krarshe looked out the window of the professor's office, down to the training room below, the countless craters his morning experiments had left behind pooling the rain water, making the room all but useless. The pitter-patter of rain against the window pane was soothing in the otherwise insufferable room.

"Almost done?" Landry asked without looking up from his work.

"Oh, umm... No, not yet." Krarshe collected more books from one of the two wooden chairs by the entrance. He looked over the titles before putting them on one of the multitude of shelves, trying to follow the convoluted organization system Landry had explained earlier. *I wish we could have just cancelled the experiments so I could go back to sleep, rather than tidying up this mess of an office.*

All of the books were on some aspect of magic, covering topics from individual spells and their uses and modifications to magic theory and the nature of mana. He hadn't seen a library this extensive since he left home.

Krarshe felt a thud against the back of his head hard enough to cause him to drop all the books he was carrying. He turned around to see he'd been hit by a book. A floating book. He watched it curiously as it floated away from him. Krarshe looked over at Landry to see if he had noticed the mysterious book, but he just kept writing. *Okay... Guess I shouldn't be surprised.* He followed after the book and reached out to grab it out of the air. As his hand approached, the book darted away, fleeing to the far corner of the room by the ceiling. Again, he looked to Landry, who remained disinterested. Krarshe sighed. He dragged one of the chairs from the entrance wall over to the corner and climbed on top of it. The book was just barely out of reach. Up on his toes, he reached as far as he could. "Al...most... Got I—" The chair tipped over just as he almost got a grasp of the book, causing him to fall into countless other stacks of books.

"Be careful with that book. It can be mischievous," Landry explained, not looking up from the book even now.

Krarshe lay upon the fallen pile of books in defeat as he watched the book fly away yet again. "I swear, this book..." he groaned.

"Cursed item," Landry said. "A mage's idea of a prank."

Krarshe crawled his way out of the mess of books and stood up. "Someone has a perverse sense of humor."

"I've been told that more than once." He gave Krarshe a smile before returning to his work.

Krarshe stared at the old man for a minute before shaking his head, irked. "You have a lot of books here," he said as he began picking up books again, trying to help pass the time.

"Mmm. I've been studying magic for a long time."

"How long is 'long'?"

"Well, maybe not that long to an elf. But just about my entire life. Ever since I retired from adventuring."

Krarshe stopped. "You were an adventurer?"

"Believe it or not, yes. When I was younger." Landry looked up from his work. "Let me show you."

Landry stood up and made his way over to a chest in the corner. Carefully pulling out a collection of keys from his pocket, he fingered through them before grasping an old, rusty one firmly. He inserted it into the chest's lock and turned it. Nothing happened. He turned it a couple more times before taking it out and looking at it more carefully. "Oh, my mistake. It's this one," Landry muttered to himself. This time, the lock opened with a click. He opened the chest and reached inside. "Here, this one..." Landry took out a necklace with an amulet attached to it, offering it to Krarshe.

Krarshe took the necklace, puzzled. "Umm... What is—"

Landry said a spell under his breath and the room grew darker. Very dark, in fact. "Put it on and grab the amulet tightly."

Still confused, Krarshe followed the teacher's instructions. As he clutched the amulet, it began to glow, growing brighter the tighter he held it.

"It's a light amulet. Or, at least, that's what I've been calling it. I found it in some ruins."

Krarshe raised an eyebrow. "Seems odd."

"Not really. Equipment gets lost all the time. Some of it is from the original inhabitants, others from... past adventurers."

Krarshe shifted uneasily. He was fully aware of the dangers adventurers encountered, and it made sense. It just wasn't something he ever really dwelled on, and didn't care to here.

"This one..." Landry said, carefully pulling out another item. It was a glass case with a large, dark blue or purple crystal was suspended in the center of it. He took the amulet back from Krarshe, and in exchange handed him the glass case. "It's a soul cage."

"Wait, a soul what?"

"A soul cage," he repeated, putting the amulet back in the chest. "Touching the crystal will rip your soul from your body, leaving it an empty husk. Never touch the crystal directly."

"What?!" Krarshe nearly dropped the case.

Landry laughed. "It's fine, it's fine. That case is reinforced with magic. It'd take a dragon's strength to break it open."

"Oh, ha..." Krarshe laughed uneasily as he returned the case back to Landry. He peered over Landry's shoulder into the chest as the teacher put the case back, seeing an assortment of other objects. "If you don't mind, why did you quit?"

Landry froze, his hand still reaching into the chest for another object. "Hmm..." He stood upright and took a few paces away from Krarshe. "I guess it'd be a good lesson..." As he turned back, Krarshe could see the teacher's typically jovial expression had grown sullen. "Do... Have you heard of a 'magic-eater'?"

Krarshe shook his head.

Professor Landry walked back to his desk and sat down. "Magic-eaters are... Well, they're a kind of demon." Landry stared at the floor, reminiscing about his youth. "And, as its name implies, it eats magic. Mana. Perhaps the most dangerous creature for us mages." He took a deep breath before continuing, "Typically, they're found in ruins, consuming lost magic equipment. Well, my adventuring party were tasked with investigating such a ruin..." Krarshe noticed his lip quiver ever so slightly. "By some miracle, I was the only one to escape."

"They all...?"

Landry nodded. "We didn't know it was there. Even if we did, it probably would have caught us off guard. I was the only mage, after all. As long as I didn't cast anything, we should be fine, right? Never would have guessed the enchanted equipment we had just bought would cost everyone their lives..."

"... Sorry. I shouldn't have asked."

Landry shook his head. "This was decades ago. And besides, it's important to learn from past experiences. Right?" His mustache raised as he smiled, but there was only sadness in his eyes. "I should get back to work."

As he picked up his quill, a knock came at the door. "Professor? Could I request your assistance?"

"Oh, right. You said you had questions, didn't you, Marcus?" Landry got up from his chair. He locked up the chest and slipped the key back into his robes. "If you'll excuse me, Krarshe. Please continue organizing the room. You're free to go at lunch time, or when you finish."

Krarshe nodded, reluctant as he was. Still, it was the least he could do after bringing up that sore subject. He continued picking up books and slotting them into the holes in the shelves. He looked up at the book hovering in the corner. *Mmm... No. I think you can just stay there.*

The hours went by. Landry never returned to the office, but Krarshe had cleaned most of the books off the floor and furniture. Only a few books sitting on a small table by the window remained. He picked them up and brought them over to the shelves. As he went to put the last book in its spot, Krarshe noticed a small slip of paper sticking out from between the pages. *Oh, was he using this book?* Curious, Krarshe opened the book to the page. The slip of paper only had 'B.B.' written on it. The page appeared to be a fire spell. "*Ra tso, ra hias, Soujiin...* Wow, this is a long spell. Didn't realize they could be that long. What is it for... Pillar of Flame? Hmm. Wonder how it would look if I cast it?" Krarshe laughed to himself before remembering that was a source of frustration for him. "Well, either way. Done before lunch." He checked for the position of the sun, but the clouds were too dark to make any guess as to its location. He shrugged. "Yeah, I think I've enough time for a nap." He put the book onto the bookshelf and made his way out of the office, grinning to himself.

* * *

Krarshe yawned as he watched the on-staff student talking with a customer. He was surprised that today, despite the endless rain, there had been several customers that had come in. Naturally, Krarshe wasn't allowed to talk to anyone. Not that he cared to, but by this point he'd hoped his afternoons wouldn't be spent at the counter, whittling away his time. At least the customers had made for some slight entertainment.

A stampede of students stormed by, trying to shield their heads from the rain with their hands. *Guess the day's over then. Can't wait to walk in this...*

The door to the store flung open. "Karshe!" Tibault came rushing into the store, flinging the hood of his cloak off his head. Uncharacteristically, alone. "Do you want to come to dinner?"

"Umm..." Krarshe's eyes shifted to the student and customer. While Tibault's outburst had drawn their attention for a moment, the student quickly brought his attention back to the products. "I can, I guess. Why the sudden urgency?"

"I got a spell right! I think that calls for celebration!"

"Uh-huh... What about Bri then?"

Tibault's gaze shifted. "Well... The place I was thinking... My older brother told me about it."

"What's that got to do with Bri?"

"It's... If I say I wanted to go... for the waitresses... Is that sufficient explanation?"

Krarshe raised an eyebrow.

"Look, I wanted to see it, but I didn't feel comfortable going alone, okay? Besides, after all that hiding from us you did, I think you owe me."

"I don't know if that's a qualification for 'owing' you," Krarshe said. "Besides, it's raining really hard. I was thinking of just returning to my inn and drying off."

"You didn't bring a cloak?"

"It wasn't raining yet when I left."

"Didn't notice the clouds?"

"I left early."

"Yeah, did you forget what time I said I had to chase him down?" Bri said, emerging from the back room.

Tibault jumped a bit at her entrance. "Where'd you come from?"

"I walked through the building? Well, anyways, what were you two discussing?"

"Oh, nothing," Tibault said, waving dismissively.

Bri looked at Krarshe for confirmation. "He wants to go to a restaurant for dinner," Krarshe replied. Tibault shot him a look.

"In this rain?"

"That's what I said too, but he insisted on celebrating successfully casting a spell or something."

"Y-yeah, but I guess we can wait for another day. With the rain and all." Tibault laughed nervously.

"Let me get my cloak and I'll join you two," Bri said.

"Guess I'll be sitting in wet clothes then," said Krarshe.

"No cloak?"

"That's actually what we were discussing when you walked in," explained Tibault.

"Oh. I guess that makes sense. I can see if someone in the dormitory can lend me an extra."

"Thanks. Guess we'll wait for you to come back then. I should be able to sneak out of here pretty easily..." Krarshe wasn't sure if the student would even notice he'd left. It didn't weigh on Krarshe in the slightest, regardless.

"I don't understand why they make you stay here until closing," Tibault said.

"Me neither. It's annoying though."

"Well, I'll be right back then. Don't leave without me," Bri said as she left out the store's entrance.

Krarshe and Tibault could see her immediately sprint past the window towards the dormitory, trying to shield herself from the rain with her hand. "Karshe..." Tibault started. "Why did you tell her?"

"I mean, you never clearly explained..."

"My explanation wasn't sufficient?!" Tibault groaned. "This is going to be so awkward..."

"If it helps, we can say it was my choice."

"You know, I may just say that."

The two bickered back and forth for a few minutes before Bri came back. She took out a cloak from under her own and handed it to Krarshe. "Here. It might not fit well, you're a bit bigger than my neighbor, but it's better than nothing."

Krarshe draped it around his shoulders. Sure enough, it came to just above his knees. "Well, it covers the important parts." Krarshe surveyed the room. "Let's go, while the on-staff student is busy."

The three, with hoods up, snuck out of the store and into the pouring rain. They made their way through the streets, splashing through the small rivers of rainwater as they flowed towards the Silver River. The streets were largely empty, save for the occasional carriage.

"Haa... I love the rain," Bri said.

"Are you mad? This is awful," Tibault retorted. "I'm wet up to my knees."

"You don't like this? It's like we're the only ones in the world!" Bri said with a twirl, arms fully extended. "Or, like we're on an adventure!"

"Umm... No."

"I don't know about that. Feels more like we're fugitives. Escaping under cover of night and storm," Krarshe said.

"That's an adventure!" Bri laughed.

"Ugh, I'm regretting this. You two are too much." Tibault pulled his cloak tighter around himself. "Thankfully, it's not too much farther."

"Let's take a detour then!" Krarshe joked.

"Yeah!"

"You to go ahead if you want," Tibault said. "I won't be joining you."

"Think about it. You can tell those waitresses you're sopping wet because you just got back from some quest."

"Waitresses?" Bri asked.

"Yeah, Tibault wan—"

Tibault's hand flew out from under his cloak, hitting Krarshe square in the chest. "Nothing. Nothing, don't worry about him. He's just being weird." He shot Krarshe a sideways glance.

Bri looked at the two boys suspiciously, but just shook her head and continued on.

"Ah, down this alley." Tibault guided them down a side street. There were a few men standing outside the door, sword on their hips.

"The Silken Courtesan...?" Bri read the sign aloud. She slowly turned around to face her friends. "Care to explain...?"

"It was Karshe's idea!"

Wow, he didn't even hesitate. What kind of name is that, anyway?

"Mmm... Why were you the one leading us then?"

Good point.

Tibault stood there, looking around as though searching for an excuse. Bri sighed. "Teva spare me. As long as you're paying and the food is good," she said, headed toward the entrance.

"See? It's fine," Krarshe said with a smile.

Tibault rolled his eyes. The three made their way into the building. The two guardsmen outside gave them a look, but didn't say anything as they entered. The room was boisterous, more than Krarshe expected in the otherwise quiet Castle Ward. *Guess nobles are people too.* They found an empty table and sat down. They had no sooner pulled back their hoods than a waitress came over.

"Can I get you three a drink?" she asked in a sultry voice.

Krarshe looked her over. She wore a long slip dress that came down just to just above her ankles. The red fabric seemed smooth, with a luster to it. There was a slit in the side that came up to mid-thigh. He couldn't tell, but it seemed as though she was standing in a way to expose as much of her thigh as possible. "Just an ale for me. Whatever is cheapest."

"S-same," croaked Tibault.

Bri glared at the two boys. "Whatever is most expensive."

The waitress bowed and headed for the bar.

"The most expensive?" Krarshe asked.

Bri shrugged. "Because you two are paying. And, because you dragged me to a place like this."

"Weren't you the one who wanted to come?"

"Truthfully, I was going to ask Karshe alone. I figured you wouldn't want to come here."

"Curses, you two. You're such boys."

"Well, yeah," both Krarshe and Tibault said in unison.

The waitress came back, carrying their drinks and a menu. The cups were glass, not the usual wood or ceramic he'd seen in other kingdoms. "Here are your drinks, milords and milady. I'll give you a few minutes for your orders."

Tibault's and Krarshe's eyes followed her as she walked over to another table. The other waitresses seemed to be acting very familiarly with some of the other patrons. *I think I'm beginning to understand why Tibault's brother recommended this place.*

"Ah-hem! So..." Bri drew their attention back, away from the waitresses. She lifted her cup and said, "To Tibault's successful spellcast. May you have more."

Krarshe raised his glass and looked over at Tibault.

"I feel like I'm being mocked here," Tibault grumbled. He reluctantly raised his glass as well.

"No, I'm quite serious. I hope you can get the hang of it."

"Just don't become an anomaly," Krarshe said. He took a drink of his ale and frowned. It was more bitter than he'd hoped from such a high-class restaurant. He continued, "It's no fun."

"Don't think I have anything to worry about there." Tibault took a drink. "Ack! This stuff is awful!"

"Glad I'm not alone on that one. This ale is terrible."

"Mine's pretty good," Bri said, sipping it again. "Probably triple the price too." She smirked.

Tibault sighed. "Well, my parents will be happy to hear it, at least. They were growing concerned at my lack of progress."

"Oh? Then you'll have good news for them," Krarshe said.

"Must be nice," Bri said under her breath before taking another sip of her drink.

"Hmm?"

"Nothing. So, Ka- Kr-arshe, what did you do today, what with the rain and all?"

"The most exciting thing I've done since coming here. Cleaning."

"What?" Tibault and Bri both said.

"Professor Landry had me organize his office."

"That sounds awful," Tibault said.

"Oh, it was. Probably more than you realize. There was this one cursed book..."

"Let me guess, it was floating?" Bri asked.

"Have you seen it?"

"No, but I've heard about it."

"A floating book? Why?" Tibault asked, reaching across the table to grab the menu.

"Some kind of cruel prank, he said." Krarshe took a drink of his ale and grimaced. "Cursed thing hid up in the corner near the ceiling. Ended up falling off a chair onto a pile of books trying to retrieve it, before he mentioned what it was."

"You didn't figure something was odd about it? Wow, Krarshe..." Bri covered her face with her hand, embarrassed for her friend.

"Hey, he said ALL of the books." Krarshe sighed. "There was a few other things he had, from when he was an adventurer."

"He was an adventurer?!" Bri said, nearly spilling her drink.

"Who?" Tibault asked, looking up from the menu.

"Professor Landry. The one old one with the really long mustache."

"I wonder if that mustache was that long when he was adventuring..." Bri mused.

"Anyways, he had some light amulet. And a soul cage."

"I feel like I'm constantly lost in this conversation," Tibault said, poking Bri with the menu before she finally took it. "What's a soul cage now?"

"Apparently some artifact that will rip your soul out of you if you touch it."

"Teva's mercy! Why'd he have something that dangerous?!" Bri asked.

"It's in some sort of container. I don't know. He just handed it to me without explaining."

"That's it. It's official. The maddener has taken him," Bri said, putting the menu down.

"Are you ready with your orders?" the waitress asked, gently placing a hand on Tibault's shoulder.

"A-a-ah," Tibault stammered.

"Oh, my apologies. Not quite yet," Bri said.

"Okay then. Please take your time," she said, gently tracing across Tibault's shoulder with her fingertips as she left, causing Tibault to shiver reflexively.

Bri rolled her eyes. "Let's get this order in before we continue, shall we? I don't know if Tibault can contain himself otherwise."

"W-what? I'm fine," Tibault said, his voice cracking.

Krarshe laughed, watching his friends banter back and forth. As three carried on, enjoying each other's company, Krarshe thought to himself how great it was that he made up with them. Then to Na'kika and the advice she'd given him. Looking at this scene now, it might have been the best advice he'd ever received.

CHAPTER 16

Krarshe was beginning to regret his choice of seating in the classroom. It was an ideal spot, somewhere he could sit quietly and admire the courtyard. His game of counting stones in the early morning had amused him more than the lectures. As the year marched on, however, the chill of Harvest air crept in through the thin glass pane, and this game was hardly worth the discomfort.

Sirnus had passed without excitement or incident, as had much of Harvest. To Krarshe's dismay, that included any meetings with Lycia. Now in the final quarter-cycle of the first half of Harvest, he had largely given up hope on seeing her. He had thought of every possible excuse and reason, over and over, to exhaustion. In the end, he decided it wisest to just not think about it. A short meeting amongst the many he'd encountered over his years of travelling. It still ate away at him, despite his resolution.

The Harvest winds blew strong, kicking up dirt and leaves from distant trees outside the city walls, and created a vortex in the barren courtyard where they were trapped. He watched as a single brown leaf escaped over the wall, settling just beyond the school's gates. The imprisoned leaves settled as the winds died, before once again being stirred by another gust of wind, and launching even more leaves from the courtyard. A few poor female students got caught up in the storm of leaves coming in the gate, the wind catching them off guard as they tried to both shield their eyes from the dust and hold down their skirts.

"I don't understand how you tolerate sitting beside the window," said Bri, sitting down next to Krarshe. "It's cold."

"It's a bit uncomfortable, but I still like it here. Gives me something to do during lectures," he said, in spite of his previous thoughts.

"Uncomfortable? I'm shivering by the end of lectures."

"And I can't feel my fingers after but a short time into it," Tibault added, sitting next to Bri. "Look, the rest of the class has moved away from the windows," he said, gesturing to the rest of the students piling into the room. The rows of tables nearest the windows were largely empty, the students preferring to crowd onto the tables closer to the entrance.

Krarshe shrugged. "Beats being clustered tighter than a stone pile."

"Not sure I'd agree..."

"Quiet down everyone!" Owyn said, entering the room swiftly, putting his books down on his desk the same way he did every day. "I have an announcement!"

The whole class started to murmur and whisper to each other. "An announcement? I wonder what it is," Tibault whispered to Bri and Krarshe in the same way the class did amongst themselves.

"I wouldn't get too excited. I suspect I know what it is..." Bri groaned. Her gaze seemed distant, like her mind was elsewhere. Before Krarshe could ask, Owyn continued.

"Starting the last five days of this quarter-cycle, and through the first five days of Second Harvest, the academy will be in recess. No classes will be held, and all students in the dormitory will need to make outside arrangements. Those incapable of doing so will need to discuss with me after class to see if special exceptions can be made."

The murmuring of the class erupted into a delayed roar of excitement, as though they hadn't understood the announcement at first.

"A break?! How is that not exciting?!" Tibault whispered excitedly.

Bri just held up a finger, before pointing toward Owyn. Almost on cue, he continued.

"Ahem! I'm not done yet. While this break may seem convenient for you students, it will serve two purposes for the academy. First, it will grant the professors time to assemble their research findings to present before the Council. Secondly, it will give us time to have repairs made to the training room..." Owyn glared at Krarshe.

"Well, that's new," Bri said quietly with a chuckle.

"At the end of this recess, there will be an exam. The first of several you will take before being allowed to move on to the advanced courses."

"Aaaand there it is..." muttered Bri.

It took Krarshe a minute before it dawned on him. Bri had failed the exam. Repeatedly. It stood to reason that she despised the exams by now. Or dreaded them.

"The exam will be conducted individually, with each student being tasked with casting a spell before myself and the other professors. Which spell will be assigned the morning of the exam, and the demonstration will be held in the afternoon. Each student will receive a different spell, and you are not to discuss your spell with the other students, whether during your preparation or after the test. Doing so will be tantamount to cheating and result in immediate failure, as well as disciplinary action."

The classroom turned quiet. All the previous excitement had drained from their expressions. As Krarshe surveyed the room, it seemed like only Armand retained his confidence. *Always smug...* Krarshe thought.

"Do try your best not to fail. The first exam is there to see your growth. It would be unfortunate to go through the bitter taste of failure on such an exam..." Krarshe thought he saw Owyn look over at him, but second guessed himself when he noticed Bri shrink back into her seat next to him. "Not that any of you have anything to worry about, of course. If you have been keeping up with the lectures and practical demonstrations, I have no doubt you will pass." Owyn walked back to his desk and produced a book. "Let us begin today's lesson," he said, pulling out a piece of chalk.

"That seemed harsh," Krarshe said as Owyn's chalk clacked and screeched across the board.

"Quite unsettling," agreed Tibault, wetting his quill as he began to write his notes.

Krarshe turned toward Bri. She sat there quietly, still cowering in her seat, staring blankly at the floor. He opened his mouth to say something to her, but no words came out. His mind raced as he tried to think of something, anything, to encourage her. In the end, he was left, mouth agape, without any tangible encouragement to offer. He sat back in his seat and looked out the window once more, forced to swallow his frustration.

* * *

Krarshe meandered around the store, inspecting the shelves of magical products. He wasn't so much interested in the store itself, but figured knowing what kind of items were used by people here seemed a better use of his time than drawing on the dusty counter with his index finger. He weaved up and down the aisles of goods, trying to avoid the supervising student as they restocked the shelves. Apparently, Krarshe wasn't even trusted enough to do that.

He pulled a scroll from the pile and opened it up. The alphabet they used for magic was still difficult for Krarshe to master, at least compared to what he used growing up at home, but he had enough time in the store to have gone over the notes Bri gave him to at least grasp the basics. *Wall of flame,* he read to himself before rolling it back up and returning it to the shelf. *Removal of water... Dry?* He thought for a moment on who would have enough demand for such a spell that they'd pay for a single-use magic scroll. "Oh! This one's interesting..." he said out loud. *Summon rain. Definitely a lot of potential uses.* "I didn't know they could use such grand spells."

"Who?"

"People aro—" Krarshe caught himself, realizing someone had snuck up behind him. He spun around to see Lycia leaning in toward him, her green eyes shimmering with curiosity from under the dull brown hood of her cloak. Krarshe coughed slightly. "A- Ahem. Just... Mages. Here. In... Remonnet?"

"Why is that a question?"

Krarshe could feel himself losing control of the situation. "N-nevermind that. I haven't seen you in a while."

Lycia drew back the hood. In the light, he could see her cheeks and nose were slightly red from the chilly Harvest air. "I-it's not that... I didn't want to come... Just... My training has kept me busy. A lot busier than I would have guessed. And more tiring. It makes the journey to Remonnet challenging."

"Oh?" Krarshe saw a golden opportunity. He could feel his heart rate quicken. "Where are you from?"

"Huh? Oh, umm..." She laughed nervously. "I'm from Valenfort. It's a small village to the south, just past the green fields, where the trees start to spring up again." She laughed again. "Sorry, I... didn't even realize I'd never talked about it."

"You come that far?"

Lycia nodded.

Krarshe decided to push his luck a bit further, his heart pounding even harder. "Wow. I feel bad now. That's a long way to travel to talk to me," he said with a smile, despite the tightness in his throat.

"Oh, no, no. I umm... I have other things to do here too. Quite a few, actually," Lycia said, frantically turning away to look at the shelves. Krarshe wanted to move to the side a bit, to catch a glimpse of whether or not she was blushing, but decided against it.

After a bit, he breathed deeply to calm himself. He decided to change topics; he hadn't had the opportunity to talk to her in a long time, and didn't want to let this time go to waste. "Has the training been going well?"

Lycia turned to face him again, mostly composed once more, and nodded. "I think so. Though I can't say for certain. I still suffer from mana exhaustion daily, or nearly so." She chuckled to herself. "Honestly, not a side of my mother I knew of."

"Now I'm curious," Krarshe pressed, laughing slightly.

"I feel like a poor slave girl! She's callous and demanding!" Lycia shouted louder than Krarshe thought she'd be capable of. "I just... Ugh. It's brutal."

Krarshe just laughed. He hadn't realized it until just now, but she seemed more confident whenever magic training was brought up.

"What's so funny? I'm sure you've vomited enough times in your own training."

"Actually, no. I can't say I know the feeling of mana exhaustion." He paused. "Not that I know of, at least."

"R-really...?"

Krarshe shook his head.

Lycia's face turned a bright crimson as she spun around. "Jeeze, you're horrible..." she said, pulling her hood over her reddening ears.

"What did I do?"

"Here I am, telling you all this... embarrassing stuff and yet... You. You've NEVER gone through any of it... Argh! You're awful!"

Krarshe laughed again. "Sorry, sorry. I just—"

"Excuse me! Miss customer," the supervising student interjected, cutting between Krarshe and Lycia. Krarshe hadn't even seen him approach. "I apologize for his abysmal behavior. Is there anything I can help you with?"

Lycia turned back around to face Krarshe and the student. Her face told Krarshe that she was just as surprised by the student's appearance. "I—Umm..." She looked around the store, clearly trying to think of something.

The supervising student sighed. "Miss. This is not a place to socialize with your kind. If there's nothing you need today, I must ask you to—"

"Oh, I need a scroll," Lycia said.

A moment passed before the student spoke again. "What KIND of scroll? Do you know which spell?"

"Umm... Yes."

"... And that is?" The supervising student was clearly getting impatient.

"A scroll of Abyssal Vortex."

The student and Krarshe both stared at her blankly. While the student seemed dumbfounded, Krarshe was just impressed at how decisive her answer was. *Is she actually here for that? What even IS that?*

"Abyssal... Vortex?" asked the student.

Lycia nodded.

The student rubbed his eyes. "Miss, I don't know who sent you here, but we do not carry such dangerous spells in our inventory. In fact, I don't believe void spells are even inscribed as scrolls."

"Oh, but I had one made by special request."

"That's not the issue... Void spells are—"

"The mages here are certainly impressive. I had my doubts too, but the instructor who was here had assured me they could complete my request."

"Oh, is that what Professor Landry was talking about the other day?" Krarshe jumped in, trying to give credibility to Lycia's tale. "He was mentioning he had made a spell scroll unlike any he'd done before. Was quite impressed with himself."

Now outnumbered, the supervising student seemed at a loss. He sighed again. "My apologies. It must be in the back. Allow me to go search for it."

"Thank you," Lycia said with a smile.

After watching the supervising student disappear into the back room, Lycia and Krarshe exchanged glances before bursting into stifled laughter.

"That was pretty good. How'd you come up with that?"

"I just picked the most obscure spell my mom has mentioned."

"Wait, that's a real spell?"

Lycia nodded. "Incredibly frightening too. Or so she says. She wouldn't show it to me."

"What does it do?"

"I have no idea."

"Huh..."

The two sat there quietly for a moment. The interjection had disrupted their previous conversation, but Krarshe didn't really want to bring it up again. He didn't want to sour Lycia's mood again.

"So, have you learned anything new in your training?" Krarshe asked.

"I've learned a few arcane spells so far."

"Oh really? Like what?"

"Nothing particularly noteworthy. This is probably the most interesting one." She gestured to the scrolls on the shelf. To Krarshe's surprise, a scroll on top began to wiggle slightly before sliding off the pile, towards Lycia's open hand. It touched the tip of her finger before suddenly dropping to the floor. "Damn it." Lycia bent over and picked it up. She sighed. "Clearly, I still don't have it mastered."

"No, no. That was incredible!"

"If only it were more useful."

"How is being able to move distant objects not useful?!"

"There's quite a bit of limitations with the spell. Distance, weight, speed. You need to be able to see it. Honestly, it feels more useful to play tricks on people than anything," she said with a wry smile.

Krarshe laughed. "That has its merits."

"What about you? How is your training progressing?"

"It's not. Well, not really. I have found a couple useful things, but I still just cast the spells they tell me to."

"At least you're getting to cast spells."

"If only they'd come out correctly," Krarshe muttered, mildly annoyed with himself.

"What do you mean?"

"Miss, are you certain there's a scroll of Abyssal Vortex here?" the senior student shouted, popping his head out from the back room.

"Oh, yes. Very much so," Lycia lied. "Just keep looking. I wouldn't want to not pay for such an EXPENSIVE scroll."

The student sighed again, audibly enough to be heard clearly from across the whole store. As suddenly as he had appeared, he was gone again.

"This could be construed as torture, you know," Krarshe said, looking at her sideways, eyebrow raised.

"Torture? I would never..." Lycia quipped, smiling.

Krarshe shrugged. "I don't particularly like him, so keep at it."

The two shared a laugh again. Krarshe wasn't sure why, but seeing her laugh made his heart race. Her bright smile, how she delicately brushed a tear from her eye after she calmed down, it was all having an effect on him.

Lycia was first to restart the conversation. "So, anything else? Have they discussed mana control yet?"

"Still no word on it."

"That seems odd..."

"Especially if it's as important as your mother says," Krarshe said. "Oh, but we do have an exam coming up at the end of this quarter-cycle."

"An... exam, huh?"

Krarshe couldn't help but notice how she averted her eyes ever so slightly. "Is... there something wrong with exams?"

"No. Nothing..." Lycia replied evasively.

"You're clearly avoiding the topic now."

"I'm sorry... It's just..." She looked around for a minute before continuing, quieter than before. "I don't know if it's right for me to say to a student, especially on school grounds..."

"I'd rather know than be left witless. The wisest decisions are made with all the knowledge one can gather."

Lycia shifted, warily looking around the room once again. "Well..." She leaned in closer, making Krarshe's heart palpitate. "My mom says this school doesn't train mages..."

"What? That seems..."

"No, I mean. They're producing soldiers. For the war. Just people they can put out there to kill people."

This wasn't what Krarshe had expected the secret to be. Before he could respond, Lycia continued.

"Because all they want are bodies to fill their ranks... Well, supposedly they try to intentionally fail exceptional mages..."

The blood rushed to Krarshe's head, making him lightheaded for a moment. The notion seemed ridiculous, but it still struck a nerve somewhere deep down inside him. "Wh—" he started to shout before catching himself. "Why would they do that? That doesn't even make sense," he whispered.

Lycia looked around again, making sure Krarshe's outburst hadn't been noticed. "Apparently, magic instructors hold a fairly high position here. In Remonnet, I mean. Each of the professors here were assigned this position for being exceptional mages."

"Assigned?"

Lycia nodded. "By the Council of Mages. And because they fear exceptional students catching the eye of the Council, the teachers here don't want to let them graduate. It'd be effectively training their possible replacements, since the Council holds ability in high regard for teaching positions. If they didn't hold a teaching position here, they would be sent out to the battlefields themselves instead of enjoying this high-paid, well-respected, and peaceful job. Of course, exceptions to this are made for those with connections to the Council for the sake of currying favor, but for the rest..."

"I'm... having a hard time believing you."

"I know it sounds absurd. And, honestly, I don't even know if it's true or not. It's just what I've heard from my mom." Lycia jumped at a crash that came from the back room, followed by some cursing from the senior student she had sent to find her scroll. In even more hushed tones, she continued, "My mom used to be on the Council. Back before I was old enough to remember things. She says she left because she couldn't abide by their approach to educating mages since the war started."

"Still... Things could have changed, right?" Krarshe asked, still struggling to believe her tale.

"That's true. It's been many decades, and the people who now occupy the Council's seats are likely entirely new. Well, at least the humans have probably stepped down by now. Or died."

"Either way, no way of knowing without experiencing the exam myself," Krarshe said more cheerfully than before, attempting to direct the conversation away from this dismal subject.

"Also true. Well, I pray you won't be targeted for failure."

"Why would I?"

Lycia raised an eyebrow. "From what you've said, at least, you're quite powerful."

"While this may be true, I also cannot cast a spell correctly."

"They won't care. Power is power to them."

"You seem quite certain, Lycia."

"I've just made up my mind about this academy. In addition to what my mom has said, they also exclude a gifted mage like you from classes, and apparently banish you to the store to wither away talking to customers."

"Actually, you're the only customer I talk with," Krarshe admitted.

"Eh?" Lycia said, surprised. "I—Y- You—" she stuttered before turning away. Krarshe could see her ears turning red. "Just... me............ huh?"

Krarshe stood there watching her before his words finally sunk in. "Oh! Umm..." He could feel his face warming. "I- I didn't mean... Umm... You're just the only customer who's around my age! And... Well... Ah! You've been the one coming to talk to me every day!"

Krarshe could see her ears turn even more red. His embarrassment was beginning to overcome him as well. He turned away from her bashfully, rubbing the back of his neck with his hand.

The adolescent elves stood there in silence, averting their gaze. The sounds of the senior student rummaging in the back room filled the store, an appreciated distraction from the quiet, awkward atmosphere.

"I- I should... go..." Lycia said, her back still turned to Krarshe.

"Y-yes. That... Yes. It's... Umm... It's getting late..."

"Well........ Bye," Lycia said curtly before scurrying out of the store.

"B-Bye..." Krarshe managed to say as the door swung closed again.

"Miss, I really don't think—Where'd she go?" asked the supervising student, once again emerging from the back room.

Krarshe looked over at him. He was covered head to toe with dust. It was almost as bad as after one of Krarshe's sessions with Landry. "... She..." He looked out the window. She was already passing through the front gate and out of his sight. "She said she couldn't wait any longer. Said she'd come back for it another day."

"Curses..." he spat. "Well, good riddance. Fucking sprites..." he muttered, turning back to the back room, patting the dust off his uniform.

Sprites? Krarshe disregarded the comment and kept looking out the window. While Lycia's words about the exam still gnawed at him, those thoughts had been pushed to the far recesses of his mind. His emotions had full control over him, as he felt lighter than ever before. As though he could burst out of the store and joyously sing to the heavens. No matter what he did, he couldn't regain his composure. This inexplicable excitement choked him. But part of him enjoyed this feeling. In fact, he hoped to feel it forever.

CHAPTER 17

Karshe stretched as he let out a great yawn, like he had so many times before in the store. His tiredness seemed independent of how much time he spent in the store; even a few hours proved to be enough for him to start falling asleep.

It was the last day of classes before their recess began. Somehow, the impending vacation made the day feel even longer than usual. He tried to pass the time by drawing in the dust on the counter, but his repeated use of this tactic had left little undisturbed dust with which to draw. It didn't stop him from trying, however, as his thoughts drifted to some spells he'd experimented with on his own before Landry had come to the training area the past few days.

Some shouting in the courtyard pulled his attention to the window. He could see students storming out of the main entrance and toward the front gate. "What in the world...?"

"Karshe!" Tibault shouted as he burst through the front of the store, followed quietly by Bri.

"Wait, what happened to the afternoon lecture?"

"They ended it early," Bri explained. "Like usual before recess." Bri walked around the store, looking over the shelves.

Krarshe couldn't tell if she was looking for something, or just out of habit. "The professors dismiss the junior students so they can give extra time for the senior ones. They usually have projects to submit instead of exams, so they give them the opportunity to get some extra assistance."

"Uh-huh..." Krarshe thought back on what Lycia had said regarding how the school operated. It seemed even less credible now.

"Wait. Are you stuck manning the store?" Tibault asked, looking around as he walked up to the counter.

"I haven't heard anything otherwise."

"That's too bad. Oh, Bri. Were you going to tell him about it?"

"It?"

"Oh, right. Thank you, Tibault," Bri said, putting a wand back on the shelf. "My family hosts a gala at the start of Second Harvest. Personally, I can't stand them, so—"

"So she's inviting us," Tibault interjected.

"Right."

"To... suffer with you?" Krarshe joked.

"Why else would I invite you two?" The three of them laughed.

"Is it formal?" Krarshe asked.

"Usually," Bri said. "My parents force me to wear a formal gown."

"That could be a problem..."

"Why?"

"I don't own anything like that. Probably not up to your parents' expectations."

"Maybe we can see if you can borrow some of my brother's clothes," Tibault said. "You're probably about his size."

"There you go. Problem solved," Bri said. "There's no escaping this gala. Trust me, I've tried."

"What, did you try to escape through the window or something?" Krarshe asked.

"Once or twice, maybe."

"Guess I'm stuck then," Krarshe said with a shrug.

"Well, first would be to make sure the clothes fit," Tibault said. "Maybe we can stop by my home and try them on."

Krarshe groaned.

"What's that for? My house isn't far."

"It's not that. I just get out of here pretty late normally. And it's a long walk to my inn, remember?"

"You should just get going now then," said a slow voice from the back room.

Krarshe spun around to see Landry slowly reveal himself, grinning. Or at least, Krarshe thought he was grinning. The beard and mustache made it hard to tell. "But—"

"It's fine, you have my permission. Now go, go," Landry said, waving Krarshe away.

Krarshe turned back to his friends, who simply shrugged. He turned back to Professor Landry. "Thank you, sir."

"You go have fun, Krarshe. That's what youth is for, no? Heh-heh. Enjoy your holiday."

Krarshe bowed and hurried out from behind the counter, following Tibault and Bri out of the store. He could feel himself smiling like a fool. It was only a few hours that he really gained, but the freedom was invigorating for some reason.

The three of them chatted as they walked out the academy gates. The Harvest sun was already nearing the city walls, and the cool breeze whipped down the streets of Castle Ward.

"So, where do you live?" Bri asked.

"Just down Emerald Alley" replied Tibault.

"That far?" Bri groaned. "Well, let's get going then."

"Where is that?"

"Oh, right. You're not from here, Ka- Kr..arshe," Bri said, catching herself to correct his name. She would still trip up on his name from time to time, but had gotten significantly better. "It's not THAT far, really..."

"It's only a few streets down from White Stone Plaza. It's really NOT that far."

"I just don't like the cold, okay?"

"And... where is that?" Krarshe asked.

Bri and Tibault both stopped walking to stare at him. "The plaza in front of the castle..." Tibault said. "You don't know many street names, do you?"

"People name streets?! What a novel idea," said Krarshe as he looked off into the distance, stroking his chin pensively.

"I... can't tell if you're joking..."

Bri coughed, interrupting the two boys. "Krarshe's inability to navigate the city aside, it's not far. Let's just get going, my hands are going numb."

"Mine have been numb for a while," Tibault added.

"... Mine are fine." Krarshe laughed.

Bri and Tibault shot him a sideways glance. Bri sighed. "Let's just go."

As they got closer to White Stone Plaza, Krarshe noticed colored fabrics hanging from shop walls and around entrances. Most were red and orange, with the occasional gold or silver. The sheets of fabric were twisted in drooping arcs along the front of buildings and across the street, from one building to another. Krarshe had noticed them the past two days or so, but wasn't sure what they were. As they passed a store, he noticed one of them had the word *Tevaona* embroidered upon it in gold lettering.

"What's that?"

"What's what?" Tibault asked.

"That word on that cloth."

"Tevaona?"

"That one."

"It's the name of the festival," Tibault explained. "You... Have you always been this ignorant?"

Krarshe shrugged. "It's my first time at this festival."

"You didn't know that streets had names!"

Bri cut in before Krarshe could retort. "It means 'Teva's Blessing'."

"... In what language?"

"I... don't know, actually," Bri admitted.

"You know, me neither," Tibault added.

"Are you sure it's not *Teva-oh-nah*?" Krarshe asked.

"I've always heard it *Te-vaoh-nah*," said Bri.

"Same."

"Hmm." Krarshe thought about it to himself. "I guess it's moot."

The three continued toward the plaza, observing the various decorations. As they got closer and closer, they started seeing more people. Most were nobles, dressed in more layers than any commoner would likely own. A sweet smell drifted in on a cold breeze from the direction of the plaza.

"Oh that smell..." Tibault closed his eyes and sniffed deeply. "I love harvest season. Especially the apple tarts."

Bri's stomach rumbled. "Please don't bring up food. I'm getting hungry."

"That's right, you barely ate at lunch today," Tibault noted.

Krarshe's stomach joined the chorus. "That smell is too good to not make you hungry. What was it again?"

"Probably apple tarts. Or a pie? I can't tell."

"Is this torture? Are you torturing me?" Bri asked, her stomach crying out again.

Tibault laughed. "How about I make us some food when we arrive at my house?"

"You can cook?" Bri asked.

"Of course. We... aren't really wealthy enough for servants. Well, not multiple."

"Do they not cook for you?"

Tibault shrugged. "My mother prefers to cook. And, she forced me to learn it too."

"Cooking isn't that complicated," Krarshe explained to Bri.

"I know that," Bri shot back. "I am a great cook. I'm just surprised that Tibault knew how to."

"Should I not?"

"You don't seem like the type to."

"I can probably cook better than you, Bri."

"Impossible."

"Shall we try it then?"

"Are you challenging me, Tibault?"

Tibault smiled. "Absolutely."

"Hmph. Okay, challenge accepted. I can't let my honor be stained. Just you wait, you won't be able to stop eating what I make."

"Same to you. Let's also have my mother try each as well, as an official judge of our three dishes."

"Wait, three?" Krarshe asked, surprised.

"Isn't your mother a bit biased?"

"She's a harsh critic when it comes to food. I have no doubt she won't give me any special treatment over the two of you."

"No, wait. Am I cooking too?" Krarshe asked again, more insistently.

"Well, it won't matter either way. Your mother will have no choice but to grant me victory," Bri said smugly.

"You may be my friends, but I won't show you any mercy," Tibault said proudly.

"How did I get involved in this?!" Krarshe asked desperately, his words not reaching either of his friends.

"Wait, wait. What's that?" Bri asked, drawing everyone's attention to the crowd that blocked the entirety of White Stone Plaza.

"I don't know. Let's go take a look."

The three of them approached the mob as they tried to peek over the shoulders in front of them. Search as they might, there were no openings through which they could slip through.

Krarshe stopped and turned away from the crowd, frustrated. "Oh! Tibault! Bri! Over here!" he called out. The two stopped and looked back at Krarshe. Krarshe started pulling a wooden crate away from one of the stores.

"Stop that! You're going to be accused of stealing!" Tibault shouted in a hushed voice, just loud enough for Krarshe to hear it over the noise from the crowd.

"It's empty. It's fine," Krarshe said dismissively. He climbed up on the box. "... What? Who are they?"

"Who?" Bri asked, climbing up on the box.

"Hey! Not you too!"

"Come on, Tibault. We're only borrowing it for a moment." She looked over the top of the crowd. "Teva's protection... What is going on?"

"What? What's happening?" Tibault asked. He looked around and sighed. "Move over! And help me up!"

Krarshe and Bri pulled him up onto the box. "Who are they?" Krarshe asked again.

"Whoa..." Tibault muttered in awe. "I don't know, but they look important..."

A large escort of mounted knights trotted in pairs down the street that led from the city's northeastern gate in Castle Ward. They wore full plate armor which shone in the quickly setting sun. Every third pair of knights held a large green banner. As the long, pointed flag waved and whipped, Krarshe could just barely make out a blue bird emblazoned on it. The bird looked to be a hawk, or an eagle, carrying a spear in one talon and a staff in the other. Krarshe didn't recognize the emblem from his travels, but he knew it wasn't the rose of Remonnet.

"Look! Look! It's a carriage!" a young boy shouted excitedly nearby in the crowd.

Krarshe looked toward where the knights had rode in from. As the boy said, a white carriage came rolling down the street, its windows covered on the inside by green curtains matching the color of the banner. The side of the carriage facing Krarshe and his friends bore the same emblem he saw on the banners.

"Momma! Momma! Whose carriage is that?"

"Hush!"

"I can't believe he'd come here personally..." commented another man in the crowd.

"Maybe it's not really him," came another voice.

"Only Talyra's king would ride in a carriage like that."

"Maybe it's an envoy."

As the carriage rattled and bounced down the cobblestone road toward the castle, the crowd became more and more restless. Krarshe could hear some people shouting profanities at the cart as it passed, shaking their fist at whoever rode within it.

"This seems like it's getting dangerous," Krarshe tried to whisper to his friends through the growing roar of the crowd.

"What?!" Tibault yelled, cupping his ear.

"He said it's getting dangerous!" Bri yelled back.

"Who is she?! Welcoming in our enemy!" came another yell from the crowd.

"Give me back my boy, whoreson!"

The crowd somehow got even more rowdy. The mass of people moved and surged like the sea. One of the knight's horses reared back, startled by an object flying out of the crowd. Krarshe wasn't sure, but he thought it was a shoe. Thankfully, the knights seemed unfazed by the hostility.

"We should go around this! Before a sword is unsheathed!" Bri shouted. "Tibault! Detour!"

"Right! This way!"

The three climbed off the box. Tibault led Bri down the road toward Feyfaire, getting jostled by angry nobles and merchants, as Krarshe shoved the box back against the wall where he'd found it.

"She's incompetent, to surrender to an enemy."

Krarshe stopped shoving the box for a moment. He wasn't sure where the barely audible voice came from, but it was oddly calm. He watched Tibault and Bri flee the scene of the crowd, and started after them.

"Indeed. She should just dispose of him while he's here."

"She won't."

Krarshe slowed down, but kept walking to not draw attention to himself. *I really shouldn't be listening to this...* he thought. But, his curiosity was overwhelming.

"Can you really abide by this?"

"... You were right."

As Krarshe passed the corner of the nearby store, he saw two men talking in the alleyway. He couldn't make out their figures well, but was able to see the sheen of short, golden hair on the shorter one. The taller one wasn't visible, but the air about him gave Krarshe an uneasy feeling. A feeling like he'd never felt before. The short glimpse of this man chilled him to the bone and made his skin crawl. The world began to feel as if it was spinning. He took a breath as he hid around the corner instinctively, steadying himself against the wall of the store.

"Will you listen to me now?" asked the taller one.

"... Yes. We need to make our move soon," replied the blonde one.

"Good. We'll discuss this later, somewhere more private..."

"Krarshe!" Bri yelled, startling him. She had apparently turned back to find him. "Let's go!"

"R-right!" He followed behind Bri. *What was that about? Whatever it was, it seemed suspicious...* He looked at Bri as she ran just ahead of him. *Should I mention it to Bri? Tibault?* As they got away from the noise of the crowd, they stopped to catch their breath.

"What was that... all about?" gasped Tibault, trying to catch his breath.

"I..." Bri took another deep breath. "I have... No idea..."

The three stood hunched there, bracing themselves against their knees, breathing forcefully.

"Okay. Well." Tibault breathed one more deep breath before pushing his curly, disheveled hair back only for it to flop back in his face. "Shall we get going?"

"Yeah... Yeah." Bri said, her usual poise and dignity returning. "I'm even more hungry now."

"Oh, that's right. I need to show you how inferior your cooking is, don't I?"

"Oh yes, milord Tibault. Demonstrate your lordly cooking to me," Bri mocked.

"You may be a high noble, but I won't forgive that insult!" Tibault laughed.

The two of them started down a small road branching off the main street, heading toward the Silver River. Krarshe followed just behind them. He watched as they joked and jabbed, laughing and smiling gleefully. ... *No. I don't want them to get involved with... whatever that was. Whatever that feeling was, it can't be good. Nor safe.* He looked at his friends quietly. *It's as* do'mro *says. 'It's wiser to avoid the squabbles of men.' No doubt it'd be better if they—no, we stay out of it.* Krarshe nodded to himself. He jogged to catch up to Bri and Tibault, joining in the jovial atmosphere of the start of their recess.

CHAPTER 18

Tibault's home was small and unremarkable, with a plain wooden door bordered by two tall windows, much like the other tightly packed houses in this part of Castle Ward. If what Krarshe knew of Tibault was any indication, the lesser nobility seemed to be only slightly better off than your average merchant, so this wasn't beyond his expectation. It felt almost more of a mark of status to own a house in the district than being a desirable location. Much like the rest of the city, orange and gold fabrics twisted in arcs across buildings in celebration of the festival. The sun's fading light paraded down the whole length of the street, illuminating it in a warm, welcoming glow. Aside from the soft roar of the Silver River but a few streets away, it was quiet, peaceful. All in all, it was a pleasant neighborhood, very cozy.

Tibault stopped as he reached for the door handle. "I'll just warn you now," he started before looking back at his two guests. "My family is a bit... odd."

Krarshe and Bri looked at each other, raising an eyebrow simultaneously. "I could have guessed that," Bri said, smiling.

"Same here," Krarshe agreed.

Tibault didn't respond to their jab and calmly opened the door. He stepped aside and gestured them in. Bri entered first, Krarshe following behind her, both looking around the house as they stepped inside.

The inside was as plain as the outside. There was a slight step up from the entrance way, leading to a small hallway which was dimly lit by the light coming from the two windows by the door and what little light escaped the room to the left. There was a staircase on the right just past the small step, and Krarshe could make out a few doors further down the hall.

"You can hang your jackets over there. And make sure to take off your shoes before you step up," Tibault said as he leaned against a wall to remove his shoes. "Otherwise, Astrid will beat us bloody."

"Who?"

"Oh, Tibby! You're home!" Krarshe turned to see a woman coming out from one of the doors at the end of the hall. Krarshe guessed she was probably in her late thirties, or early forties, but it was hard to guess. Her long brown hair curled and twisted down past her shoulders and draped itself across her red and white dress. Like Tibault, she had a smattering of faint freckles across her nose and cheeks. "And you brought friends!"

"Mooooooooom!" Tibault whined. "I told you to stop calling me that!"

"... Tibby?" Bri whispered into Krarshe's ear. He could hear her start to chuckle.

"What's wrong with 'Tibby'?" Tibault's mom protested. "I could call you what I used to if you'd rather."

"No! No no no no no!" he shouted, waving his hands in front of her desperately as he ran toward her.

She laughed. "Relax, I wouldn't do that to you. Not in front of your friends." She turned to behold the two guests. "So. Tibby. I believe introductions are in order."

Despite the dim light, Krarshe could still see a red hue spread across Tibault's cheeks. Tibault cleared his throat. "This is Bri," he said, gesturing to Bri. Bri gave a small curtsy. "And this," gesturing to Krarshe, "is Karshe."

"Krarshe," Bri corrected. Krarshe had intended to let the mispronunciation go, but Bri was apparently still very proud of her getting it right.

Krarshe just shook his head dismissively and bowed. "Either is fine."

"Hmm. Krarshe, was it?"

Again, hearing his name pronounced perfectly on the first attempt startled Krarshe. "Y-yes."

"Hmm. Interesting. I haven't seen many elves in Remonnet."

Krarshe could feel his body relax. "There's certainly not many."

"Well, you both may call me Claire. I hope my family and I can exemplify the hospitality and generosity of a noble family of Remonnet," Tibault's mom gave a small curtsy. "Now, come into the parlor. I'd love to hear more about you both."

Krarshe and Bri removed their footwear and began to follow Claire into the hallway.

"Actually, mom," Tibault started. "We were getting hungry, and—"

"Oh! Shall I make something for you all?" she asked, suddenly excited.

"No, no. That's okay. We were actually discussing our cooking skills on the way here and—"

"And TIBBY here challenged us," Bri said, cutting into the explanation.

"A cooking competition? Sounds fun!"

"Could you be an impartial judge for us?" Tibault asked.

A wide smile spread across Claire's face. "Of course! I'd love to!" she shouted, clapping her hands together with glee. Quickly, though, the smile melted away from her face, leaving behind a stern look that Krarshe couldn't have even imagined her making before. "Just understand, I'm a harsh judge. I don't want to hurt your friends' feelings."

"We'll be fine," Krarshe said. Bri nodded in agreement.

Claire studied the three of them for a moment. Her jovial smile returned in an instant. "Okay then! I'll get Astrid to start the oven for you. Come, let me show you around the kitchen and our pantry. Astrid! Could you come down here?! Come, come, this way."

Claire led them through the open doorway on the left, the dining room, and through a pair of double doors. It opened into a large kitchen, large enough to compete with one in a restaurant. A large window spanned nearly the whole back wall of the room, letting in an incredible amount of sunlight compared to the dark hallway. Claire flew through the kitchen, showing them where to find pots, pans, and cooking utensils of all sorts, many of which Krarshe couldn't even guess at their purpose. She boasted about the two ovens the kitchen had, and the elaborate flue that supported them. Krarshe noted her enthusiasm felt as though she was trying to impress someone.

As she led them around the corner to another pair of double doors, a woman entered the kitchen. "You called for me, milady?" Her plain gray dress and graying hair was contrasted by a stark white apron. Krarshe shuddered as he felt her cold eyes fall upon him.

"Could you start the ovens and stove for our guests, Astrid, dear?"

Astrid didn't say a word, just bowing solemnly and turned to her task, pulling wood from a pile beside the chimney.

"Okay," Claire said, pulling Krarshe's attention back to the tour. "This," she said, dramatically pulling open the double doors around the corner, "is our pantry." Krarshe looked over the shelves of foods, spices, and anything else one could think of using in their food preparations. "We have meat and fish stored in the ice box there," she said, gesturing to a large box in the corner of the pantry.

"What's an ice box?"

Claire turned to Krarshe, surprised.

"He's from some rustic village up north," Tibault explained.

Claire smiled understandingly. "This box is a magic item, imbued with an ice spell. You can put food into it to keep it cold, thus keeping it from spoiling so quickly."

Krarshe raised his eyebrows. "Wow. That's amazing."

"Modern magic certainly is, isn't it? Just be careful reaching into it, the sides are quite cold," Claire explained. "Well, that's the end of the tour. I'll be in the parlor if you need anything. Let me know when your dishes are finished, okay?"

"Okay, Mom."

"Thank you very much," Bri said.

Krarshe bowed slightly.

Claire left the kitchen, followed silently by Astrid.

"Your mother's nice," Bri said.

"Oh? Just wait..." Tibault said with a knowing smirk. He rolled up the sleeves on his shirt and tucked them neatly to hold them in place. "Well, time to show you what real cooking is!"

* * *

"So, what do we have here, Tibby?" Claire picked up a fork and knife and looked at the plate in front of her.

"Seared and salted silverfish, paired with sautéed bush beans and carrots, and sliced tomatoes." Tibault stood there proudly, already the victor in his own mind.

"Ugh, I hate bush beans," Krarshe complained, staring at the wiggling green bean at the end of his fork. He was more entertained watching it dance than he was interested in eating it.

"You can't just cook toward one person's tastes," Tibault quipped.

"The fish is okay, I guess," Bri said, mouth full, finally able to sate her hunger a bit. "Maybe a bit too salty."

241

"And a bold choice to use tomatoes." Claire picked one up with her fork, looking it over. "Tough skin at this time of year, Tibby." She pulled it off her fork with her teeth and began to chew.

"Well, I—"

Claire held up a hand, halting Tibault's response. She spit something into her napkin. "Too tough. The beans and carrots seem nicely cooked, and have a proper texture." She ate both in one mouthful, chewed slowly for a bit and then swallowed. "Could have used more seasoning. Now..." She cut into the fish and inspected it closely. Krarshe and Bri had stopped eating for a minute, watching Claire's assessment. Tibault's earlier confidence seemed to be breaking down, clearly getting a bit nervous as his mother looked over the focal point of the dish. "You should have seared this longer. There should be a crisp edge here, but it's lacking that entirely. Just because it looks seared doesn't mean it's done yet." She took a bite, and immediately spit it into her napkin. "Too much salt. This isn't some salted meat for adventurers."

Krarshe watched as the final remnants of Tibault's pride evaporated. Tibault slowly pulled out his chair and plopped into it. He put his face in his hands, just sitting there. *He was right,* Krarshe thought. *She's a harsh critic.*

Claire took a sip of her glass of water and swished it around briefly before swallowing. "So, who's next?"

Bri glanced at Krarshe before sighing. "I guess I'm up." She stood and walked through the double doors leading to the kitchen. She emerged with three plates, placing them on the table in front of each critic.

"Well, this is new. What is it?" Claire asked.

"It's actually a recipe I came up with on my own. It... doesn't really have a name. I just call it beef in brown sauce."

Claire raised an eyebrow. She looked down at her plate of brown goop with bits of meat and vegetables in it. "This looks like a stew." She stirred the mixture with her spoon, then lifted it and watched the brown sauce drip slowly back to the plate. "Sort of."

"I love stews. They inspired this dish."

"I guess I'm not surprised to see potatoes with this," Krarshe said, remembering the comments Bri made at lunch when they had first met. He looked across the table at Tibault. He seemed to have recovered slightly from his mother's harsh words.

"A pseudo-stew?" Tibault laughed.

"Just eat. The stew first, then your words," Bri retorted.

Krarshe took a spoonful and shoved it in his mouth. His eyes widened. It was good. Very good. He took another spoonful, and another. "Wow. This..."

"Is quite delicious," Claire cut in, having just finished her spoonful. "The meat is properly cooked. The strips of thinly sliced beef carry the perfect amount of this sauce. The traces of sliced, sautéed onions and garlic really bring out the savory flavor of this sauce. The reduction in the sauce gives it a perfect, sticky consistency to cling to the beef and potatoes." She stuffed another spoon of it in her mouth, smiling as she relished the bite of food. "What spices did you add to this sauce?"

Bri smiled. "Oh, you know. A bit of this, a bit of that." She looked over at Tibault, who looked even more rejected than he had previously. The combination of his mother's harsh words toward him and the praise she showered upon Bri had decimated his pride, leaving nothing in its wake. "I can share the recipe with you later if you'd like."

"Oh, please do. One thing I would change, however, much like Tibby, you used too much salt. I'd use less and add more black pepper. It should enrich the taste even more."

Bri bowed. "Thank you for the advice. I will take it to heart."

Claire ate a few more bites before putting the plate aside. "One contestant left," she said with a smile. "I hope you have something unique from your homeland, Krarshe. I always wondered what types of meals elves enjoyed."

"Oh, it's nothing special. I had it a lot while travelling," he explained as he headed to the kitchen. He emerged momentarily, placing the three plates in front of the three.

Everyone stared at their plate in perfect silence. The only noise heard was that of Astrid moving around above them upstairs. Claire was the first to speak.

"What... in Teva's name... is this?"

"It's beef."

She continued to stare at her plate blankly.

"Umm... Karshe? Did you... just burn a cut of meat in the oven?" Tibault looked at his plate inquisitively.

"I cooked it."

"This is cooked?" Bri asked, turning the charred black slab on her plate over with her fork.

"Is there something wrong with it?"

"Umm..."

The three were startled by Claire slamming her hands on the wooden table, causing all of the dishes to jump slightly with a clatter. "This... This is not cooking!" She stood up violently, knocking her chair over. "This is not cooking!" she repeated, louder than before. "I hesitate to even call this food! This is an abomination! An insult to every chef and livestock everywhere!"

Krarshe raised an eyebrow. He picked up the charred lump from Bri's plate, looking over the hard object. "Seems fine to me." He bit off a piece with a crunch, black char crumbling onto the table. He chewed it a bit and, to the horror of his friends and Claire, swallowed it. "Tastes fine too."

Claire stared blankly at Krarshe for a minute, blinking repeatedly. She then picked up her chair, sat back down, and breathed deeply. She brushed her curly brown hair back out of her face and composed herself. "Krarshe," she started calmly. "This is... unquestionably... the worst thing I've ever laid eyes on. I regret beholding it for even a moment, as it will undoubtedly stain my eyes for the rest of my life. For this insult —No, for obliterating this poor cut of meat, I demand an apology. Apologize to every cow in existence, and swear upon your life, and the lives of your children's children's children, that you will NEVER step foot in a kitchen again. In fact, you should not be allowed within a shipspan of one, on penalty of the Hungerer's annihilation. May Teva have mercy on your soul."

The three students sat there staring at Claire, dumbfounded. "Umm... That seems to be a tad bit excessive," Krarshe replied after a moment.

"No. It's not," Claire said flatly. Krarshe waited a minute, expecting her to continue, but she just sat there, her forehead resting gently against her steepled fingers, eyes closed, as though she was praying.

Krarshe looked at Tibault and Bri. They just looked back at him. Tibault quietly snuck Krarshe's plates off the table and back into the kitchen. When the so-called food was gone from Claire's view, Bri spoke up. "So, who won?"

Claire breathed deeply again before opening her eyes, cheerful once more. "Without question, you, my dear." She smiled at Bri. "Your dish was truly marvelous."

Bri didn't even try to hide her smug grin. She looked at Tibault. "A fair competition," she said, offering her hand mockingly.

Tibault rolled his eyes. "Yes, yes. Okay, I take back what I said." He stood up and shook Bri's hand.

"What about me?" Krarshe asked.

"You, don't talk," Claire shot a look at him, a brief flash of her previous irritation surfacing again before disappearing as quickly as it had appeared. Clearly she was still upset by his cooking.

The door around the corner opened and shut. Krarshe could hear a man groan.

"Oh, Dear! Tibby brought some friends!" Claire said, hurrying to the front door.

"From the academy?" said the man as he stepped up into the hall and into view of the dining room. His hair was dark, a disheveled mess of waves. His clean-shaven face exposed its soft features. Paired with the gentleness of his tired eyes, every bit of him gave off a calm, kind feeling.

Bri stood up and ran out from behind the table. "I'm Bridgette Bulliere, a friend of Tibby's," she said hurriedly with a curtsy. Tibault glared at Bri, while his father gave a slight bow. "You can call me Bri."

"A pleasure to meet one of House Bulliere, Miss Bri." He turned to Krarshe. "And an elf? How rare."

Krarshe followed Bri's example and hurried to the other side of the table. "Krarshe, sir," he said with a bow.

"Is it uncommon for elves to have family names?"

Krarshe hesitated before answering. "I'm just a commoner."

"Ah, I see. I didn't realize elves shared that in common with us." He looked up for a second. "But wait. A commoner? At the academy?"

Maybe I should have claimed to be some noble from a far-off land... Krarshe sighed. "It's a long story. I wouldn't want to bore you."

"Dear, don't pester the poor boy."

He laughed. "Fine, fine. A pleasure to meet both of you. I'm Bernard," he said, bowing once again. "So, what's all this?" he asked, gesturing to the dining room.

"We were competing. In cooking," Tibault said.

"Well, two of us were..." Bri said, giving Krarshe a sideways glance.

Bernard took notice of Bri's comment. "You didn't participate?" he asked as he took off his coat. "I would have loved to try elvish cuisine."

"No. You wouldn't," Claire said sharply.

Bernard froze, then looked at Tibault. Tibault put up his hands and shook his head. Bernard nodded nearly imperceptibly before changing subject. "So, what about my dinner?" he asked with a laugh.

"I'll make you something, Dear."

"Fantastic! Well then, if you two are okay staying for a bit, I'd love to get to know Tibault's friends more."

"Of course," Bri said.

"Let's take this to the parlor," Bernard said, heading for the door next to the staircase. He murmured something that Krarshe couldn't make out. A moment later, several candles ignited, bathing the hallway in a warm orange glow. "There we go. A bit too dark in here for my eyes."

"I forgot you were a mage," Krarshe said. "That startled me."

Bernard laughed. "We both are, in fact," he said, looking at Claire as she walked through the door to the kitchen. "Truthfully, it's thanks to magic that we have this lifestyle. I earned this title on the battlefield."

"You must be quite skilled."

"More lucky than skilled," he joked. He opened the door to the parlor and muttered the spell again, lighting the candles across the room. There were several ornate chairs and a couch encircling a beautifully carved table, the finish of which reflected the dozen or so candles in the room. "Come, sit." He gestured to the gathering of furniture as he sat down in one of the chairs.

Krarshe hurried toward the couch, having never sat in such a lavish seat. The seat sank comfortably as he sat, cradling his body. "Oh... This is nice."

Bri sat in the chair adjacent to the couch. "What? The couch?"

Krarshe nodded. "I've never sat on anything but hard wooden chairs. This is luxurious..." he said, letting his head roll back as he closed his eyes, immersing himself in the soft, cushy sensation of the couch.

"I hope you don't mean like the ones at the academy," Tibault said, taking a seat next to Krarshe on the couch.

"Sometimes worse," Krarshe said, looking at Tibault without lifting his head. Tibault grimaced.

"I'm glad you're enjoying yourself," Bernard said. "Now, I have so many questions. I've never had the opportunity to speak with an elf, if you don't mind indulging my curiosity."

Krarshe's gaze shifted to the ceiling. *This could be an issue...* Krarshe lifted his head up. "Well, I don't mind answering. But I'm much more curious about you."

"Me?"

"I, as well," Bri said. "Since you mentioned it, I'm curious about how you earned your title. And about life as a full-fledged mage."

Bernard smiled. "I'd be happy to tell you. So, it all began ten years ago..." He leaned in and began to recite his tale. Bri and Krarshe listened attentively as he wove the tale, undoubtedly embellishing it as he went. While Krarshe wasn't certain of its authenticity, it didn't matter. He was glad to keep the focus off himself, and thanked whatever deity it was that urged Bri to distract Tibault's father.

* * *

Krarshe sat at the dining room table, playing with his spoon, putting pressure on the tip to lift the handle and spinning it around in a circle. Luckily, Bri and Bernard had continued talking about magic for hours, thus freeing Krarshe from needing to fabricate any stories about his homeland. Tibault and Claire had helped Krarshe find a suitable outfit in Tibault's brother's closet for the gala. It fit shockingly well, but took forever to put on. Krarshe already knew he'd probably put it on wrong the day of the gala, and had resigned himself to asking Tibault to fix it. When they had returned to the parlor, Bernard told them to stay for dinner, to which they agreed. Krarshe was eager to see what Claire could do, after her critiques earlier.

Claire burst through the doors to the kitchen, carrying two plates, which she placed before Bri and Krarshe. Astrid skillfully carried the remaining three plates, which she put before Tibault and his family. "Thank you, Astrid," Claire said. "Now, eat up and tell me what you think."

"Looks beautiful as always, just like you," Bernard said.

"Oh, you." Claire kissed her husband before sitting down in her seat.

Krarshe wasn't sure what he was looking at. The white sauce coated the meat entirely, hiding its color and texture. A light sprinkling of herbs covered the meat and vegetables. It smelled delicious. He spooned a bit of the sauce and saw it was slightly stringy as he pulled it.

"Oh, mmm! This is incredible! What is it?" Bri asked. She kept her polite posture, unlike Tibault who was already shoveling mouthfuls of food into his mouth like his father.

"The sauce uses cheese and milk as the base," Claire explained. "I'd be happy to show you how to do it some time. You need to be careful not to burn it."

"Absolutely!"

Krarshe stirred it briefly before finally tasting it. His eyes lit up. It was exactly as Bri had said, delicious. He cut into the meat and ate it also. He recognized the unmistakable texture of chicken as he bit into it, the creamy sauce mixing with the taste exquisitely. The bliss was immeasurable. Truthfully, this cheese sauce would probably pair well with just about anything. The vegetables were the same, the divine taste of the cheese was a perfect match.

"Better than your cooking?" Claire asked, looking straight at Krarshe.

"Definitely," he said, swallowing a mouthful of food. "I never said I was a good cook."

"I don't know if that constitutes cooking," Bri joked.

"Let's leave that where it belongs, lost unknown to the ages," Claire said, returning to her food.

The five of them ate in silence, enjoying the food. The quiet meal was quite the departure from Krarshe's usual dinners at the Easy Lute, full of music and the clamor of patrons. It was relaxing.

"Where do you two live, if you don't mind my asking," Bernard said as he wiped his mouth off on his napkin. His eyes darted to the wide window facing the street. Krarshe turned to see that it was getting dark and the street lamps were being lit.

"I live on the other side of Castle Ward, just a bit from the city walls," Bri said.

"I'm staying in Feyfaire."

"Feyfaire?!" Tibault's parents said in unison.

Krarshe nodded. "Was cheaper than Castle Ward."

"That's really far. Do you need an escort?"

"I've walked there later than this. I'll be fine."

"Are you sure?" Bernard pressed.

Krarshe nodded.

Bernard turned to Bri. "I know it's not that far, but what about you, Miss Bulliere? I'd feel terrible if something happened to you. Especially with the ruckus this afternoon."

"In White Stone?" Bri asked.

"You saw it?"

"On our way here. We had to walk around it."

"Oh my. Was something happening?" Claire asked.

"Do you know what it was, Dad?"

"Sounds like the king of Talyra was here with his escort," Bernard explained. He took a sip from his glass and set it down gently. "I don't know if that's true, but it makes me nervous if it is."

"Teva's protection..." Claire muttered quietly.

"After that recent battle near Varenne Grove, I fear Her Majesty, the Queen, may be offering up her surrender," he said somberly.

"I can't imagine that being true," Bri said.

Bernard shook his head. "We suffered quite a number of casualties." He paused for a moment. "But so did they... Hmm..." His view grew distant, his mind clearly turning ideas and possibilities over again and again. "Hmm. Maybe you're right. I don't think she'd surrender so easily, not with the company of troops returning from Aebrodora."

"I trust she knows what she's doing," Tibault chimed in. "She's led well."

Bernard looked at his son, then smiled. "I agree, though I know not all think such." He stretched with a great sigh. "So, are you sure you don't want an escort? Neither of you?"

"I'll see her home," Krarshe volunteered. "If it'll allay your fears."

Bri nodded. "If anyone here could protect me, it'd be Ka-Krarshe. Though I'd fear for the city if it came to that..."

Tibault's parents gave a confused look. "Karshe's magic is... something else," Tibault explained.

"Oh. Yes, elves. I guess that makes sense," Claire said, nodding.

"I'll entrust my honor with you then, Krarshe," Bernard said. "Ensure my honored guests make it home safely, yourself included."

Krarshe gave a slight bow and smile.

The rest of the dinner passed by quickly, as they made small talk. Claire had offered them tea, but Krarshe and Bri declined. As they got ready to leave, the servant Astrid offered Krarshe a cloth satchel containing the formal attire for the gala. After the delicious dinner and pleasant company, he had almost forgotten it was the reason for coming here. He thanked her and he and Bri said their goodbyes, then set out into the night.

"That was delicious," Krarshe said to Bri as they walked down the street, now completely dark aside from the street lamps. There was no moon or stars to be seen, indicating oncoming rain.

"His mother is quite the chef. I'd say she is probably better than my family's cooks."

"Cooks?" Krarshe asked, emphasizing the 's'.

"... Yes."

"Wow, your family must be really rich."

Bri shrugged. "They've been advising Her Majesty's family since the empire collapsed." Bri started to rub her shoulders and shivered. "It really is cold out here. I should have brought a cloak or something."

"I suppose so. It's already mid-Harvest."

"You suppose?"

"I guess the cold doesn't bother me as much. Maybe a bit uncomfortable, but not much else."

"You're so strange. Aren't elves supposed to have weaker constitutions than most?"

"I don't know."

Bri stopped and stared at Krarshe.

"What?" he asked.

Bri just shook her head and groaned. "I just don't understand you." She started walking again, more quickly than before. Krarshe couldn't tell if she was annoyed or just cold, but he did his best to keep pace with her.

As they passed through White Stone Plaza, Krarshe could see some people still mulling about. The chatter seemed to be lingering conversations about this afternoon. "They were nice," Krarshe said, thinking back on their dinner.

"Hmm?"

"Tibault's parents."

"Oh. Yeah. Really nice." Bri's pace slowed, eventually coming to a stop. "I'm a bit envious, honestly."

"Aren't you high nobility?"

Bri shook her head. "We are, but that doesn't matter. I'd trade a title for a family like that without a second thought."

"It's unwise to wish without careful consideration."

"I have considered. I have considered it plenty." She looked straight at Krarshe, her dark brown eyes glistened with the light of the street lamps. "I still wouldn't hesitate, even for a moment."

Bri held Krarshe's gaze for several moments before Krarshe turned and started walking. "Okay, okay, I get it. I don't question your decision. But are they really that bad?"

"It's this way."

Krarshe turned to look at Bri, pointing down a street Krarshe had walked past. "Uhh... Right."

Bri laughed and continued in step with Krarshe. They continued down the maze of streets, in a part of the city Krarshe had never been to before. There were fewer and fewer houses, and each became larger and larger. There were even ones with grassy yards and trees within their stone walls. Krarshe never knew there to be such extravagant houses in this city.

They eventually came to a large gate, flanked by armored guards on either side. At her approach, the guards stood at attention. "Welcome home, mistress!" they said in unison. Bri gave a dismissive wave as they hurried to open the gate.

As the gates opened, Bri turned back to Krarshe. "You'll see and understand my certainty at the gala." She gave him a smile, tinged with sadness. "Thanks for escorting me. I'll see you at the gala," she said, with a small bow. She turned toward the gate without meeting his eyes again and walked through.

"Bye," Krarshe said softly with an unseen wave, watching her walk as the gates slowly closed once more, with a loud clang and a click of the lock.

CHAPTER 19

"Do people really wear this?" Krarshe shifted uncomfortably in his formal dress. "This is awful. I'm pretty sure it's choking me too. And why does it have so many layers?!" Krarshe groaned. "And I thought the school uniforms were formal. This feels excessive."

Tibault tugged at the neck of his shirt before fixing the ruffled bit of cloth tied around it. "I've never been fond of these cravats either. But it's part of being a noble, suffering through it," he said, running his hand through his slicked back hair. He must have done it a hundred times since they left Tibault's house, as though it were habit. "At least, that's what my dad says."

"Seems silly."

"Well, yeah, it is."

Krarshe waited a moment, expecting Tibault to continue his response, but he never did.

"I'm glad to see my brother's clothes worked out so well."

"I did try them on when Bri and I visited, remember?"

"I know. I'm just saying."

"Personally, I'm glad I could figure out how to put this on. There's so many layers!" Krarshe gestured, pulling the outer coat aside to show the vest and shirt.

"At least we won't be cold."

"I suppose, but this is ridiculous." Krarshe sighed. He knew he was just complaining with no hope of resolution. At least it was only a single night he had to put up with it.

"At least you don't have to wear this regularly..." Tibault said, as if reading Krarshe's thoughts. "Are you sure we're going the right way?"

"Fairly certain this is the way we went," Krarshe said, thinking back to a few nights ago when he walked Bri home.

"Only fairly?"

Krarshe stopped to look at Tibault. "Look, I know my sense of direction may not be the best..."

"Uhh..." Tibault looked away uncomfortably.

"... But I'm... It's this way." Krarshe started walking again, more confidently. "... I think."

"I knew I should have asked Bri where she lived." Tibault covered his face with his hand, sighing. "This is going to be like that time you tried to bring us to the Golden Flagon, isn't it?" He continued to follow Krarshe down the twisting streets of Castle Ward.

"I got us there, didn't I?"

"Only took you until it got dark..."

"Not my fault the sun sets earlier this time of year," Krarshe said with an indifferent wave. "And the food was good, right?"

"It was okay. The beer was better."

"After having tasted rum, everything tastes too bitter."

"You've had rum?"

Krarshe nodded. "Was right after that bruising I got."

"Huh." Tibault turned forward again and walked in silence. Despite the nonchalant response, Krarshe could read the jealousy on Tibault's face. He was always bad at hiding his emotions, but that made it easier to interact with him.

Countless carriages clattered down the stone streets, ferrying nameless nobles to their festivities. The harvest festival was at its peak, and even in the usually quiet Castle Ward district, there was music and revelry. Not quite as unruly as it was in Feyfaire, however; Krarshe had to avoid countless drunks stumbling through the streets to get here, dodging all manner of drink and fare that seemed determined to dirty his borrowed attire. Despite the hassles, he was slightly excited to take part in his first festival. And a great deal nervous.

"Tibault."

"Hmm?"

"Have you ever been to a gala like this?"

Tibault shook his head. "No. Well, no, that's not true. I've been to one. Years ago. But never like this."

"Like what?"

"The Bullieres are a very powerful and established noble family. They've held their authority since Remonnet laid their claim to the empire."

"So you're nervous too?" Krarshe asked.

"I'd be lying if I said I wasn't." He took a deep breath. "Not only for myself, but my family. Our honor hinges on my conduct here."

Krarshe raised an eyebrow. "That seems exaggerated."

"It's not. Public appearances are... They can determine your success as a noble. Your whole family's success..." Krarshe could see Tibault shake nervously. He swallowed hard. "Must be nice to not be a noble. Though I suppose you'll have your own struggles tonight."

"Struggles? How so? I mean, I know I need to behave appropriately to not embarrass Bri as her guest but—"

Tibault pointed to his ear. Krarshe looked at him for a moment, puzzled. He reached up and touched his own, pointed ear. Only then did it occur to him what Tibault meant.

"You're an elf. Those struggles."

"Oh. Right." Krarshe laughed awkwardly. "I almost forgot..."

"That you're an elf? Karshe, are you drunk already?"

Krarshe shook his head and raised his hand. "No, no. I meant I forgot some people might take issue with that. I guess I've been around you and Bri so long that I forgot."

"Just remember, Bri and I aren't like most nobles. Unlike them, we're friends." Tibault turned to face Krarshe and smiled.

Krarshe noticed a few carriages lining up in front of a gate, slowly being guided inside. "Oh. I think it's that house."

"Think?!"

"At least, I'm fairly sure..."

Tibault groaned, exasperated. "Sure, fine. Let's just go ask one of the—Whoa..." Tibault's eyes widened as he stared up at the massive house. "Y-you're sure it's this one?"

Krarshe looked through the bars of the gate at the huge structure. It wouldn't be too much of an exaggeration to call it a castle in its own right. It must have been nearly twice or thrice the size of the entire academy grounds, and that was without including the estate's auxiliary buildings and gardens. "I'm sure. I remember the fountain over there," Krarshe said, pointing toward an elaborate, multi-tiered fountain just before the gardens.

Tibault stumbled a bit, grabbing into Krarshe suddenly to catch himself. "Okay. Okay... Right. Well, le—" Tibault's voice cracked. He cleared his throat before trying again. "Let's go, shall we?"

Krarshe and Tibault approached the gate. As carriage after carriage stopped and let off their guests, Tibault tried to guide Krarshe to arrive between them. Krarshe watched men and women, young and old, be let out of their carriage by their footman. The garb seemed as stuffy and convoluted as what Krarshe and Tibault wore. *Guess we look the part, at least.*

As a carriage left, Tibault pulled Krarshe with a yank. "Come on!" They came before the foremost guard just as the next carriage started to move.

The guard looked at them as they approached, his eyes resting upon Tibault but a moment before falling heavily on Krarshe. "Names?" he asked after a few seconds, his gaze shifting to a scroll of parchment he had.

"Ti—" Tibault's voice cracked again. "Ahem. Tibault Dumont."

The guard inspected his parchment a minute before looking at Krarshe. "And you?"

"Krarshe."

The guard looked up from his list, his eyes narrowing.

"That's it. Krarshe," Krarshe clarified.

His eyes returned to the list, skimming through the names as quickly as he could. The carriage behind the two boys was already letting out their noble passengers. "Kurarussh?" He looked up at the elf boy.

Tibault and Krarshe exchanged glances. "Yeah, that's me."

Just as the boys had done, the guards exchanged looks. He shrugged. "Elves..." he said with a hint of disgust. He nodded to the other guard manning the gate, who opened it and gestured them inside. "Just don't cause any trouble."

That seemed unnecessary... Krarshe thought, nodding and smiling his practiced smile.

"And I'm sure you'll keep an eye on the sprite," the guard added as Tibault passed by him. Tibault gave an awkward smile without really responding.

When they were a distance from the gate, Tibault leaned in toward Krarshe and whispered, "Don't mind that shit-eater."

"What?"

"Calling you a... a sprite."

"What of it?"

Tibault put a hand on Krarshe's shoulder and stopped. "That... doesn't bother you?"

"I don't even know what it means," Krarshe admitted. Krarshe had heard the word tossed around a couple times, but he was never able to deduce its meaning.

Tibault gave him a confused look. "It's... Umm... You know..." He leaned in closer to Krarshe again. "It's a rude way to refer to an elf. You've really never been called that here?"

Krarshe thought for a moment. In his few cycles in this form, he couldn't recall any instances of being called it directly. Maybe a couple times, but he never took it personally. Krarshe shrugged and shook his head.

Tibault breathed deep. "Well," he started, glancing around at some of the other guests entering the estate. "Just don't let it bother you if someone does that here."

"Honestly, I can't see it being an issue. Words are just that: words. They only have what power you grant them."

Tibault chuckled. "Where'd that come from?"

"My grandfather used to say it."

"Your grandfather again, eh? You like to pass off his wisdom as your own, don't you?"

"What would wisdom be if it couldn't be passed on?"

"Okay, okay. That's enough words of wisdom from Karshe," Tibault laughed. He faced the entrance of the mansion. "Well," he took a deliberate breath. "Let's go face this gala then."

"We face it together," Krarshe said with a reassuring smile. "At least until I find a pretty girl to chase after." His smile grew wider.

"Pssh. Sure you will," Tibault retorted. "You have the tact of a toad."

"I'm moving up in the world, I see."

The two continued joking and laughing as they entered, the tense air all but dissipated.

* * *

Krarshe and Tibault walked through the wide double doors into the light of the grand hall. Spheres of light held motionless at each pillar of the room, with a larger orb near the center of the ceiling two stories up; the brilliance of it all was such a sudden change from the dark of the evening streets that they both had to shield their eyes. As his eyes adjusted, Krarshe was awestruck by the countless guests scattered throughout the first floor and along the curved staircases and balcony of the second floor.

Krarshe couldn't make out if there was anyone up on the third floor balcony from the ground, but it seemed to be more dimly lit. The floor had an ornate silver and bronze design whose sheen reflected the numerous glowing orbs, giving the space an even brighter aura and sense of elegance and affluence. Countless tapestries and portraits lined the walls, paired with elaborate furnishings and adornments. Just what Krarshe could see here on the first floor of the grand hall was probably worth more than all the money that had ever passed through his hands.

Krarshe and Tibault both moved off to the side just past the entrance and continued to study the room. Most of the guests were older, though there were a few children clinging to their parents. The men all wore formal vests and coats like their own, though some wore more elaborate garments. The women all had some variation of the same dress, overflowing with ruffles and frills. There were a few who wore more revealing gowns, exposing their shoulders, their hair covering the exposed part of their backs. It took a moment, but Krarshe noticed those women were usually younger and didn't appear to be accompanied by a man. Rather, they seemed to be accompanied by SEVERAL men, for the moment at least.

All of the guests seemed to be mingling in a reserved way, talking or flirting, as servants brought glasses around to guests. Under one of the balconies, there were minstrels playing, though they seemed to serve as mere background noise for the social gathering. The floor looked prepared for dancing, but everyone was busy with their conversations. Seeing it reminded Krarshe of his conversation with Burmir. *I could see how he'd find this a bit dull, especially compared to a tavern.* As Krarshe and

Tibault slowly made their way deeper into the room, they could see banquet tables filled with food set along the wall opposing the musicians. A few people were clustering there, eating small servings of food while enjoying the company of other guests.

"Well, at least there's food," Krarshe commented, nodding toward the tables.

"I'm not particularly hungry..." Tibault groaned. "Rather, I feel like I'm going to vomit."

"You were fine a second ago."

"I wasn't actually inside a second ago. Let alone surrounded by all these nobles."

"You're a noble too, you know?"

Tibault turned away, hunching for a moment before audibly swallowing. "I should go outside."

"You'll be fine. Come, let's go sit down over there."

Krarshe guided Tibault over to the steps leading up to the balcony. Tibault sat on the steps, trying to regain his composure.

"You don't have to be so nervous," Krarshe said, shielding Tibault from view of most of the hall.

"I—" Tibault swallowed again. "—can't help it. I don't do well in formal gatherings. I feel so... out of place here."

"How do you think I feel? I'm not even a noble. The clothes I'm wearing aren't even mine!"

A couple coming down the stairs must have heard him, as they both looked over at him before wrinkling their noses and edging toward the far end of the steps.

"Look. We'll just hang out here, out of the way, until we find Bri. Then it'll be the three of us, like usual. You'll be okay."

Tibault breathed deeply. "Yeah, okay. I can do this."

"You can do this, Tibby."

Tibault glowered at Krarshe. "I swear to Teva, if you call me that again..."

Krarshe laughed, harder than he probably should have at a formal gathering. It seemed a couple people by the food took notice, but they didn't seem to mind. "I'm going to go see what food there is, then I'll be back."

Tibault rolled his eyes. "You and food."

"What can I say? I like to sample new foods."

"For what good that'll do. Your sense of taste must have died years ago."

"I didn't say I was a GOOD cook, just that I was capable of it."

"I'm not starting this debate again. Just go look," Tibault said, rubbing his brow with his thumb and forefinger. "And tell me if there's anything good. In case my stomach settles."

Krarshe nodded and headed for the tables. He slid past a few gatherings, more clumsily than usual due to the uncomfortable clothes he was wearing. When he arrived, his eagerness quickly vanished. The table seemed to be filled with small starter dishes and samplers. A few cooked vegetables, some fruit, mostly things Krarshe had eaten countless times before. As he reached the end of the row of tables, his spirits picked up again. There seemed to be some sort of pastry, one he wasn't familiar with. They were small and seemed to contain a golden filling. And there was a whole mountain of them. With the current price of wheat, he couldn't even fathom how much these all cost. Looking around briefly, he quickly grabbed one and took a bite. The flaky casing crumbled as he bit into the slightly warm, syrupy filling. The sweet taste of warm apples filled his mouth as he let out an involuntary "Mmmm". He hurriedly finished his pastry and grabbed another, stuffing it into his mouth. Each bite was followed by the involuntary sound of satisfaction.

As he reached for another, he heard someone click their tongue and mutter, "Dirty sprite. Who, in Teva's name, invited such a disgusting creature?"

Krarshe's hand froze before slowly falling to his side. He forgot where he was. Forgot who was around him. He wasn't back at The Easy Lute, or at lunch with his friends. He was at a formal gathering for nobles. At Bri's invitation. Accompanied by a lesser noble. Krarshe didn't have a name to uphold, but Bri and Tibault did. *I get it now, Tibault,* he thought. He saw a stack of small plates at the very end of the table. Calmly, he grabbed two and put a pastry on each, and slowly maneuvered his way back to where he left Tibault.

Tibault was still resting his face in his hands. He didn't look as ill as before. "How are you feeling, Tibby?"

Tibault's posture didn't change as a swift kick caught Krarshe in the shin. "I told you not to call me that." Tibault picked up his head. "A bit better. Find anything good?"

Krarshe handed him a plate. "It's delicious."

"A hand pie?" Tibault asked, raising an eyebrow.

"Delicious," Krarshe repeated more insistently.

"I mean, yeah, it's a pie. I feel like this is more of a dessert. Was there no dinner food?"

"Delicious," Krarshe repeated yet again, enunciating each syllable.

"You're such a child." Tibault took the plate and bit into it. "Oh wow..."

"Right?!"

"... Okay. You win. Delicious." Tibault took another bite.

Krarshe sat down next to Tibault on the step, biting into his third hand pie. "I get it now, I think," Krarshe said, muffled by a mouth full of food.

Tibault turned to Krarshe, cocking his head to the side slightly. "Get what?"

Krarshe swallowed. "Nothing."

"That's probably the most true statement you've ever made," Tibault said with a smile before returning to his hand pie.

"They let vermin into this gathering? Bit embarrassing for House Bulliere." Krarshe and Tibault turned to see Armand talking to two other boys while gesturing.

"I didn't think you'd be invited," Tibault mocked, uncharacteristically. "Who did you have to bribe?"

"Tch! Please. A rag-noble like you wouldn't even pass for a servant here," Armand said, walking down the stairs to the main floor. He turned to Krarshe. "I'm surprised a sprite like him wasn't arrested for just stepping foot on the premises."

Tibault stood up, fist clenched. Thinking quickly, Krarshe stood and put a hand on his shoulder, stopping Tibault from taking unsightly action. "Let me show you something I learned," Krarshe whispered in Tibault's ear. Krarshe stepped forward. "Oh, my apologies, Lord Armand! I realize I must have slighted you in some way by not greeting you sooner! This lowly elf, Krarshe, bids you fair greetings," Krarshe made a grandiose bow. As he righted himself, he took note of a few other nobles who had turned to watch the exchange. He stepped forward with a smile and extended his hand. "May I have the blessing of shaking your lordly hand? It would mean the sky and heavens to me."

Armand and his two friends laughed. Krarshe could see Armand's eyes dance around the room, taking note of those watching as Krarshe had just done. He was cornered, Krarshe knew. "Of course, I am not so haughty as to deny such a courteous request." Armand stepped forward and shook Krarshe's hand.

Bzzzt.

Armand released Krarshe's hand. "There, I pray that lived up to your hopes," he said.

There were a few snickers. More than a few. From some of the onlookers. After a short moment, Tibault joined in, stifling a laugh. Krarshe smiled. "Of course." His eyes looked up slightly, to the top of Armand's head.

Armand's facade fell as his gaze turned more serious. "What are you—" He was interrupted by the frantic touch of one of his friends. "What?"

His friend leaned in and whispered. "Your hair, Armand."

"My hair?" Armand asked, confused. He reached up to his head. "What's wrong wi—" He stopped mid-sentence as he felt his wavy blond hair standing on end. There were slight flickers of static electricity tagging his fingers as his hand traced each strand.

The snickers in the crowd turned to laughter as Armand's face went from shock to horror. Krarshe couldn't contain his amusement as his smile grew even wider. A few other nobles were taking notice of the events by the stairs now, joining in either laughter or whispered gossiping.

"Y-Y-Y-YOU! FILTHY FUCKING SPRITE!" Armand howled. "You did this, didn't you?! DIDN'T YOU?!?!" He stepped up to Krarshe aggressively, getting face to face with him. Krarshe expected a fist to catch him in the face, but he couldn't help but keep smiling.

"What do you mean? How could I have done... that?" Krarshe asked, glancing up at Armand's hair again. "All I did was shake your hand, after all."

"You..." Armand snarled. "You dreg! You vile sprite! Hungerer find you and your whole sprite family!" He turned sharply and fled toward the entrance, head down as he tried to flatten his hair. Every time his hand ran through it, flicks of electricity followed, pulling the hair up again.

The laughter continued for a few minutes before it gradually dwindled and people returned to their conversations. Krarshe could tell by some of the gestures that a few discussions were centered on Armand's accident, giving him a sense of accomplishment.

"What was that?!" Tibault asked after he settled down.

"Hmm?"

"You did something, didn't you?"

Krarshe smiled. "Maybe."

"No getting out of this, Karshe. What did you do?"

"Oh, you know, just something I picked up during class," he said with a shrug. "Or, with Professor Landry, specifically."

"Oh... Wait. But, I didn't hear you say anything."

"Hmm?"

"Karshe," Tibault started before leaning in. "Was that... a spell?"

Krarshe looked away. "I don't know what you're talking about."

"Stop avoiding the question!"

"I mean, you didn't hear me cast anything, right?" Krarshe asked. Tibault nodded. "Then how could it be?"

Tibault sighed. "That's what I'm trying to figure out, but you keep AVOIDING it."

Krarshe turned back to the steps. His hand pie was still on the steps where he left it. "Oh. Right." He picked up the plate and took a bite of his pie. "Mmmmm... Still warm," he managed to say, mouth full.

Tibault sighed again. "Fine. I give up." Accepting that he'd never receive a straight answer, he followed Krarshe's example and resumed eating his hand pie.

* * *

The next hour or so was largely uneventful, aside from Krarshe's second visit to the food tables. The music continued to fill the hall with a cheerful energy. As more guests drank their fill, a few gathered the courage to dance. Krarshe watched from his seat on the stairs, catching glimpses of fluttering dresses in the gaps between other guests as men and women twirled and spun on the grand hall floor. It seemed complicated, and Krarshe was more than content to just watch.

Suddenly, there was a commotion by the staircase in the far corner of the room from where they sat. Krarshe and Tibault turned to see a beautiful young woman coming down the steps, more elegantly than either had ever seen. Her rich violet gown billowed gracefully with each step, the silver embellishment glittering in the light.

"Whoa. She's beautiful..." Tibault said, his vision captured by the allure of the young woman.

"Yeah..." Krarshe said, too captivated to articulate himself better. "Wait..." Krarshe regained his senses after studying her a moment longer. "Tibault, that's Bri!"

"What? No way..." he said, trailing off. "Maddener take me, you're right!"

Both of them stood up. "I don't think I've ever seen her like this."

"Me neither," Tibault admitted. "I know she's high nobility, but this... I didn't expect this."

A crowd of young men surrounded her at the bottom of the stairs. It was hard to see what was happening behind the wall of men, but eventually she emerged, daintily offering her hand to each man as she passed. Each took her hand with a bow and a brief exchange of words which Krarshe couldn't make out. Introductions were his guess.

She made her way across the room, the beautiful, delicate daughter of a noble, but Krarshe could see the truth. Her gentle gaze wasn't that of delicacy, but of displeasure. She was doing the dance she practiced, but there wasn't a hint of sincerity in her greetings. Until her eyes fell upon Krarshe and Tibault. Bri's eyes lit up and a big smile crossed her face. She turned to the throng of young men and exchanged some words while pointing toward her two friends. She then gave a deep curtsy before turning and hurrying over to Krarshe and Tibault, garnering the two boys a dozen scornful gazes.

"Thank Teva you two are here," she said. Her exposed collarbone heaved with her chest as she breathed heavily, more out of breath than Krarshe would have guessed from that distance. "I wasn't sure how much more I could put up with."

"Just that brief exchange?" Krarshe asked.

"Teva, no. I've been putting up with this all evening. Those are just the new arrivals."

"Who were they?"

"Suitors, I'd guess," Tibault said, looking over at the crowd of disgruntled men. "Based on the looks they're giving us."

"Mostly," Bri admitted. "A couple were just looking to cozy up to me for political clout."

"Why does it feel like they're out for blood now?" Krarshe asked.

"What?" Bri turned to look back. "Oh. Them. I wouldn't worry about it. They're not dumb enough to start an incident."

"An incident?"

"Told them Tibault was the son of a duke, and Krarshe was foreign royalty."

"You what?" Tibault and Krarshe asked in unison.

"It's fine. They won't question my word. Though..." Bri looked Krarshe up and down. "Maybe it's a bit difficult to believe him, with those clothes." She paused. "You two look good, though."

"Thanks," Tibault said. "You... You too."

"You were just looking at my chest, weren't you?"

"W-what? N-no, no."

"You're the worst." Bri turned to Krarshe. "Right?"

"Huh?" Krarshe's eyes shot up to meet Bri's. "Oh, yeah. Yeah. Sure. That."

Bri punched Krarshe square in the shoulder. "Teva spare me these idiots. I swear, you boys are all the same."

"Sorry..." Krarshe said, rubbing his bruised arm. "I—You just—You look..."

"Incredible," Tibault finished Krarshe's sentence.

"That."

Bri gave a hollow smile. "Thanks."

"No, no. We mean it. The dress looks beautiful on you, and the way your hair is done is very pretty," Krarshe said, trying to keep his eyes above her shoulders, away from danger.

Bri sighed. "Thank you. Genuinely this time. Can't say I agree with the hair comment though. Having it in a bun is kind of annoying. I don't like that I had to do it to expose my back either."

"You really don't like the formal dress, do you?" Tibault asked.

"I love the dress. I just don't like being paraded around like some toy to attract attention for my family." Bri tried to put a stray strand of hair back up into the neat arrangement, but it just fell in her face again. She groaned. "This stupid hair."

"You should leave it. I never fuss with my hair," Krarshe said. "Admittedly, it's cute too."

Krarshe could see Bri blush slightly. "Fine. I'll just leave it. I'm tired of trying to get it to cooperate."

"That's the point I'm at too, and we only got here not too long ago," Tibault said. Krarshe hadn't noticed, but the slicked back hair had slowly come undone, having almost returned to the mess it usually was.

"Your hair is clearly in charge of itself," Krarshe joked.

"It's impossible to win," Tibault laughed.

"Lady Bridgette," an older noble said, halting the conversation. "I hope I'm not interrupting anything."

"O-oh. N-no. Not at all," she said.

Krarshe watched as Bri shrunk back. Seeing it sparked a memory, his first encounter with her in the academy's store. He hadn't seen this timid side of her in a long time.

"I just wanted to convey my thanks and appreciation to your family, for this wonderful gala and for the assistance your father gave me."

"Y-yes. Of c-course. I will l-let him know," Bri stuttered with a curtsy.

The man smiled before returning a slight bow. As he left, Krarshe asked, "What was that?"

"What was what?"

Krarshe paused. "Nevermind."

The three returned to their talk. Tibault told Bri about their interaction with Armand an hour earlier. Krarshe was subjected to Bri's interrogation, and, much like Tibault's, he avoided a direct answer. Krarshe talked about the hand pies, which led to them talking about their cooking competition some days ago. Rather, about the charred meat Krarshe had produced. Their conversation drifted from one topic to another, from Bri bringing them up to the balcony to explain the layout of her house, to pointing out who a multitude of nobles were. All of the names were new to Krarshe, but Tibault seemed to recognize a few of them. Eventually, Krarshe convinced them to move the conversation back downstairs next to the hand pies for entirely personal reasons. Hungry reasons.

As they talked, joked, and laughed, the events with the older noble repeated themselves time and again. Someone would approach Bri to discuss something with her family, and she would shrink back into the little mouse from the school store. At first, he dismissed it, but as it happened time and again, Krarshe felt that curiosity gnawing at him.

"Bri, do you notice that your personality changes?"

"Changes? When?"

"Any time one of these old men come talk to you."

"Old men? Oh, the other nobles. I guess I do change a bit."

"A bit?" Tibault pressed. Apparently, he had noticed the change in her too.

Bri nodded. "You could blame my upbringing, I suppose. All of the etiquette my father forced upon me."

"What do you—"

"Pardon me, Milady Bridgette," a young nobleman said, yet another interruption. "Might I have this dance?"

The disruption gave Krarshe a moment to notice the music had become more prominent. Or, rather, a lot of the chatter had stopped. More people were dancing than there was not too long ago.

"Oh. Umm... Sorry, I was just about to..." She turned to Tibault.

"Absolutely not. I'd definitely vomit out there," Tibault said.

Bri's face contorted in disgust. She quickly grabbed Krarshe by the hand. "I just promised a dance with this man, so I must apologize," she said to the young noble. Krarshe caught the boy sneering at him before Bri pulled him onto the dance floor.

"Wait," Krarshe tried to protest. "I don't know how to dance."

After taking a central place amongst the dancing guests, Bri stopped and whipped Krarshe to face her. "It's easy. Just put your hand here..." she said as she guided his free hand to the small of her back, "and then just follow my lead. And try not to step on me."

Krarshe looked down at his feet, trying to measure distance before the gap between his and Bri's body quickly disappeared. "Easier said than don~~~e!" His words were drawn out as Bri quickly took Krarshe in a twirl, pulling him along with her movements.

Krarshe could feel his heart begin to race as they danced, there in the center of all these nobles. The world around them was a blur of blues, reds, and golds; the light that lit the room glowed brightly, and the reflection off the floor added to the disorienting chaos. There were a few times where he could feel himself step on something. The music seemed distant now, engulfed in the confusion. He wished she didn't drag him out here. He wished Tibault was suffering this instead of himself, as cruel as it was to think.

He was about to release his grasp of Bri when he heard her speak softly to him. "Relax. Just listen to the music and I'll do the rest." Krarshe's vision focused in front of him, meeting Bri's clear, dark brown eyes. It was the first time he noticed their height difference, as he looked down at her. This small girl, with such a confident gaze. "You trust me, right?"

Krarshe breathed deeply, calming himself, and smiled. "Wholeheartedly." He stopped worrying about the rest of the room and just felt her movements, listened to the music, and trusted her guidance. The chaos that entrapped him a mere moment ago disappeared. The room still whirled around him, but the image of Bri's poise and composure remained his steadfast anchor. *So this is dancing,* he thought. *It's... actually kind of fun.*

This continued for a few minutes before Krarshe noticed a shift in the music, seamlessly changing to a new song. Krarshe panicked for a moment and looked at Bri, but her calm demeanor didn't change. Rather, her dancing changed as seamlessly as the music. This might have been the first time Bri ever revealed her experience as a noblewoman. Content to continue following her lead, Krarshe relaxed and danced along with her.

About half way through the song, Krarshe began to notice a few nobles watching them. He turned his attention away from Bri to look around the dance floor. The number of guests dancing had dwindled. Before being pulled around in a twist, Krarshe could make out even more people watching the two of them, several of which were the men Bri had abandoned earlier for the company of himself and Tibault. A few were whispering something to each other, sneering at him as they did it. Krarshe could feel his nervousness rise again. Trying to remain calm, he turned his focus back to Bri. Unfortunately, it had the adverse effect, as he noticed her allure again. This further exacerbated the issue as he could hear a few of the young men mutter insults of jealousy.

It wasn't long before it felt like the two of them were the only pair dancing, everyone's eyes falling upon them. Krarshe tried to push the thought out of his mind, but it lingered, smoldered, and eventually engulfed him.

Not a moment after the song began to change, Krarshe stopped abruptly, catching Bri off guard as she was yanked back by the suddenness of it. Krarshe released her hand and waist, and gave a deep bow, trying to make it look planned. Bri luckily followed up with a curtsy of her own as they made their way off the dance floor. Sure enough, as they left, Krarshe was able to see clearly that there was no one left dancing. Instead, everyone was just watching the two of them. Krarshe was never a fan of being the center of attention, but especially so here, where he was both the only elf and commoner and in the company of a young lord and lady. That incident with the hand pies affected him more than he realized.

"Krarshe, what was that?" Bri asked, catching him by the shoulder as he made for the safety of the staircase. "Are you okay?"

"Yeah, I'm fine. I just... I wasn't feeling comfortable out there."

"You did fine, there was nothing to worry about. And you only stepped on my foot a few times."

"It's... I don't know. It felt like people were watching us," Krarshe said. He wasn't sure how to put it into words, exactly. It was just a feeling.

"What in the world was that out there?!" Tibault came hurrying over through the crowd.

"Tibault!" Bri rebuked. "You did fine, Krarshe. Don't worry abo—"

"No, not the dancing! The glowing!" Tibault explained in as hushed a voice as he could manage with his hysteria.

"Glow?" Bri asked. "What glow?"

"Yeah, what do you mean?"

Tibault pulled them over to the side. "You two didn't notice?" Bri and Krarshe shook their heads. "You two looked to have some sort of blue glow emanating from you."

Krarshe and Bri both exchanged puzzled looks before turning back to Tibault. "I don't know what you're talking about," Bri said.

"Same," Krarshe said.

"You sure?" Tibault pressed, looking sharply at Krarshe. "Especially after what you did to Armand..."

"Wait, you did that?" Bri asked, turning to Krarshe. Her face said she was wanting an explanation, but Krarshe wasn't about to give her one.

"I hold that what happened to Armand was divine justice. But... even if I did have something to do with Armand, this wasn't me." *At least, I don't think so...* thought Krarshe.

"Well, it got everyone's attention regardless." Tibault sighed. "I thought we were trying to remain inconspicuous..."

"Here," Bri started, cutting past the two boys. "Let's just go up on the balcony. There's a spot where we can avoid most of the guests."

Without a word, both Tibault and Krarshe followed her upstairs. Krarshe had enough of this party, he just wanted to spend some time with his friends away from all the looks. Annoying Armand was fun, but whatever the anomaly was with the dancing was beyond his understanding. He was content to spend the rest of the night with as little attention as possible.

* * *

Fortunately, the rest of the evening was quiet. Krarshe and his friends managed to avoid interacting with guests, aside from a few nobles paying their respects to Bri. They talked about a multitude of things, and Bri was able to get a maid she was friendly with to bring them some food directly up on the balcony. None of it compared to the hand pie for Krarshe, but it was all still good. It was several hours before any of them realized how late it was.

"Oh, I think the party is coming to an end," Tibault noted. "There's only a few guests still downstairs."

"Guess you're right," Krarshe said, peering over the edge to get a better look. "This was fun. Or, well, the latter half, I guess."

Bri smiled and nodded. "Probably the only fun gala I've been to. Come, I'll see you out. The guards might give you trouble this late."

As they reached the bottom of the balcony steps, a man called out to them. "Bridgette. There you are. I was wondering where you ran off to." The man nodded a goodbye to two other, older men and walked over to the three of them. Krarshe noticed Bri seemed to seize up, almost as if she'd been caught by city guards while picking someone's pocket. The man stood before them, taller than either Krarshe or Tibault. He didn't seem to be particularly old, even with Krarshe's difficulty guessing one's age, but the lines in his forehead and around his mouth made him appear so. The lines, combined with his solemn expression and humorless eyes, gave him an unnerving sternness. His light brown hair was slicked back, his face clean-shaven; the whole visage reminded Krarshe of Professor Owyn. "It's unladylike to not introduce your guests."

Bri flinched. Krarshe saw her try to right her posture and turned toward the man. "T-Tibault, Ka-Ka... Krarshe. T-this is m-my f-father, Gaspard Bulliere."

"Bridgette. Stop stuttering."

Bri flinched again. She breathed deeply and repeated, "This... is my father, Gaspard... Bulliere."

"And they?" her father asked in a slow, monotonous tone.

"This... I—" she stopped and cleared her throat. "This is... Tibault Dumont."

Tibault gave a frantic, rigid bow. Bri's father gave a slight nod. "Ah, yes. The Dumont family. Your father just received his title not a decade ago, yes?"

"That—" Tibault's voice cracked. "That's correct, sir."

"Mmm, yes..." Gaspard turned to wave at another guest as they left and continued without turning back to face Tibault, "I suppose your parents will continue to serve admirably in... whatever it is that they do." As the other guest exited the front door, he turned back to Bri. "And this... other young man?"

Bri swallowed hard before the second introduction. "This is Krarshe," she said, saying Krarshe's name slowly to avoid stumbling. After her father continued to stare at her for a moment, she added, "Just Krarshe."

Krarshe bowed as Tibault had and said, "It is a pleasure to meet you, my lord." When he righted himself, he saw Gaspard hadn't moved. Rather, he just stared intently at Krarshe, his eyes silently filled with scorn.

Without removing his gaze, he said, "To think, my own daughter would befriend a peasant. And an ELF, no less... Perhaps I raised her without teaching her how to properly evaluate people."

"T-they're both great mages!" Bri retorted. "Krarshe is probably the most powerful mage in the school! Including the teachers!"

"Silence!" her father shot back, turning back to her swiftly enough to send a few strands of hair into disarray. Bri immediately shrunk back like a scolded dog. "You dare to talk back to me in such a tone? After you've been traipsing around instead of studying? Off playing with..." Gaspard gave Krarshe and Tibault a sideways glance, "... Miscreants... like these? Need I remind you of your place, as a Bulliere? You have a name to uphold, as my daughter. And I WILL have you uphold it, if you wish to keep this name..." With each scathing word out of his mouth, Bri flinched and cowered more and more.

By the time he finished his tirade, Bri looked to be on the verge of tears, her exposed shoulders shaking uncontrollably. Krarshe turned to Tibault. He was frozen with fear, and trembling not unlike Bri. The few guests and staff around the room had stopped as well, watching the commotion.

Gaspard took a deep breath, calming himself. A vein clearly bulged on his forehead, exposing his anger despite his calm visage. As he guided the stray hairs back into place, he said, "I cannot believe you'd invite these people to this estate. But I guess I shouldn't be surprised that you would do something like that."

Krarshe heard a small hiccup from Bri. He couldn't see her face, but he knew what was coming. And he wasn't going to just watch this scene anymore. "I'm most sorry, sir," he said, drawing her father's attention. "It seems that my presence has inconvenienced you. But rest assured, we were just leaving. Thank you for the hand pies, they were quite delicious." Without giving Gaspard the chance to respond, Krarshe grabbed Tibault and Bri and dragged them out the front door. As he left, he thought he heard something about a sprite.

Once out the door, he pulled them off next to the fountain and sat them both on one of the stone benches that encircled it. Bri immediately broke out into tears. Tibault retched a few times but, to Krarshe's surprise, managed to hold on to the contents of his stomach. Krarshe didn't say anything to either of them, and instead just stood off to the side, trying to act as a barricade to hide them from the vacating guests.

After a minute, Bri croaked out, "I hate him..." She hiccuped a couple times before repeating, "I fucking hate him."

"Your father?"

Bri just nodded slowly, her lower lip still quivering. "Teva, why am I such a failure..." she sobbed, the tears cascading down her cheeks again.

Krarshe had heard these words from Bri before. At the time, he wasn't sure what to do but offer empty words of encouragement. But this was different. He knew Bri now. He walked over and sat down next to her, throwing a comforting arm around her shoulders. She leaned into his embrace as she continued to cry. "I said it before, and I'll say it again," Krarshe said. "You're not a failure." Her crying grew louder for a moment before subsiding back to muffled noises. He let her settle down for a minute before continuing. "Your spells are incredible. You're one of the kindest, most caring people I've ever met. And I've met a lot of people." He rocked her side to side a bit, trying to draw her attention away from her thoughts.

"You're one of the strongest people I know, Bri. Both mentally and physically... I should know, with how many times you've hit me."

He heard Bri choke on a giggle before snorting back some of her mucus. "And you always deserved it," she muttered quietly before snorting again.

"Every time," Tibault added. It seemed he'd recovered.

Krarshe laughed. "You okay now, Tibault?"

"Yeah. Still feel a bit queasy, but better than before."

Bri sat upright, sniffing still. She wiped the tears from her cheeks with her palms a few times before Tibault pulled out a handkerchief and handed it to her. She took a shaky breath as she dabbed her eyes before saying, "I hate when this happens."

"Your dad?" Tibault asked.

"We almost got through the night without seeing him, but of course he'd come find me," she said, about to break into tears again. Bri continued, her voice starting to shake again, "The night was going so well... And then he HAD to ruin it for me. Again!" She fell into sobbing again.

"Is this what you meant when I escorted you home the other day?" Krarshe asked.

Bri nodded. "It's like he just wants to ruin my life!" she cried. "He always does this!"

"Should I go punch him for you?" Krarshe asked. "Though, last time I did that, I broke my hand..."

Bri calmed down for a moment. She hiccuped again, then said, "Thanks, but that'd probably make it worse."

"Yeah, a broken hand isn't fun, let me tell you," Krarshe joked. Bri elbowed him, causing him to let out a grunt. "Add another hit to the tally."

"You're awful at cheering people up, you know that?" Bri croaked, smiling at him.

"Truthfully though, your father is... pretty disagreeable," Tibault said.

"I would have said abhorrent," Krarshe replied. "Honestly, Wild Brow is downright jovial compared to him."

"Why do you think I moved into the dormitory?" Bri asked, wiping her tears with the handkerchief again. She let out a shiver, prompting Tibault to start taking off his coat.

"Wait, let me," Krarshe said. Tibault sat back down on the bench. "I'm too warm with all this clothing anyway." He removed his coat and offered it to Bri.

"Thanks, both of you. These dresses aren't really made for the cold." She draped it over her exposed shoulders and pulled it tight around her.

Krarshe sat back down next to her, turned to face her as best he could. "Bri. Listen... Don't pay your father any mind." He put his hand on her shoulder. Her dark brown eyes, still glistening with tears, looked deep into his brilliant blue ones. "You ARE a great mage. And an even better person. Better than he'll ever be at either. Okay? So disregard that dreg."

Tibault shuffled closer to Bri. He bumped his shoulder against hers and nodded. "What he said."

Bri's sullen look slowly turned into a smile as she looked away. She hid her face with one hand as she pulled the coat tighter with the other. "Thank you..." she said, practically a whisper. She quickly broke free from Krarshe's grasp and stood up. She stretched and walked away, tracing the edge of the fountain with one hand. "The stars really are beautiful, aren't they?"

Krarshe and Tibault exchanged confused glances at the sudden change of topic. They both shrugged and leaned back to look at the sky. "They really are," Tibault said. Krarshe just sat there quietly.

"I really hope I pass this time."

Krarshe and Tibault both looked at Bri again. She was still gazing at the sky.

"I'm tired of my only value to him being a marriage asset," she continued.

"You'll pass," Krarshe said. "I know it."

"Yeah, no doubt. You're the best mage in class," Tibault added.

Bri's eyes sank. She stared at the ground quietly for several seconds before speaking softly. "... I hope you're both right."

CHAPTER 20

"Did you do anything exciting during your break?"

Krarshe looked over at Landry. He had been milling about the training room mindlessly as the elderly teacher sat quietly reading a book. While he was still scheduled to come to the training facility, Krarshe wasn't allowed to cast any spells because the stone floor and walls had been repaired in preparation for the exams this afternoon. It was nearly midday when Landry finally broke the silence with his question. "I went to a gala."

"Oh? That sounds fun," Landry said, his mustache raising slightly as his mouth curled into a smile beneath it.

"It was. Or, most of it was." Landry gave Krarshe an inquisitive look. "I'm not particularly good at handling nobles. Too prim and proper for me," Krarshe explained.

Landry nodded. "Speaking truthfully, I'm the same. I'd rather toil away in my office."

"I really hated the clothes I had to wear also. So stuffy. And all of the waitresses at the inn I stay at were making a big fuss about them."

Landry's eyebrows raised. "Oh?"

"Yeah. My regular waitress, a catfolk girl, was obsessed. Her excitement was... Well, it was kind of cute, honestly. Just a bit excessive."

"Catfolk can be like that. Especially if she's your regular server. They tend to get attached to people they spend a lot of time with. At least, that's what I've found in my years of experience," Landry said, his gaze distant as he mused to himself. "It's a remnant of their ancestry."

"Huh. I didn't know that," Krarshe said. He waited to see if Landry would add any more, but he didn't. "Did you partake in any festivities yourself?"

"Oh no, I was quite busy." Landry patted the large, leather-bound book in his lap. "Even without classes to teach, I had to go through my research findings and prepare them to present to the Council later. You students aren't the only ones under pressure this quarter-cycle."

"What is your research on?" Krarshe asked, less out of interest and more just trying to pass the time.

Landry smiled again. Without a word, he raised his thin hand and pointed a bony finger at Krarshe.

"Oh. Right. Maybe the recess was too long," Krarshe said with a laugh. "Do all of the professors do research?"

"All except Owyn. He's busy with the fledgling mages."

"What do they research?"

Landry shook his head. "That's a secret. While I may know generally what they're studying, I'm unaware of the details. Much like my research with you, I haven't shared my findings with any of them." He looked up towards the sun, shading his eyes from it with his hand. "They'll find out when the findings are presented to the Council." He stood up unsteadily, pushing off his knee with his free hand while the other clutched the book. "I'll guess it's just about time for the junior students' exam. You can run along to the store for now. I'll see you tomorrow. No, wait. The following day. I forgot today was our scheduled meeting day. Doesn't seem right without being covered in debris." He laughed his slow, drawn-out laugh.

Krarshe nodded. "I'll see you then." He made his way through the door and into the hall of the academy. On his way to the store, he passed the other teachers making their way to the training room. Each was carrying at least one book, though a couple carried two. Krarshe couldn't make out what they were talking about, but they seemed to talk quieter as they passed him. Owyn leered at him as he walked by. Krarshe still felt his scorn was unwarranted, but he'd just grown accustomed to it.

He decided to check in with his friends as he approached the classroom and maybe offer words of encouragement. It was never his strong suit, but probably better than nothing. As he peeked in, he was met with a room in disarray. Some students were in their seats, poring over their notes while others had their eyes closed and mumbling to themselves. A few were briskly pacing around the room silently, their minds clearly elsewhere. *I guess they're more nervous than I thought.*

Krarshe entered as quietly as he could and made his way towards Tibault and Bri. Tibault seemed to favor reviewing his notes and reciting the spells to himself. Bri was kneeling on the floor by the window, her palms pressed together similarly to the priest he'd visited after he got hurt. Neither one seemed to notice his entrance as he continued to watch them quietly. After a minute, he spoke up. "Good luck, you two."

Tibault jumped slightly before turning to him. "Curses! Don't startle me like that!" Tibault looked around a bit before returning to his notes. "When did you even get in here?"

"Just a moment ago," he said, looking over at Bri. She still hadn't moved. "You ready?"

"No. No way. I can barely cast spells during our practical training." Tibault rubbed his forehead as though trying to clear his doubts.

"Well, don't get too stressed out about it."

Tibault looked over at Krarshe again. He breathed deeply. "Well, thank you for the support."

"How long has she been like that?" Krarshe asked.

Tibault glanced over at Bri. "I don't know. Maybe since I started studying."

"Hmm..." Krarshe slid next to Bri. She was still as stone, her breathing slow and deliberate. He leaned in next to her ear and said, "Good luck, Bri."

She jumped more than Tibault had, stumbling back towards the bench as she swung her hand up to protect her ear. "Teva's mercy! Krarshe! Curses!"

Krarshe laughed. "Sorry, sorry. I just wanted to wish you good luck on the exam. Not that you'll need it."

Bri groaned. She put her hand on the bench and pulled herself to her feet. "Wish that was true. I honestly feel at this point that only Teva's guidance can get me through this."

"You don't need divine assistance. I said it the other day, and I'll keep saying it until you know it yourself. You're a great mage. Have confidence in yourself."

Bri looked away with sullen eyes and said, "Multiple attempts at this say otherwise..." She gazed across the room, watching the other students study before turning back to Krarshe. "... Thanks," she said with a weak smile.

"Bri. I mean it. If you don't pass, then it's impossible for anyone."

"Krarshe... You truly are awful at encouraging people."

"What? How?"

Bri rolled her eyes. "Think about what you just said, and then think about how long I've been here."

"Do you two mind? I'm trying to study!" Tibault shouted at them.

"Tomas. To the exam area." Krarshe turned to see the heavier professor in the doorway. A boy jumped up from his bench before nervously making his way out of the door, following the teacher.

"What was that?"

"Exams are done in private, remember?" Bri said. "He's up first, I guess. At least he'll be done first too."

"Still unlucky," Tibault muttered, not looking up from his notes.

Krarshe watched Tibault study for a moment. "Well, I should probably leave you two to prepare. Again, best of luck."

"Thanks," Bri and Tibault both said in unison. Bri sat down and stared out the window as Krarshe had so many times, apparently not feeling the need to study.

"Fun, isn't it?" Krarshe said as he headed to the door.

"You know, it kind of is," Bri responded, slightly more cheer in her voice than before.

* * *

Krarshe wandered around the store, waiting for the end of the day. There was a senior student who had disappeared to the back room the moment he arrived, carrying a stack of books. When Krarshe had looked back there, the student seemed to be working on something feverishly, flipping through the books he'd scattered across the floor. With nothing else to do and no customers, Krarshe spent his idle time amidst the shelves of magical goods.

As he shuffled up and down the aisles, he tripped over a stack of boxes that had been left at the corner of the shelving, nearly falling to the floor. "Ow! Curse these damned boxes. Ugh." He tilted the top-most box and found it was actually light. Lifting the wooden lid, he saw it was empty. "Who leaves a bunch of empty boxes around?" Krarshe asked aloud to no one in particular, more due to embarrassment that he tripped over them than anything else. He crouched down and picked up the stack that was nearly as tall as him and started toward the back room before he was struck by an idea. He put the boxes down quietly and crept over to the side of the store. From there, he could see the senior student was still working on whatever assignment he was trying to finish, completely oblivious to the world around him.

Okay, Krarshe thought. *Let's do it.*

He grabbed the stack of boxes and headed out the front of the store, opening the door as quietly as he could. As he stepped out into the courtyard, he barely caught the door with his foot as it nearly swung closed. He eased it back into position and made his way around the back of the store.

He could hear the sounds of spell casts from over the wall as he approached. He set down the stack of boxes in the corner of the school building next to the training area wall as gently as possible. Jumping up a bit, he managed to grab on to the top of the box and hoisted himself up onto the stack. The boxes were a lot more narrow than he realized initially, leaving little room to maneuver as he tried to position himself on top of them. He steadied himself against the school's wall as he tried to stand up. The boxes shifted slightly as he reached a crouched position, causing him to brace himself against both walls and stop. He steadied himself and took a breath before slowly bringing himself to a full standing position.

Okay, hard part: done. He looked up. It was still out of reach at full height. *Mmm... Maybe not.* He wished he had a few more boxes, but that was out of the question at this point. He knew he had to jump but the thought of doing it on this flimsy tower made him nervous. *Just one good jump.* He crouched slightly before leaping and reaching for the top of the wall. The boxes shifted as he held his breath. Luckily, they stopped before falling over. He relaxed, knowing he avoided outing himself. Bracing himself against both walls with his feet, he inched his way higher, pulling himself up with his arms as he gained height. His feet slipped and scraped against the cold stone walls as he kept scrambling up them, eventually pulling himself up to rest on his elbows. From there, Krarshe pushed himself up as high as he could, swinging a foot onto the ledge before fully getting himself on top of the walls of the enclosure. *That was WAY harder than I expected...* he thought, taking a moment to catch his breath. He looked back to make sure no one saw him atop the wall before positioning himself so he could watch the exams while staying out of sight of those inside. It seemed he was just above the teachers, with a view of the center of the training area. It really was a perfect spot.

"That'll do," said a familiar voice from the base of the wall. "That concludes your exam. You're free to go home for the day."

Krarshe ducked down as he saw one of his classmates turn and bow in his direction and make his way out of the training area.

After the clang of the door closing sounded, he heard Landry's voice ask, "So, what did you think?"

"Seems promising. He could use a bit more practice, but I have high hopes," said a voice Krarshe had heard before, but couldn't identify.

"I have no doubt he'll perform admirably in time," said Professor Owyn. "For now, let him continue in my class."

"Agreed," said another unfamiliar voice. Krarshe thought it might be the heavier teacher, but wasn't sure. He barely remembered most of the teachers, let alone their voices. "I'll fetch the next student."

The door opened again with a metallic creak before clanging shut again. The other teachers sat quietly, aside from occasional mutterings and scritching of quills. After a couple minutes, the door opened again and another student took his position in the center of the room.

"Let's see..." Owyn commented. "Ah yes, Felix. You can begin when you're ready."

"Oh, that's an interesting one..." commented one of the teachers.

"That spell again? How dull," Landry commented quietly. Krarshe wouldn't have been surprised if the comment was missed by the student.

"*S-se E-Esf—*"

"You can't cast a spell like that, Felix. Just do it like we've done in class," Owyn said, interrupting the nervous casting.

The boy took a deep breath and started again, "*Se Esfiru hinoras, suesoo shu zeraus dzam mea'anom.*" He took another breath before continuing, "*Sem te se yanrum shu hiaso'odum, dun suesoo yanhadis!*"

A gust of wind blew past Krarshe and into the center of the training room. Dust and leaves were caught up in a gale that whipped around his classmate. It swirled around him for a moment before exploding outward, throwing a few leaves off in all directions. After the explosion of wind, the air grew still again.

There was some murmuring from just over the wall before Owyn spoke up. "Very good, Felix. That'll do for today. You're free to go home."

The boy bowed nervously and left the room in the same manner as the first boy. "That was good," said Landry.

"He's coming along nicely," said a voice Krarshe hadn't heard yet today. "The spell felt a bit slow, and potency was lacking, but he'll be fine, I'm sure."

"Is it enough for a passing mark?"

"I'd say yes."

"As would I."

"That's a plurality then," Owyn said after a moment. Krarshe could hear his quill scratching away.

"I'll be a moment again," said one of the teachers as he left.

This... seems straight forward. How is Bri having issues with this? Krarshe wondered.

After a minute, Krarshe saw a head of messy brown hair enter the room. "Tibault, yes?" Owyn asked as Tibault took his position. "You may go ahead when ready."

Ooh! I get to watch Tibault so early! Krarshe could see Tibault visibly shaking, clearly nervous. *I hope he doesn't vomit...*

Tibault took a few breaths before taking his stance. He held out his open palm to the far wall. *"Chiian dzam nia'e, Iiasu, se chiian dzam gra zehinga, sem tsaru fanyisn!"* A small orb of light began to glow just in front of Tibault's outstretched arm. Krarshe could hear the surprise in the muffled voices of some of the teachers below. After a moment, the orb began to flicker before going out entirely.

"Ah, that's unfortunate. You can give it another attempt," Owyn said, unusually flat for the sympathetic words he spoke.

Tibault took a deep breath before reciting the spell again. This time, nothing happened at all.

"Don't be too disappointed," he heard Landry say. "There is always next time."

Krarshe couldn't quite make out Tibault's expression through the messy brown hair, but he could tell by Tibault's posture that he was distraught. He just nodded slowly.

"You're free to go home for the day. I'll see you in class tomorrow," Owyn said.

Tibault slowly made his way out of the training room. *I'll have to go cheer him up later.*

"Is that the one who was looking into imbuement?" asked one of the teachers. There was a moment of silence before he continued. "Wonder how long he'll last here." A few of the teachers laughed.

"With his skill level, he'd be better as a researcher. He'd be worthless on the battlefield."

"Can't even conjure up a simple light spell." More laughter followed.

"Maybe he could be used as a shield for a real mage." More laughter.

Krarshe wasn't sure what he was listening to anymore. It seemed so contrary to the words Landry had just uttered a moment ago. What was most unsettling, however, was the laughter. He expected this from the condescending tone from Owyn, but didn't realize the other teachers weren't any better.

A few more students came and went. Their skills varied widely, though most seemed to do fine, based on the teacher's reactions. A small handful struggled like Tibault did, which was met with ridicule after the student left.

Krarshe was shocked at Armand's exam, which was a repeat of the first spell they had cast on the first day. The effect wasn't much better than the first time he'd seen him cast it, but the attitude of the teachers was completely different. They lavished praise upon him, saying that he'd certainly be one of the best mages in the kingdom, or perhaps even find himself a seat on the Council. It made Krarshe sick to see the smug look on Armand's face. Before long, it was Bri's turn.

"Miss Bulliere. Here again, I see," said Landry. "As always, I wish you luck in your exam."

Bri didn't even acknowledge the teachers. She walked solemnly into position and took up her stance. She raised both hands in front of her, palms facing forward.

"Let's see, what spell is it this time?" said one of the teachers. "Oh. Hmm. Very well then. You may begin when ready."

"*Ra tso, ra hias, Soujiin, hias shu krangra dzam mea'anom, se me hinoran! Hias, grunda e ja...*" A flame appeared just in front of her right hand. "*... Krangra, grunda e jacho...*" Another flame appeared before her other hand. Krarshe leaned in closer, watching the flames grow in side. This spell was already longer and more complex than the other students'. Bri continued, "*Naruen se zadzu meaa hiatsan. Sem tsaru motsa shiim. Naru'a, motsa shiim...*" The two flames began to rotate in front of her, slowly at first but then speeding up until they formed a large flaming ring, then quickly becoming a disc. "*Hias dzam ze'anarun!*"

The spinning disc of fire erupted, shooting a giant pillar of flame forward with a cacophonous roar. The flames spread against the back wall, curling around the edges and along the storage areas on either side. Krarshe could feel the heat of the flames from his perch. Bri held the spell for a good ten or fifteen seconds before the flames slowly subsided. The back wall was blackened, a sight Krarshe recalled from his time in the training area.

There was silence for a minute as Bri tried to catch her breath. She wiped her forehead with the sleeve of her white jacket before finally turning to the teachers. *That was INCREDIBLE!* Krarshe thought, struggling to stop himself from yelling down to her in congratulations. *I told you there was nothing to—*

"... Hmm. If you'd like, you can give it another attempt," Owyn said.

WHAAAAAAAAAAAT?!?! Krarshe nearly jumped from the wall into the training area. His sensibilities came back to him and he crouched back down. *What the fuck is he even talking about?!?! That was unbelievable!!*

"I—" Bri took a few more labored breaths, "I don't... think I can..." She was clearly exhausted after that spell, her breathing ragged as though she'd just run across the whole of Remonnet.

"That's disappointing, especially after all that effort you put in. But, very well then. You may return home for the day," Owyn said in his rehearsed way.

Krarshe watched as those words tortured Bri. He could see her purse her lips as she fought back against the sting of them. She gave a small nod of understanding and quickly made her way out of the room.

Wait, they actually failed her? Again?! After THAT?!?!

"That was... quite a spell," said one teacher.

"Yes indeed," said another.

"I'm surprised she managed to cast it, truthfully," added a third.

Exactly!

"How much longer is she going to keep this up?" Owyn asked with a sigh. "It's getting more and more difficult to fail her."

... Huh?

"I thought for sure she'd be unable to cast this one," said Landry. "I found the most complex spell from my evocation class. She's far too exceptional."

Wait... No. No, I can't be hearing what I'm thinking...

"If she'd just withdraw from the school, we could stop having to put up with this farce time after time."

"I just pray she does not realize the breadth of her skills. That would cause problems for us," said Landry, with a bitter tone Krarshe had never heard him utter.

No... No no no no no! Curses, you have to be kidding me... Krarshe slunk down, the reality of the situation was evident now, a reality he had hoped and prayed was false. *Lycia was right.*

Krarshe could feel his blood begin to boil. He remembered the pain Bri went through, the tears she shed just the other day, the torment she suffered time and again. It was all them, these so-called teachers. All of it. Krarshe lowered himself down to his tower of boxes, no longer interested in the exam. No, not an exam. This was a sham, a mockery. Krarshe grit his teeth, frustrated, uncertain of what he should do. What he could do. He didn't bother returning to the store, he just left for the day, disheartened.

CHAPTER 21

Despite his anger and frustration the day before, Krarshe found himself again in the classroom. He sat in his usual seat by the window, but his eye was on the entrance. As student after student entered, he could identify who passed and who failed just on mood alone. Armand was cheerful for once, seemingly gloating to his group of friends. Even Krarshe could see the few of them who put on smiles were fake ones.

Gloating to your friends who failed, huh? Krarshe rolled his eyes.

Tibault walked in, more slowly than usual. Krarshe already saw how he did, but his posture made it all the more obvious. Tibault flopped into his seat and put his head down on the table.

"That bad, huh?" Krarshe asked, feigning ignorance.

"I don't want to talk about it."

"Don't worry about it. Based on their faces, I suspect a good number of students failed," Krarshe said as he nodded toward the rest of the class. Tibault let out a muffled groan.

More students arrived as time went by. Eventually, Professor Owyn came in and called for everyone to return to their seats.

"I'd like to congratulate those of you who did well on the exam yesterday," he started as a few students were still sneaking to their seats. "I hope you continue to make progress so that you can advance out of the beginner class. For the rest of you, do your best to keep practicing and taking notes in class. Just remember..."

Krarshe leered at Owyn in disgust and then turned toward Tibault. He seemed to still be dejected, his eyes glazed over. Krarshe couldn't tell if he was listening or not. *Wait... Since when can I see Tibault unobstructed?* He looked down at the empty seat between them. The one usually filled by their other friend. "Where's Bri?" Krarshe whispered.

"Huh?" Tibault grunted, coming back to his senses.

Just as Krarshe was about to repeat his question, the door to the classroom opened. Bri walked in, or rather, staggered in. Her face was expressionless, not even reacting when Owyn addressed her tardiness. Shuffling, she made her way to her seat between Krarshe and Tibault. She sat down quietly, her hands resting upon her thighs, and stared blankly at the table in front of her.

Krarshe watched her for a moment, but she was still as stone. "Bri, you okay?" he asked quietly, trying to not draw attention to them. Bri didn't react at all. Unlike Tibault a moment earlier, her eyes were clear, focused, but that made it all the more concerning.

"Bri?" Tibault asked.

"You see," Owyn spoke up. "When you lack punctuality and focus, you will be doomed to fail. Time and again."

Krarshe looked up to see the whole class watching Bri. He looked toward Owyn. His lips were curled into a wicked smile, sharper than the rest of his features.

"Perhaps, Miss Bulliere, you could pass if you listened for once, hmm?" Owyn added.

Krarshe heard a few chuckles from the students. He turned to Bri. Her eyes shifted to the floor between her knees, her hands clasping the hem of her skirt tightly, her whole body quivering slightly.

hic

Bri's shoulders shook even more, as she hunched forward and twitched with each hiccup. Despite her best efforts to hold back the tears, Krashe saw a single, silvery tear streak down her face and drip to the tip of her nose. Tibault draped an arm around her shoulders, trying his best to comfort her.

"Let Miss Bulliere be a lesson for you all. Now, for today..." Owyn said, turning back to the chalkboard.

Krarshe wasn't sure if it was the result of seeing Bri's distress, Owyn's casual dismissal, or the fact that it all stemmed from what he saw during the exam, but something within him snapped. His temper flared, his eye twitched as his face turned from concern for a friend to an enraged sneer. He couldn't stand it anymore. He was done.

"E-NOUGH!!" Krarshe shouted, slamming his fists on the table in front of him as he stood. The entire room jumped at the bang. Owyn had visibly jumped as he recoiled toward the blackboard.

"W-w-what... What is the meaning of this, Krarshe?" he asked, still shaken. He composed himself and asked again, "Is there something that you felt you needed to interrupt the class for?"

"Don't give me that shit!" Krarshe yelled back. "Class? What class?! There is no learning here, you fucking dreg!"

Everyone looked confused. Except Owyn. "Mister Krarshe, if you have issues with my teaching methods—"

"Shut your fucking mouth, you spineless slug!" Krarshe interrupted him. He couldn't stand Owyn's smug responses anymore. "Don't you dare say that. Don't you DARE fucking say that! You fail half of this class! For what?! Because they actually have any fucking talent?! You lying piece of shit! You and every other fucking *krun* claiming to be a teacher here. Hungerer take all of you..."

Krarshe felt a hand on his arm. "Krarshe... Stop..." Bri said softly. Krarshe could still see the remnants of tears in her eyes. His rage flared again.

"If I need to have you removed from the premises," Owyn started, "I can call for the city guard to step in." Owyn's face remained even tempered, but his eyes were smiling. The evil smile Krarshe had seen time and again. The condescending look that made this man the most detestable creature Krarshe had the displeasure of knowing.

"You..." Krarshe's breathing was ragged. His fists were clenched so tightly they were going numb. He saw the frightened look on the students' faces, on his two friends' faces. "You..." he repeated, trying to think of what to say. He couldn't think of anything. He had no power here, unable to get the revenge against Owyn he sought without affecting his classmates. He held himself up against the table, head hanging defeated. "I'm sorry, Bri. Tibault," he said quietly. He wasn't even sure they heard him. He raised his head once more, glaring at Owyn. "I'm done."

"Good, then if you'll sit back down, I—"

"No. I'm done... with this fraudulent school. Done with these phony teachers. Done with Professor Wild Brow here. I'm done. With all of it."

"Wh- Wh- What?!" Owyn's facade cracked. "What did you call me?!"

"You're a fake. A phony. All of the teachers are, but you are the chief of them. A failure of a mage, more concerned with his own shit reputation because he couldn't compare to the skill of his own students. Scared they'll surpass him," Krarshe said, staring straight into Owyn's eyes. "You don't want mages, you want pawns, people to fill the battle lines and die for you so you can keep this cushy lifestyle."

The students all turned to look at Owyn. He froze for a moment before speaking. "P-preposterous! Wh-Why would I," he swallowed hard, "an esteemed professor at this prestigious school be afraid of my own students?" He gave an uneasy laugh.

"You gave disproportionately difficult exams for students who excelled."

"W-We give e-exams to adequately test them!"

"You do it in hopes they'll fail. You said it yourself. What were your words again? During Bri's exam? It's getting more difficult to fail her? You wished she'd withdraw from the school so you didn't have to put on that charade? Weren't those YOUR words after she left?!"

"I—" Krarshe caught Owyn's eyes dart to the class before continuing, "I n-never... Wait. What evidence do you have? The exams aren't open to other studen—"

"You gave her a spell from the advanced class, a spell even the other teachers were astonished at. AND SHE CAST IT PERFECTLY!" Krarshe slammed his hand on the desk again. "And you had the audacity to fail her. Not because she failed, but because you didn't want her to pass. You said those words yourself after she left!" Owyn was left speechless, cornered like a wild animal. "The same goes for over half of this class!" Krarshe shouted, gesturing to the rest of the students. "Those who failed had complex spells, compared to those who passed. And yet you lavish praises on the few who passed, and then belittle those who fail! Call their dreams of other schools of magic an embarrassment to the academy, laughing at their struggles. This whole school is a cesspit..." He looked over at Tibault and Bri. They were watching him, shock and awe all over their faces. "... And I won't be a part of this any longer. Bri, Tibault, I'm sorry, but I'm leaving. When I find a real teacher, I'll find you. ... I pray you both find Wisdom in my absence."

Krarshe slid past them and made his way to the door. Owyn remained stunned as he left. Before closing the door, he took another look at his two friends, the two he spent over two cycles with, laughing, crying, struggling alongside. Then he turned to the class. "Wisdom find all of you. Wisdom to realize what this place truly is. Wisdom to know there is better out there for you than this." With that, he left, closing the door behind him.

He had barely gotten halfway across the courtyard when he heard the door slam open behind him. "You lowly elf scum!" Owyn yelled. "You think you can insult this institution?! Insult me?! And just leave?!" He stomped after Krarshe, who disregarded his boisterous insults.. "I will have you answer to the city guards! An elf, infiltrator, Thalas'anir spy, sent to disrupt our institutions! You and your co-conspirator friends will be beheaded!"

Krarshe's patience was nearing its end. He just breathed heavily and increased his pace.

"Listen to me, you fucking spr—" Owyn grabbed Krarshe's wrist. *BZZZZT!* Owyn's legs gave out immediately as he pulled his hand back reflexively from the electric shock he received. He breathed heavily as he looked at his twitching hand.

"Do... not... TOUCH... me..." Krarshe said looking back at Owyn, his brilliant blue eyes flashing with white-hot rage, hotter than a bolt of lightning. He turned forward again, leaving his former teacher quaking where he sat. Leaving the hate-filled bricks he once called a school. Leaving the friends he'd miss desperately.

* * *

"... And so, that's what happened?" Valerie asked, leaning against the door frame of Krarshe's room.

Krarshe nodded. He looked at his school uniform, thinking whether they were worth taking with him. They had cost a lot, and he didn't have many clothes, but something about them gnawed at him. He reluctantly stuffed them into the sack Valerie had brought him. He grabbed his traveller's cloak from when he was a merchant and held it up; it was a bit long for him now. He took the faded black fabric in both hands and, with all his strength, tore the bottom off it. He looked at it again and draped it over himself. It was still quite long, but short enough to work.

"Well, it's not my place to say if it was the right or wrong way to approach that. But, what's done is done. What do you plan to do now?"

"I have an acquaintance in a nearby village that's also studying magic." Krarshe looked around the room, checking if he had forgotten anything. The sack was only half full. He hadn't realized just how few possessions he had. "I'm going to see if she'll take me under her tutelage as well." He slung the sack over his shoulder and made his way into the hallway past Valerie.

"Well, I'm sure we'll miss you. Speaking of... What are you going to say to Na'kika?"

Krarshe stopped, looked back at Valerie for a moment, then faced away again. "I... Could..." Krarshe hesitated. "Do you think... YOU could mention it?"

Valerie stood there silent for a minute. Krarshe could feel the look she was giving him burning into the back of his head. "No. No way. You're not just disappearing on her."

"Val..."

"No. You should at least have the decency to say goodbye yourself."

"If I say anything to her, she'll either stop me from leaving or demand to come with me. You KNOW she would."

"... Still. It's not right."

Krarshe turned to Valerie. Her gaze was downcast. "I know. I feel like we both realized this the last time it came up." Valerie didn't respond, so Krarshe continued. "Just... Tell her I'll be back to visit. That I promise to visit."

Valerie turned back to Krarshe. "You damn well better, or may the Wanderer find you. ... I still think you're an idiot for not saying anything."

"Oh, and see if you can find someone to teach her to defend herself."

Valerie's brow furrowed as she cocked her head in confusion. "That's... a weird request."

"Just... thinking back to that one night... I know she has you and the rest of the staff, but still. I can't help but worry about her."

"Well..." Valerie brought a finger to her lip as she thought. "I think... I might know a man."

"Oh, here." Krarshe stopped and dropped his bag onto the floor. He rifled through his belongings until he pulled a gold rose from his coin pouch. "If they ask for payment," he said, tossing the coin to Valerie.

She caught it and looked it over. "You really are a good person, you know?" she said with a soft smile. "Even if you ARE an idiot."

Krarshe smiled. "Thanks. For everything," he said with a small bow, picked up the sack and headed downstairs. As he approached the dining hall, he peeked around the corner. Na'kika was nowhere to be seen. He pulled his hood up and adjusted the sack he was carrying and, as quickly and quietly as he could, made his way out the door.

He walked about half way down the street before he turned back, a final look at the place he'd called home for two cycles. It really hadn't been that long, but now, it felt as though it had been a lifetime.

As he walked the streets of Feyfaire, a vagrant as he had once been, he felt a strange sense of emptiness. Travelling was nothing new to him, but this time it was different. This time he'd grown to know people. He'd been a part of their lives, just as they were a part of his. As a merchant, every interaction was fleeting. Rarely did he see the same person twice. Any time in the caravans he'd been part of were spent largely alone in your own cart. In the few cases where you socialized with your fellow merchant, it felt as though they had their guard up. Like they knew the interaction was transient, never letting themselves become too involved. He must have instinctively done the same, rarely giving details about his own life, rarely opening up to others.

This was different though. Before he realized it, he'd opened himself up to Na'kika, Valerie, and the rest of the inn's staff. He'd grown to know Tibault and Bri, and their families, as they had grown to know him. Krarshe choked up for a bit as he walked, thinking about everyone he'd met. *Not that they know me truly. Perhaps I still have my guard up.* He stopped and thought for a moment. *I have to visit all of them.*

Krarshe sighed. He'd never been this sentimental before. It was odd. But he kind of liked it. He enjoyed having people he could call friends. A place where those friends awaited his return.

"Well," he said aloud. "Each step is a new journey. Right, *do'mro?*" He smiled to himself as he set out toward the village of Valenfort, in search of his new master.

EPILOGUE

Owyn paced nervously to and fro in the empty hall, eyes affixed to the polished, ornate flooring. He stopped and looked at his visage in one of the golden vases that lined the hall. He was a mess, unkempt, disheveled. The bags under his eyes were prominent reminders of his sleepless nights since receiving his summons. He attempted to smooth out his hair into his usual ponytail, but his hands were shaking uncontrollably. He swallowed hard and reached into his pocket for his already-damp kerchief, dabbed pointlessly at the sweat accumulating on his brow, and stuffed it back into his pocket. "There. That's presentable," he said to his reflection, trying to calm himself.

The door at the end of the hall opened. "The Council will see you now," said a scholarly man as he emerged from the doorway.

Owyn breathed deeply, tugged at his coat, and promptly walked past the humorless scholar and into the dimly lit circular room. He walked up a few steps onto a podium at the center. Owyn kept his gaze downcast as best he could, but threw glances at the thirteen seats that towered over him on all sides.

The light in the center of the room grew brighter, causing him to wince and shield his eyes.

"Owyn Lavaud," came a voice from ahead of him, in the shadows beyond his sight. "You stand accused of flagrant misuse of your position. How do you plead?"

Owyn corrected his posture, trying his best to not squint against the bright light. "Not guilty."

"The Council granted you the position of educator under the assumption that you would utilize it to further the strength and power of Remonnet. How, then, does one proclaim innocence after the mass-withdrawal of those he has been tasked with educating?"

"It was not the fault of the educator," Owyn argued.

"No? Who then?"

"One of my former students. Surely you would understand if you read my report on the matter."

"The Council has read your report, do not speak to us in such haughty tones," another voice shot back. "One problematic student does not forgive the withdrawal of twenty-five others over this past half-cycle."

"If the Council has read my report in full, then you will understand why—"

"Yes, we have, but your claims are without merit," the second voice said, interrupting Owyn.

"But, in conjunction with Landry Chapuis' findings—"

"I have read Landry's research, Owyn," said a third voice from behind him. "The student in question certainly has an abnormal mana pool, and has a strong affinity for lightning magic, but these findings do not substantiate your claim that this one student has 'tainted blood'. His name alone is not evidence of association with malevolent entities."

"But I am CERTAIN of it!" Owyn shouted back, spinning around to look at his faceless prosecutors.

A sigh could be heard to his left. "Owyn Lavaud, you understand the severity of such a claim, yes?"

Owyn nodded silently.

"Then you must have evidence of equal severity for the Council to take action. Not just raving like a madman because you failed in your duty to us."

"I wish to provide experiential evidence that was not included in my report," Owyn said.

There was some murmuring around him. "Very well," the first voice said finally. "You may present it and we will judge on its merit."

"Upon his departure, he attacked me." There was more murmuring from the shadows. Owyn smiled as the first councilor tried to regain order. He continued, "When I grabbed him, I felt a jolt of electricity pass through me, enough to bring me to my knees. When I looked up, I could see it. The lightning in his eyes."

There was an eruption of whispers at this information. After a minute, the first voice spoke. "Your claim is that he attacked you with a castless spell, then?"

"Yes."

"That would certainly be compelling. IF it is true, of course."

"If I may interject," said a new voice. "My son knows the student in question and has told me of a similar experience."

"You may continue."

"My son knows of this Krarshe from his class with Owyn. He says at a gala hosted by House Bulliere that he received an electric shock when shaking the boy's hand."

"I was there to witness the effects," said another voice. "It was... mysterious to say the least."

The room again erupted into whispers. Owyn could feel the tides shifting in his favor now. He clenched his fist, confident in his path. Just one more push. "Members of the Council! I put forth that this elf, Krarshe, is not an elf. Instead, he is a half-breed, dragonborn, intent on disrupting Her Majesty's plans! A dangerous agent of our enemies!"

This set the Council off into a shouting match about the veracity and severity of this claim. Owyn smiled, satisfied with his approach.

The deliberation was interrupted by the banging of a gavel. "Silence! This petty arguing dishonors the Council! The Queen's Council!" After everyone quieted down, the first voice spoke again, "Let us discuss this in a civil manner. Owyn, you have made your case. Please wait outside for our decision."

Owyn bowed with a devilish smile. This was the best case he could hope for. The Council was certainly on his side now, with Queen and queendom on the line. He stepped down from the podium and out of the room to wait.

It was several hours before he was called back into the Council's chamber. He stepped up to the podium once more, this time brimming with confidence.

"The Council has made its decision. While your claims have severity, there is little empirical evidence for them aside from your word and the word of a councilman's child."

Owyn's confidence began to melt away.

"As such, you are hereby suspended from your position at the academy."

Owyn backed away in disbelief, the words ringing in his ears. This wasn't what Owyn thought would happen. He was so confident that he'd riled up the patriotism in the council.

"During this suspension, you are to procure evidence of this boy Krarshe's origins, whether he is half dragon, demon, or devil. Whether he is of the elemental plane, or is a fallen deity. Whatever the case may be, bring forth evidence of this, and you shall be reinstated."

Owyn was speechless. He wasn't so distraught now, with an avenue back to his respected position. But even so, this was a monumental task.

Before he could speak, the lead councilor continued. "Failing this, you will be expelled from your position and found in contempt of the will of Her Majesty, the Queen, and of this kingdom. Do you understand the verdict of the Council?"

Owyn swallowed hard. He could feel his palms beginning to sweat. "Y-yes," he said with a nod.

"Very well. Then you are dismissed."

Owyn bowed and once again left the room. Once the door closed behind him, he slammed his fist against the gold-inlaid wall of the hallway. "Five curses on them!" he spat.

"I guess it didn't go well."

"No..." Owyn said through clenched teeth.

"Did my father give my testimony?"

"He did, Armand," Owyn said, turning around to look at his student. "Apparently it wasn't enough."

Armand sighed, leaning against the wall. "So, now what?"

"Now, I find him."

"Hmm?"

"I need to capture him. To get evidence of his tainted blood," Owyn said, scowling.

"I'm sure we can do it easily enough. I don't think he would have gone far," Armand said.

Owyn shook his head. "It doesn't matter. I WILL find him. And I WILL see his head on a pike before this is over," he said, storming off toward the exit. "Upon my life, I swear it."